TATIANA'S WAR:
A PRIVATE WAR III

Tatiana's War: A Private War III

By Perry Cockerell

Illustrated by Judith Gosse

ALLIANCE
PUBLISHING

Alliance Publishing LLC

Dallas, Texas

Printed in the United States

CONTENTS

PREFACE

TATIANA'S WAR: A PRIVATE WAR III is the final book in the "Private War" trilogy series. The fictional series begins in *A Private War* as a story following combat journalists who covered World War II during the European and African campaigns. The series introduces journalists Oliver Smith, Cub Miller, and Ed Nelms, the publisher of the *Birmingham Defender* in Alabama. Oliver and Cub are sent to Africa and Europe to cover the war where they send daily dispatches back to the newspaper. In England, Oliver and Cub meet Tatiana Phillips, the daughter of a newspaper publisher in Chicago. Together, they look for stories covering the contributions of the black soldier in the European Theater.

The story is combined with another tale of Andre Williams and Booker Thompson, who grew up together in Mountain Springs, Alabama. After Andre loses his family in a tragic fire at the age of five, he is aided by Sister Camille, a nun with the St. Peter's Catholic Church, who privately educates him until Andre and Booker volunteer to serve in the Army with some assistance from Booker's Uncle George.

The two plot lines merge during the war in France when Andre is court-martialed for accidentally shooting Booker. The prosecutor, Captain John Thomas, is convinced the shooting of Booker is no accident and is connected to the fire that killed Andre's family when he was young. Andre is defended by Captain Jesse Weinstein. Weinstein and Thomas battle over the guilt or innocence of Andre in a difficult prosecution.

Tatiana's War: A Private War III begins immediately after the end of *Andre's War: A Private War II* and follows how the combat journalists learned to adapt to their civilian life following service in the war. Set in 1948 the reader will be surprised to find that final sequel becomes political satire on the most current state of affair in America while struggling to deal with deepest questions of the universe.

Perry Cockerell
September 2022

PART A:
BACK TO WORK

Chapter 1

1948
Birmingham, Alabama

NELMS FINISHED CRITIQUING ANDRE'S FIRST article for the newspaper and turned to Cub Miller.

"Are you daydreaming?" he asked.

"No."

"Then what are you working on?"

"The 320th"

"The what?"

"My presentation about the 320th Barrage Balloon Battalion," said Cub.

"For what? The war is over," Nelms said.

Oliver interjected: "We're all giving presentations at St. Peter's about our time in the war."

"It is a far distance from where we were," Cub said.

"That's redundant," Nelms said.

"What is?"

"Far distance. Each word implies the other. Use long distance instead."[1]

"I learn something new every day," Cub muttered.

"So, who's responsible for this debacle? Are you all Catholics now?" Nelms asked. "I have a newspaper to run!"

Oliver stepped in to cure the breach. "Just a presentation about World War II and the African American contribution."

"Why don't I know about this? Who's doing this?" Nelms asked.

"Cub, Tatiana, and I are talking about the black fighting soldiers and the journalists who covered the war in Europe, Jim Crow issues, things like that."

"You mean the entire staff?" Nelms sounded gruff. "Is anyone working today? We're barely profitable."

"Just the four of us. It won't take long," Oliver said.

"You should talk, Ed. You covered the Harlem Hellfighters in World War I."

"I just might. What else do you have for me, Kemosabe?"

"The presidential election."

"What about it?"

"Truman isn't on the ballot in Alabama," said Oliver.

Cub mused, "How can that happen?"

"The Dixiecrats don't want to be bound to vote for the Democratic nominee," Oliver said.

"They want to help Strom Thurmond," Nelms said.

"There is a petition to put Truman's name on the ballot," Oliver said.

"What else?" asked Nelms.

"The House Un-American Activities Committee is investigating the communists in the government," Oliver said.

"Oliver and I are working that," Tatiana said.

Nelms turned to Tatiana. "What about the the governor?"

"He's visiting with a British lord from England," she said.

"Who is it?"

"I don't know … yet," said Tatiana.

"On to the world of entertainment. Tatiana, did you write a review about *Love in Syncopation* and *Miracle in Harlem*? I never heard back."

"I saw both of them but I have haven't written a review. Do you still want them?" asked Tatiana.

"If I paid for the tickets then I do."

"Sure thing. There's a new movie called *Boarding House Blues* with Moms Mabley. There's also *Joan of Arc*, *The Three Musketeers*, and *The Treasure of the Sierra Madre*," Tatiana said.

"How many times can you retell the story of Joan of Arc?" Nelms asked. Nelms turned to Andre. "Andre, cover the Auburn and Alabama rivalry. The last time they played was …"

"1907. I'm on it."

"Mr. Nelms …" said Brandeesha, in a low-cut dress as she walked in the office with her perfume preceding her. "A lady from the Birmingham Society of Professional Journalists called and wanted to know if the *Birmingham Defender* would participate in the Griddle Iron play. It will be the first year for the newspaper to participate."

"What is the Griddle Iron play?" Andre asked.

"A comedy show by local journalists who make fun of politicians," Brandeesha said.

"I don't sing or dance. I have a newspaper to run. Tatiana, you take charge of that. You're in charge of entertainment now, " Nelms said.

"I can help," Oliver said. "Just don't make me sing."

Andre added: "I know a few people who know how to put on a play."

The room grew quiet.

"Brandeesha, work with Tatiana on the show," Nelms said.

"Not me," Brandeesha said as she turned to leave. "I'm not working with the dragon queen."

Paint chips fell from the walls.

"I don't know what has come over her," Tatiana said embarrassed and looking for support.

It was time for the meeting to end.

"That's enough for today. Everyone, see you Friday," Nelms said. "Tatiana, you stay behind, please. I need to talk to you."

Oliver glanced over his shoulder at her. She raised her eyebrows at him and looked puzzled.

Back in his office, Nelms got to the point. "Tatiana, about the reviews. The country is coming out of the Depression and I want you to make your reviews funny. Use irony, something clever. Be outrageous as long as it's in good taste. Use your imagination and create something no one has ever done before. Think outside the box. We have to keep up the distribution of the paper. Sales are down."

"You mean write entertainment articles?"

"Yes."

"*Love in Syncopation* has music and Big Band sound. Lots of dancing. *Miracle in Harlem* is about a lady who is swindled out of her store. These are good movies but no one is going to buy the paper just to read about them."

"We have to do something to interest the public."

Tatiana was not interested in entertainment news. She was into politics and things that could change the world.

"What about Oliver and me writing opinion pieces on what is going on in the state and nationally?"

"We tried that once with Oliver," Nelms said. "No luck."

"But now that we're married ..." Tatiana said.

"Unusual. There is no other black couple working together in the industry like that. Let me think about it."

"Okay," Tatiana said.

"One more thing."

"What is it?"

"We've been approached by a buyer to sell the paper."

Silence.

"By whom?" Tatiana asked.

"You don't know?" Nelms said.

"No."

"Your father."

"My father! Mr. Nelms, I knew nothing about this."

"It might be by someone who knows our financial condition. Or it could be someone pulling strings."

Nelms was hoping for insight. But Tatiana truly knew nothing about this.

"Or maybe he wants you working for his paper again and the only way to do that it is to buy mine," Nelms said.

"That couldn't be the reason, Mr. Nelms. I would have known about that," Tatiana said. "I don't know how this could have fallen between the cracks."

"Things don't fall between cracks. They fall through them."

"What?"

"The cracks are the openings between slats, like on a boardwalk. Things fall through the cracks but nothing can fall between them because that is where the slats are."[2]

"Mr. Nelms, you never cease to amaze me."

"Thanks. We are in trouble and we have to do something or we will not survive. The new 'television' is competing with the business. Why should they buy a newspaper if they can see the news on a screen in their living room? Or they don't trust us, or we're not giving them what they want. Something is changing in the whole industry."

Tatiana had no reply.

Chapter 2

"THAT WAS A GREAT ARTICLE you wrote Andre."

Andre smiled.

"Where did you find all the names?" Tatiana asked.

"Mr. Nelms gave them to me."

"Why those names?"

"He wanted to see if I could research. We had many meetings. He kept saying: 'Verbose, you are too verbose. Less is more. More is less. People can't read all of this.'"

Coffee smell permeated the break room. Oliver was there.

"What would we do without coffee in the morning? What is this about Nelms?"

"It's a new idea I have," Tatiana said as she walked over to Oliver. She bumped him as he was pouring the coffee and it went all over his hands.

"Been there," Oliver said.

He wiped his hands with a cloth, gave the coffee to Tatiana, and poured his own cup.

"You want some, Andre?"

"Sure. Thanks."

"Here you are."

"Curb service," Tatiana said. "Why don't you do that at home?"

"I will. Starting tomorrow. Break a leg," he said to Tatiana as he walked out, pushing the door open.

"You are going to be in the play, " Tatiana said.

"Of course, I am," Oliver replied, smiling.

"Uh-huh," Tatiana said.

Oliver smiled to himself as he walked out looking at her.

"The word limit is a good thing. It forces you to be brief," said Tatiana as she returning to talk with Andre.

"What are you working on now? How is your head? Let me see. That looks awful. How did you do that?"

"My friend Lanny Ellis and I – we served in the war together – we went to see the Barons and stayed out too late. I slipped on the stairs outside of our apartment after the game."

"Who won the game?"

"The Barons. They were supposed to have a new player named Willie Mays, but he wasn't there."

Andre told her about his dream, the play and the strange ending when the soldiers were hung after a military trial presided by President Andrew Johnson. Then he dropped a bomb on her: "I dreamed that the prosecutor who tried me during the war was the leader of the Ku Klux Klan and was hung."

Tatiana's eyes opened wide.

"That's ridiculous. Captain Thomas went after you at your trial but he wasn't a White Supremacist."

"I know. I can't believe I dreamed that."

"You must have been in a deep state of sleep," Tatiana said.

"It was a deep state," Andre said.

"Have you ever heard of the 'Deep State'?" Tatiana asked.

"No. Since you are new in this profession I want you tell you this before you hear it from someone else. The Deep States doesn't exist."

"I've never heard of it."

"You will and it doesn't exist. Just remember that."

"What brings this up?" asked Andre.

"Oliver's and my friend Roy Otwell, who covered the war in Europe, dropped in the other day and mentioned the Deep State. Otwell said that this time it was real but I don't believe him. It's a joke played on cub reporters. Don't let anyone play you with that game."

Andre smiled.

Oliver walked in. "Do you need to be rescued?"

"No, why?" Tatiana said.

"Your favorite governor is on television," he said.

"I hope he has his wife with him."

Tatiana looked at Andre.

"Let's talk about this again," she said. Tatiana got up from her seat. "Ouch," she said.

"What?" Andre asked.

"Nothing. I thought I felt something."

Chapter 3

ANDRE WENT TO HIS DESK and sat down.

What would he work on today? He had already tossed one sheet of paper. Paper is expensive. He couldn't do that again.

He put another sheet in his typewriter and began to type. Then he stopped and pulled it out. A second sheet ruined.

"Not that," he said to himself, thinking of a possible story.

He pulled out a third sheet and tried again. No luck.

"Having trouble starting?" Cub asked sitting at his desk across the room. Cub wore a light brown double-breasted three-piece suit with a black tie and a beige handkerchief in his coat pocket, complemented by a brown felt hat. Nelms insisted that his reporters be well-dressed.

"Do an outline and don't type until you have enough information to finish the story," he advised. "You can't just start typing what's on your mind and expect it to go anywhere. You never know where you will end up. You have to put your thoughts together with a beginning and an ending or you will be throwing paper away all day. I know."

"How did they print newspapers before the typewriter?"

"They had typesetting printers."

"You know we have class today?" asked Andre.

"Yes," Cub said.

"How did they write the Bible back then without making mistakes in their scrolls?"

"They carried those stories in their minds for years before they wrote them down. They had it just right before they started started writing."

"No telling what this world would be like if they made one mistake in their scrolls," Andre said. "A small edit and the entire world would change."

"Andre, you have a visitor," Brandeesha yelled across the newsroom. *Oh, that voice.* "You want me to send him back?"

Private Lanny Ellis, Andre's friend from the Great War, walked into the newsroom.

"Hey, buddy, Sherry sent me to check on you after last night. That was quite a fall."

"I'm okay," Andre said.

"You had us all scared."

"I'm good. Do you want coffee?"

"Sure."

Andre sat down at a table in the break room and Lanny sat across from him.

"Are you writing now?" Lanny asked.

"Yes, much better than proofreading," Andre said.

"That's important."

"It's important but no one wants to do it. If there's a typo in the newspaper, the reporters cringe. Do you know how that works?"

Lanny did not.

"They place the articles in strips of wet paper on a warming device and then I read it for typos. If it's good, then they take it and set it in a proof and then print the proof."

"Sounds like an important job."

"Yeah, if I don't catch the mistake then the Editor calls me in his office and I catch hell," Andre said. "Reporters hate typos in their articles. You'd think it was the end of the world."

"Do you have time for lunch?" Lanny asked.

"Yes."

"Okay, see you at the Fritz Café."

Chapter 4

"BOOK CALL," BRANDEESHA YELLED, her voice carrying through the newsroom like a missile.

Cub was standing at Oliver's desk.

"Incoming," he said. "Duck and cover."

Everyone stopped writing or typing and went to the table where there were free books. Oliver and Cub opened up two boxes and spread the books around the table.

"What do we have here: *A Farewell to Arms, The Sun Also Rises, For Whom the Bell Tolls*, all in one book. Is this a Hemingway promotion?" Oliver asked.

"Let me take that," Tatiana said.

"Here's one – *Joan of Arc* by Mark Twain," Cub said.

"Let me have that," Tatiana said.

"*Tales of the South Pacific*," Oliver said, picking up the book off the table. "Publication date January 28, 1947."

"What is that about?" asked Tatiana.

"*Lost Horizon*," Cub said, picking up another book. "By James Hilton. A vacation in Shangri-La."

"Captain Weinstein told me about that book after my trial," Andre said.

"Roosevelt loved it … he names everything after it … his retreat in Maryland is called Shangri La and they named a Navy ship that name," Oliver said.

"There isn't a ship named that," Brandeesha said.

"Yes, there is," Oliver said. "It is an Essex-class aircraft carrier built in Norfolk Naval Shipyard and commissioned in 1944, nicknamed the Tokyo Express. After the Doolittle Raid, President Roosevelt answered a question where the planes were launched for the raid and he said 'Shangri-La,' so they named a ship after that. Doolittle's wife christened the ship. There's a photo of the champagne splashing with all the admirals and the press looking on.[3] I remember the picture being in the newspaper when I was in Paris."

"Let me have that then. It reminds me of Paris," Tatiana said, taking the book from Cub.

"Tatiana, you're taking everything," Andre said.

"No, I'm not. There are fifty books still on this table. Here, take this one, *A Connecticut Yankee in King Arthur's Court.* The guy falls and hits his head and goes back in time to King Arthur's court and Lancelot rescues Guinevere. You know the story. Twain is an easy read with all of his descriptions and double verbs."

"That's just great," Andre said. "A story about a guy who falls and hits his head and goes back in time."

"Cub, take this one, *Cooking on Your Outdoor Grill,* or this one, *Fishing in Alabama,*" Tatiana said.

"Here Cub, *Camping in America,*" Oliver said.

"You want to know all there is about grilling in Alabama?" Cub said. "The review will be easy: Bring plenty of barbecue sauce when you visit Shangri-La!"

"Stop that. This is serious," Tatiana said.

"Yes, it is. It's serious," Cub said.

"Let's read these in two weeks and all report back," Tatiana said.

"You can't read all of these in two weeks," Oliver said.

"I'm a fast reader."

"Okay. One month," Oliver said.

"What are you picking out?"

"Whatever is left," Oliver said. "Not much left. Let's see, *Travels with Dewey.* Here's another one. *The Truman Way.* All reality. Fiction for Tatiana, reality for me."

"This will be fun," Tatiana said.

"What is this? It's only twenty-five pages," Andre asked while Tatiana handed him a book.

"*Clisson and Eugénie* by Napoleon Bonaparte," Tatiana said.

"Never heard of it," [4] Andre said.

"That might make a good play," she said.

Silence.

Andre picked up a book called *Investigative Reporting.*

Brandeesha walked back in the room. "The train is leaving at 1:30 for your presentations that start at 3. You have to take the company car. Mr. Nelms said he's going to attend the lecture and I'm driving everyone."

Brandeesha walked out.

"Great," Tatiana said. "Our driver is a guided missile."

"A handy thing to have in a war," Oliver said. "Let's go."

Chapter 5

"So why are you still hanging around Birmingham?" said Lanny to Andre walking through the buffet line at Fritz Café.

"Just work," Lanny said. "So, what's going on with you?"

"I just started. I've been proofreading," Andre said. "Now they're letting me write. I'm covering the Auburn-Alabama game."

"That's really good."

They sat down to enjoy their lunch and after few minutes Lanny asked: "Hey, I've wanted to ask you for a long time. Are you ok after Booker passing away? I mean that was tough luck."

"I wondered when you were going to bring him up. I always wondered who really shot Booker," Andre said.

"It could have been every soldier's gun out there," Lanny said. "There were a lot of weapons fired. Who knows?"

"Did you pick up my weapon after you saw Booker?" Andre asked.

"I could have. My rifle quit working. Some of the soldiers picked up German weapons and used them, and then the next thing, the Allies would shoot at us. They could tell when a German rifle was firing."

"Were you questioned by the JAG officers after Booker was shot?"

"Yes. Everyone was."

"Were you transferred out of France after you were questioned?"

"Yes. We all were transferred after we volunteered to be in the first integrated fighting unit that would fight into Germany."

"That explains it."

"Explains what?"

"The rifle that they tied to me that killed Booker was not my rifle," Andre said. "There was some talk about the serial number at the trial. Then you guys were transferred out so you were not available to testify at my trial. I never should have been tried."

"Why wasn't this figured out during the trial? Can you get the trial set aside or something?"

"I was found not guilty, so you don't have to set anything aside," Andre said. "It's just that I don't like being charged with something I never did."

"Let's talk about something else," said Lanny. "Tell me what you are doing in your world."

"My world? You wouldn't believe it if I told you."

"Try me," said Lanny.

"Ok. Did you ever mention to me the name Deep State? Do you recall saying that to me? I mean do you know what it is and is it real?"

"Deep State? Not me. I don't know nothing about no Deep State. You're crazy, man."

"I guess I dreamed about it," Andre said.

"You're always dreaming," Lanny said.

"Ok."

"I never said anything about the Deep State," Lanny said.

"That's probably Hoover's imagination."

"Hoover?" Andre said.

"That's a joke. The Deep State doesn't exist."

"I need a story, and that one came to mind and sounds interesting. I don't know why."

"You dreamed it, remember?"

"So, what is it?"

"If I tell you, you can't print any of this. The "Deep State" is some kind of conspiracy where the U.S. government is being run by some outside influence. The president is just a figure head … some say the communists run the government … something like that. It has been thrown about for years."

"How do you know?" Andre asked.

"I don't, really. Some guy with the GCJ that works in the same building that I do talks about it all the time. He's a sci-fi nut … kind of strange … people laugh him off. No one believes it's real. He says this time it is real."

"Can I talk to him?" Andre asked.

"I guess," Lanny said. "If you want to hear about Saturn and Jupiter."

Chapter 6

CUB AND ANDRE LOOKED FORWARD to their weekly journalism class at St. Peter's. Father Sanders had already written nineteen sentences on the chalkboard. As he walked in, the students became quiet and were ready to listen. "Let's see, the last time we were in class we were talking about light years and whether we were alone in the universe. Linda Beckwith, you asked that question. I wondered what prompted it."

"I read last's year's newspapers and came across the 1947 *Roswell Daily Record* that said a flying saucer landed on a ranch in New Mexico."

"You can't believe everything you read. That's fake news," said Father Sanders. "That is beyond this class."

"You mean the flying saucer is not real?"

"I'm saying that story is not correct. It is in someone's imagination. There will always be people floating conspiracy theories that there is an evil influence controlling the world, and they will look for someone, particularly a new or naïve journalist to peddle that kind of information – which is disinformation."

"But someone thought it was real. Otherwise it wouldn't be in the newspaper," Linda said.

Father Sanders smiled and turned to the chalkboard. "You do have a lot to learn. Okay, for the first sentence. It reads:

> *Every writer has heard the axiom, write like you speak.*

"Mr. Miller, is this correct?"

"You're going to put me on the spot again?" responded Cub from his seat on the back row.

"Why, yes, you are the real journalist here."

"Well … I think it looks good to me."

"What about you, Andre?"

"Looks good to me, too."

"Does everyone agree?"

"No," said Linda.

"What should it be?" asked Father Sanders.

"I think it should be: 'Every writer has heard the axiom, write as you speak.'"

"That is correct," Father Sanders said. "Careful writers use 'like' with nouns and pronouns. Here are some examples: *I look like him. It looks like a disaster.* Use the conjunctions 'as,' 'as if' or 'as though' to introduce clauses."

"What is an axiom?" asked a student.

"Look it up," Father Sanders said, and he picked up a dictionary on his desk and carried it to the student's desk.

"It means a statement or proposition that is accepted as true," said the student.

"Is it a noun or a verb?" asked Father Sanders.

"Noun."

"What is a clause?" asked another student.

"You don't know what a clause is?" asked Father Sanders.

No one responded.

"A clause contains both subject and verb such as 'you speak.'"

Father Sanders returned to the chalkboard. "Let's do the second sentence. It reads:

They spent the day laying in the sun.

"Is this sentence correct?"

No response.

"No one wants to take a stab? Okay. The verb 'to lay' means to place or put. The verb 'to lie' means to rest or decline. So, the sentence should read:

They spent the day lying in the sun."

"Huh," Cub said.

The students laughed. Father Sanders turned around to see the response.

"Okay, the last sentence is:

She's one of those people who wants to run everything.

"Does anyone see a problem here?"

Silence.

"Sentences like this cause confusion even among skilled writers and editors. So, if you change 'wants' to 'want' then bravo to you!"[5]

"Huh," Cub said again.

The students laughed again at Cub's response.

"The problem with this sentence is that when you see the word 'one' you jump to the mistaken conclusion that it is the antecedent for the verb 'wants,'" Father Sanders said. "The sentence really reads like this: 'Of the people who want to run everything, she is one.' The correct antecedent is found in the structure 'people who want.' "[6]

"I'm lost," said a student.

"We will take this up again at the next class," said Father Sanders. "You won't be lost in the universe. There is only one real world."

Chapter 7

THAT EVENING, THE *BIRMINGHAM NEWS* and the *Birmingham Defender* sent people to begin work on the Griddle Iron play. Being competitive papers, they would come together each year to make fun of local and national politicians. This year would be the first integrated show - black and white journalists acting in the same show. There would be no segregation.

"We're happy to have representatives from both newspapers," said Betty, the Director of the play.

"I understand it is the first time the program has been integrated. This is so wonderful. I am so proud of this. We will enjoy each other and become lifelong friends!"

Silence.

"Now for starters, I am not a reporter so I don't know all the ins and outs of the newspaper business and how you do this and that and write this and that – but you guys sure do have opinions!"

Betty laughed awkwardly at her own attempted joke.

"Okay. Well, I do know how to put on a play," she said, laughing again. Everyone was looking at her. She looked around to stares.

"We don't have a script yet so we are going to set up a script committee to come up with the play. Now let's begin. I'm so excited!"

"What's her problem?" Andre said.

"Andre, be nice," said Sherry under her breath.

"Do you really want to be in this?" Mary whispered to Sherry.

"It will be fine," said Sherry.

"Is she crazy?" Cub asked.

"Cub, stop that. Be nice," Tatiana said.

"Sorry," Cub said. "Where do I go to surrender?"

"Do you know what 'stage left' means?" asked Betty.

No response.

"How about 'stage right'?" asked John.

No response.

"This is John, my assistant. We work together at the First African Baptist Church on the plays there. It is Andre's church," said Betty.

No response.

"Now, Oliver. Can I call you Oliver?"

"Yes. That is my name," Oliver said.

"That is so funny! Isn't that funny, John?"

"Yes, it is funny. He says his name with so much strength and a deep resonance and speaking voice. Are you a commentator?" asked John, walking up to Oliver. "My, you are so tall."

Oliver just looked at John, who came up to about Oliver's chin. Oliver was annoyed.

"Hey, you, move away from him and go back over there where you belong," Cub said, walking over to move John away from Oliver. Cub used to throw hobos out of the Second Street Barbershop during his days shining shoes.

John swiftly walked back to beside Betty. "*Excusez-moi,*" he said, holding his hands up like he was delivering a line in a play.

"What's wrong with him?" Cub asked.

Silence.

"We gotta get him a woman," Cub said.

Laughter.

"Okay. Let's start again. I think we got off on the wrong foot," said Betty.

No one responded.

"Okay. Let's take a deep breath and give each other a big hug and go around the room and introduce ourselves."

"My name is 'No hugs Oliver Smith' with the *Birmingham Defender*."

"That is so funny!" said John.

No laughs.

"*Je suis désolé*," said John, pronouncing the words slowly and emphatically.

"Tatiana Smith, *Birmingham Defender*. I can do a hug." John walked over to Tatiana and gave her a hug.

"We know who you are," said Betty.

"Roger Murray, *Birmingham News*."

"Brandeesha Yancey with the *Birmingham Defender*. Yeah!" She raised a clinched fist. "No hugging zone here."

"Barbara Harris, *Birmingham News*. This is all we could send today."

"Cub Miller, *Birmingham Defender*."

"Andre Williams, *Birmingham Defender*."

"Sherry Williams. I'm with Andre. I don't sing and I don't do plays but Andre wants me here. I don't know the first thing about a play. And this is Mary," said Sherry, introducing her friend to the group.

"I don't know a thing about plays, either," Mary said. "Sherry roped me into this."

"I did not."

"She's always doing that," said Sherry.

Some laughter.

"Okay. Tonight, we won't rehearse," Betty said. "It is so great that we have representatives from both newspapers here. I am so excited. John is excited. We are all excited. Let's give us all a big hug again!" No takers.

Chapter 8

THE PHONE RANG AT ANDRE'S desk the next morning. Quite exhausted from the prior day – the meeting with Nelms, book call, lunch with Lanny Ellis, the journalism class and then the play practice. He had quite a lot on his plate but would not be prepared for his first call.

"This … is … the … *Deep … State.*"

There was a pause.

"Who is this?" Lanny said slowly in a deep, low voice.

Andre smiled. He knew who called.

"Come on, man. You didn't fool me."

"Gotcha. You couldn't tell. Are you ready?"

"Ready for what?"

"Have I got a source for you, and he's dying to talk."

"He is?"

"As long as it is confidential."

"It will be. I need a story," Andre said.

"We'll see you at the Fritz Café at noon."

"I'll be there. I'm all ears," Andre said.

Around 11:45 am Andre put on his long black raincoat to weather the cold and rain outside.

"You have a scoop?" Cub asked.

"Maybe. If I do, I have to look the part."

"Here, wear my hat. Now you look the part." Cub adjusted the hat and brushed off Andre's coat. Andre looked like a spy.

In the restaurant Andre looked through the restaurant windows and saw Lanny and his friend appear and walk in. Lanny had on a dark grey suit and a thin black tie. His friend had on brown pants with black work shoes and a sweater and a tie. The collar did not fit completely over the tie.

"Andre, this is Hans McClannahan. He can answer all of your questions."

Hans wore thick, plastic-rimmed glasses. Hans took off his overcoat and put it behind his chair. They sat down and a waitress brought them water.

"Nice to meet you," Andre said. "Lanny says you know about the Deep State."

"Shhh. Be quiet. Don't say that around here. Someone could be listening."

Andre looked around. People were eating. It was loud and noisy. He couldn't imagine anyone listening.

"What does that term mean?" he asked.

"Let's order first," Lanny said. "This is on the *Birmingham Defender*, right?"

Andre said nothing.

Hans acted like he had never ordered off a menu or even been to a public restaurant. After ordering he put down the menu and said: "Some people think that there is a secret government operating within the federal government to keep certain elected officials in line or remove anyone who shouldn't have been elected."

"For real?" asked Andre.

"I told you he knows what he's talking about," Lanny said. "I wouldn't bring a guy down here who didn't know what he was talking about."

"They take down people who have gotten too big for their britches and don't have the correct ideology, famous people, wealthy people, even the little guy who falls out of line," Hans went on. "The Deep State removes politicians it doesn't like and replaces them with their own indoctrinated politicians. When the Deep State candidate doesn't win, the Deep State orders the elected official removed from office. They have the power to have a former president indicted in state court based on violations that are barred by the statute of limitations in order to prevent him from running for office again."

"And how do they do that?" Andre was skeptical.

"Through harassing them with fake news, innuendo, harassing investigations, trumped up criminal charges, campaign violations, charging them with lying to investigations if they can't get them to plead guilty to crimes they are investigating then they go after them for interfering with their investigation of a phony crime. They call these 'process crimes.' They are carefully trained in doing that."

"I don't believe there is a Deep State," Andre said as he started to leave.

"Don't get up. Just wait. It gets worse," Lanny said, putting his hand on Andre to get him to sit down.

"These people in the government don't like the term 'Deep State' because that implies they are doing something wrong," Hans said. "They like to use the terms 'shadow government' or 'steady state.'"[7]

"Who are they?"

"They are marsh creatures. Modern-day seditionists who will overthrow a president if they don't like him. There is no accountability. They think they are doing the right thing and everyone else is wrong."

"Where do they come from?" asked Andre.

"Many are home grown and support communism. There is a Communist Party in this country. The Kremlin has been trying to take over the U.S. government for years. They have been influencing the public through the media and through spies, political groups, and in Hollywood. That is what Congress is investigating now with the State Department and in Hollywood."

"Are you a lawyer?" asked Andre, sitting back down.

"No. I worked at a law firm."

"What else can you tell me?"

"There is no limit to what the Deep State can do. It is embedded in the federal government. If the Deep State doesn't want someone prosecuted then they exonerate them prior to investigation. They will write out an exoneration letter before they interview the witness. If they want a witness exonerated they will not put them under oath. But if the Deep State wants someone in prison because they don't like their opinions, will throw everything they have at them to remove them."

"How do we find out who these people are?"

"It's every journalist's dream to uncover the Deep State actors. But you have to be careful because there are Deep State actors in the media."

"You are helping me?" asked Andre.

"Yes," said Hans.

"Didn't I tell you he knows what he's talking about?" Lanny said.

They continued to eat lunch while Hans told stories of Deep State action. "I need to go. I have to be home early tonight," he said. Hans put on his coat and a small magazine fell out of the pocket.

"What's that?" asked Andre.

"It's Learner's Digest. There's an article about a gospel they uncovered. Here, you can have it. Read the article about the lost gospel of Thomas. They found it in Egypt a few years ago and have been translating it. It says that these are the hidden words of Jesus that Didymos Judas Thomas wrote down that is different from the other books in your Bible."

"Ok. I will look at it. Thanks," said Andre.

"I said he knew his stuff, buddy," said Lanny.

Back in the office, Andre sat down at his desk to think. Should he type something or wait?

"Working on a story?"

Nelms walked by Andre's desk.

"Hardly. I just met with someone."

"Are you and Cub going to the journalism class?"

"Yes."

"Are you getting anything out of it?" Nelms said as he walked off.

"I learn something new every day," Andre said.

"Good," Nelms said.

Chapter 9

JIM FOLSOM WAS ELECTED THE 42nd governor of Alabama in 1946. He promised to "clean out" the Capitol by using a hillbilly band and brandishing a mop and bucket. He would drain the marsh in Huntsville. He was born in Coffee County in southeastern Alabama and was one of the first governors to advocate a moderate position on integration and improvement of civil rights for African Americans.

Folsom believed that as long as African Americans were held down by deprivation and lack of opportunity then other poor people would be held down alongside them. He attended several universities but never obtained a college degree. He served in the United States Merchant Marine and thereafter became an insurance salesman.

By 1946, Folsom was a widower with two children, having lost his wife in 1944 from complications from a pregnancy.

One day as he stood on the back of a flatbed truck doing a campaign speech in Berry, Alabama, he saw twenty-year-old Jamelle Moore in the crowd. He was captivated.

"They sure have a lot of pretty girls in Berry, Alabama," Folsom said to the crowd. After the speech he went over to Moore and said, "Hi, beautiful, can I buy you a Coke?"

"You don't waste any time, Governor," she said.

"Let's go over to the drugstore," he said.

They dated for two years and in May 1948 they eloped in Rockford, Alabama, where they were married by a probate judge.

That evening the governor and his wife entertained a British lord and lady at dinner in the governor's mansion. After his guests were seated, Folsom was heard in another part of the house, thundering, "Where is that G--d---ed limey?"[8]

The governor appeared with a glass of iced tea filled with straight bourbon. Sitting down heavily at the table, he proceeded to drink and drink, reeling off raucous stories as his aristocratic guests picked daintily at their food.

Then, on an impulse, Folsom kicked off his shoes and began wiggling his toes.

"That is an old Alabama custom," said an aide.

"Oh, we didn't know," the lord replied.

The governor got drunker and drunker and finished the meal with a loud "Aw, sh--!" and fell backwards, unconscious, onto the floor in his chair.[9]

That evening Tatiana was at the governor's mansion along with other reporters waiting for something. A tip, a snippet. Something unusual.

Chapter 10

"How was the event with the governor tonight?" Oliver asked as Tatiana walked into the room.

"Nothing from him. The British lord came out of the mansion and told us that the governor was the 'most remarkable man' he had ever met."

"What did he do?"

"Who knows? There's no story there but it would be a nice blurb on a gossip column, which reminds me, Mr. Nelms told me that the paper might be purchased and we talked about ... or I brought it up ... that you and I could do an opinion column together."

"What brought that on? I did editorials and didn't like it and went back to news reporting."

"He wants something to stimulate sales. He said the paper is in trouble."

"A column from both of us will do that?"

"It's something new and outside the box. There are no other black journalists who are married who have a column together. We would be the first."

"That is outside the box. Are you hungry? Do you want to go out for dinner or stay home?" Oliver asked.

"I want to stay home," Tatiana said relaxing on the bed.

"You know, Oliver, we're fortunate that both of us have good jobs. Most people are struggling coming out of this Depression."

"You're right about that."

"We have no big expenses and no mouths to feed other than our own."

"Are you saying something?"

"No. I was expressing my opinion."

"Maybe you should be an opinion writer."

"I'm not sure anyone wants to hear my opinions."

"Yes, they do."

Tatiana ignored him. "Mr. Nelms dropped a bomb on me this morning."

"A bomb? Like a hydrogen bomb?"

"That's not funny. That was horrible what happened in Japan. You should not make fun of what happened in Japan."

"I wasn't doing that. You said 'bomb' so I was …"

"Yes, but no one deserves a bomb dropped on them, no matter what they have done and no matter how you disagree with them. That is such an awful thing for you to joke about."

"I didn't realize I was doing that. As bad as the bomb was, it won the war. Truman had to do it. He had no choice."

"Maybe so, but it was a terrible thing to do and you should not make light of that."

"Okay, we're getting off subject. Just what did Nelms say to you?"

"He said it is my father who wants to buy the paper," Tatiana said.

"Now that is a bomb," Oliver said. "Did you know this?"

"I told him I knew nothing about it. I still should have been warned."

Chapter 11

BETTY WAS TOTALLY INTO BROADWAY plays and musicals but she knew nothing about politics. It would be a stretch for her to direct journalists in a play making fun of politicians. She would be out of her element. Being recommended by Andre and with the endorsement of others at the *Birmingham Defender*, she would have a chance to lead a production outside of a church setting. Whether she could put this production together would be a test for her and others in the Griddle Iron play.

"Did anyone come with ideas for the play?" she asked at the second practice.

"We have the election going on. We can make fun of Truman and Dewey. We should make fun of Police Commissioner Bull Connor. No telling what stunts he has pulled this week," said Barbara.

"And we have Governor Folsom. That should give us plenty of fodder," Tatiana said.

"We have a lot of jokes about the governor that we can use," said Roger. "I cover him with the Capitol group, and our city editor has a lot on Connor you could use. You could do a whole play around him."

"Oh, but I'm interested, and I hope you are, too, in incorporating a Broadway play," said Betty, who would do anything to bring attention back to Broadway.

"Just a thought," said Roger.

"Now there is a musical playing right now on Broadway called *Angel in the Wings*," Betty said. "Anyone going to New York anytime soon?"

No response.

"Well, well, aren't we prepared today!"

No response.

"Okay. There's another musical on Broadway you might like called *Finian's Rainbow*, and it's set in the South in the fictional state of Missituckey."

"What is it about?" asked Barbara.

"It is about a racist white senator who turns into a black man and then through magic and enlightenment he is sings with two black men."

"Roger, you want to play the white senator and sing with Oliver and me?" Cub asked.

No response.

"Okay, if you don't want to do that, here is one called *Allegro* by Rodgers and Hammerstein," said Betty.

No response.

"Here's another one, *Brigadoon*, about a town that appears for only one day every 100 years," said John.

No response.

"Does anyone want to be here?" asked Betty.

Grumbles but no affirmative response.

"How about a play about Joan of Arc?" asked John.

"Where did that come from?" asked Betty.

"I saw Mrs. Phillips with a copy of that book," John responded.

"I'm reading it," Tatiana said.

"The movie is out right now with Ingrid Bergman," said Roger. "You could parody the movie."

"How many times can you tell the story of Joan of Arc?" asked John.

"We've never done Joan of Arc," said Betty. "Yes, everyone knows the story, but what about the music? We'd have to create our own, I guess."

"That's just great – a musical about Joan of Arc," Brandeesha said. "I can't imagine who is going to star in it."

"How about Tatiana?" asked Betty.

"I've never been the lead in a play. I'm really someone who likes being in the background," Tatiana said.

"Great. Tatiana the Great, the journalist who interviewed Eleanor Roosevelt and showed up late. Whoopee. Now she's going to be Joan of Arc," Brandeesha said. "I'll bring the matches, if she shows up on time."

"That was rude," Tatiana said.

"Tatiana, it is up to you," said Betty.

"Thank you. I would be honored," Tatiana said.

"Yeah, right, don't make me gag," Brandeesha said under her breath.

Chapter 12

MARYELLEN STEPPED OUT ON THE porch to retrieve the paper.

It was the best part of her morning. It was cold outside. She walked over and sat on the swing. The coffee was brewing, and she could smell it.

Aunt Myrtle followed her. She was spending the weekend. Then George came out with two cups of coffee.

"George, how nice of you!" said Maryellen.

"Just doing the Lord's work early. If the wife is not happy in the house, then no one is happy in the house."

"Thank you, George," said Aunt Myrtle.

Maryellen went to pick up the newspaper as soon as the boy on a bicycle threw it on the yard in the early morning.

"I hope Oliver has an article in the paper this morning," she said as she walked back to the swing perusing the paper.

"I know what you're thinking," said Bruce as he sat down on the porch swing. "Does Oliver have a byline?"

"No. I was thinking … is Tatiana pregnant?"

"I could have guessed that," said Aunt Myrtle.

"Me, too," said George.

Soon a jogger came by their home and stopped and walked up to them.

"Oliver! What a surprise. What are you doing?" asked Maryellen.

"Staying in shape in case I have to go back to war."

"Don't say that. You are not going to war again. This country will never be at war again," said Maryellen.

"I know," Oliver said. "So, your Aunt Myrtle is here. What are all three of you doing?"

"Just hanging out," said George.

"How is Tatiana? Is she pregnant?" asked Maryellen.

"We are in the Griddle Iron Show. Tatiana has the lead," Oliver said.

"I can't wait!" said Maryellen. "Why don't you bring Tatiana over some night. I haven't seen her in a long time. Have you two talked about having kids? You know how George and I want grandkids. Don't we, George?"

"You said it," said George.

"I'm not ready for this conversation now," Oliver said.

"We are not ready for life, either, after we are born," said Maryellen. "We are not ready to go to war when we go to war, and when the war ends, we are not ready for peace."

"I'm ready for peace," said George.

"I'm ready for breakfast," said Aunt Myrtle.

They all laughed.

"I guess none of us are ready for what life brings us," Oliver said. He was bending over catching his breath and stretching his legs before jogging back home to go to work.

"I dream of you and Tatiana bringing kids over here," said Maryellen.

"Dreams?" Oliver asked.

"I think about it," said Maryellen.

"Be careful what you think about," said George.

"And dream about," said Aunt Myrtle.

"I have to go now," said Oliver.

Oliver headed back home. He was in perfect shape and good health. At home, Tatiana's chickens were making noise in the backyard. She had already left for work. Oliver checked the pens and there were three eggs for Tatiana's business: Tatiana's Fresh Eggs.

Chapter 13

AFTER THE MORNING MEETING, OLIVER walked into Tatiana's office.

"You had three eggs this morning."

"I forgot to check. Thank you."

"You're welcome. I saw Mom this morning. She wants us to come over for dinner. Did you hear from your father?"

"I haven't."

"Are your parents coming here sometime?"

"If I have a baby," Tatiana said.

"Mother dreams of you having a baby."

"Dreams?"

"She thinks about it, she says."

"Dreams are serious business," Tatiana said.

Cub walked into Tatiana's office.

"What is serious?"

"Everything is serious," Tatiana said.

"That depends on what 'is' is," Cub said.

"You always say that," Tatiana said.

"Let me show you this. She won the war for the Allies," Cub said, holding out a comic book showing Wonder Woman.

"Who won the war?" asked Tatiana.

"She did – Wonder Woman," Cub said, pointing to Wonder Woman fighting in World War II. "I thought that was you when I saw that."

"No, you didn't," Tatiana said.

"I mean every word I say," Cub said.

"Mean what?" Oliver said.

"The paper should run comics in the back," Cub said. "Tatiana is in charge of entertainment. She could do that."

"That's silly," Tatiana said.

"I know people who go straight to the funnies before they read the news. That might be something to take to Mr. Nelms."

"I read the comics when I don't want to be depressed reading the headlines," Oliver said.

Tatiana pondered that for a second. "You're right, Cub. For the first time, you're right."

Brandeesha walked in. "Mr. Nelms needs to see you, Mr. Miller." Then she saw the Wonder Woman comic in Cub's hand. "What is this?" she asked.

"Wonder Woman," Cub said.

"Looks like Tatiana the Great," Brandeesha said and walked out.

Tatiana looked at Brandeesha but said nothing. Then she grimaced to Cub and Oliver, mouthing the words without saying them: "I have no idea why she said that."

Chapter 14

ANDRE WAS AT HIS DESK when Tatiana walked over.

"I heard you met up with your war buddy the other day. Are you working on a story?"

"I don't know if it's a story yet."

"How are you coming with your book?"

"It is a book about investigative journalism."

"You will be introduced to that phase of journalism soon," Tatiana said.

"Have you ever heard of the Deep State?" asked Andre.

Tatiana smiled and laughed. "Oh, Andre, where did you come up with that? There is no such thing. That is a joke played on new reporters. With all the complaints being made out there that journalism is dead, this is a joke to see if journalists are really working and doing their own research."

"You mean you have heard of the Deep State?"

"Oh my gosh. Not that again."

"Oliver's friend was here a while back floating that term around. I hate that term: '*the Deep State,*' it sounds so sinister and stupid. I's a myth that there are government officials in the agencies running the government and they use the media to push their agenda. Some call it a shadow government."

"You mean like a 'steady state'?"

"That too. The conspiracy nuts hate the term '*the Deep State*' because it implies that they are doing something wrong."

"There is some truth to it?"

"None whatsoever."

"My source said the government is full of communists who are infiltrating our society and Hollywood," Andre said. "He says the government has been secretly investigating it for years and is about to go public with hearings to expose communism in the State Department and in Hollywood."

"You mean the House Un-American Activities Committee?"

"Yes."

"That committee is a witch hunt and is destroying the lives of people with allegations and innuendo."

Andre began typing away. Tatiana, still curious, wanted to know more about Andre's source.

"You really know how to type. Andre, tell me: Where did your source say the Deep State operates?"

"Within the federal government." Andre stopped and looked at her.

His fingers were on pause. Andre could type without appearing to ignore her. He hated it when he was on a roll and someone came to his desk to chat; it disturbed his train of thought. If he were alone, he could write his story. How could he get his work done in a newsroom with all the conversations and the sounds of typewriters? Journalists must have the ability to concentrate, to write, to type, to create, to eliminate all mistakes and turn in the story on time. The English language is the most complicated language on earth because there were no rules. The exceptions were the rules. There was nothing logical about it in either speech or how it is written. And please, no typos in print. That is the cruelest form of punishment to see a typo in a story.

"That is ridiculous, Andre. This is a wild tale. See the pattern. You fall for anything that comes from someone's mouth. What is this on your desk?"

"Learner's Digest."

"What is in it?"

"Some article that my contact was reading. He said they found the lost gospel of Thomas."

"The lost gospel of Thomas?" asked Tatiana.

"Yes."

"What's in it?"

"I don't know. I haven't read the article."

"Do you mind if I take the magazine?"

"No. My source works for the FBI," Andre said, typing a sentence. Now he was in a real conversation and there could be no more multitasking.

"And what does he do for the FBI?"

Andre didn't know what to say so he said, "I can't tell you." He didn't know.

"Protecting your first source. Very good. I will tell you that I don't believe that the Deep State exists. Maybe in the future or the past, but not now. Come on, let's go get coffee."

In the hall, Tatiana said, "Don't you see what is going on Andre?"

"No."

"Did your war buddy bring this source to you?" She opened the door to the break room and walked to the coffee machine. Someone had started a new pot.

"Coffee is brewing." Tatiana poured a cup. "I can tell you that the government does not leak information to the press. Your friend didn't come to check up on you. He's luring you into something.

You have to be careful here. He could be playing you. Find out what he is up to. Trust no one."

She finished and gave the cup to Andre.

"I didn't think of that," Andre said.

Tatiana sat down at the table across from Andre.

"You know, Andre, if you're talking to someone at the FBI then he is probably breaking some rule so I would give him a cover name to protect your source. He could be fired for talking to you."

"Thank you."

"Be careful with people who suddenly appear in your life. Journalists are easy targets and can be manipulated if they don't know what they are doing."

"Yes, I understand."

"Now that that is settled. What I came to talk to you about was that I've been thinking about what you went through growing up and during the war. I think the story of you and Booker and the fire and your family would make a great human-interest story. I would like to find out more about your family, and Booker, too. He must have been a character. Do you want to talk about it?"

"Booker was quite a character. Totally opposite of me."

"For some reason I am drawn to him. What can you tell me about the fire?"

"You want to dig that up? I don't know much about it, but my Aunt Clara knows about it. George Thompson would know. They were there. I try not to think about it."

"I know what you mean," Tatiana said. "When you become a journalist, you begin to study the things you write. If you do it too much, then you identify with the story. You study it so much you dream and visualize it and then it becomes part of you. You can even have the same psychological impact as the ones you're writing about. You might not even realize it. I think that is the same thing you went through with your childhood and the war."

"That's true," Andre said.

"We don't have to talk about the fire at your home. Tell me about your friend, Sister Camille. What do you know about her? She is the one who rescued you after the fire and taught you all these years?"

"She has been a friend since the fire. I don't know that much about her. She and the other nuns rescued me when I was six years old. She likes to talk about how the world will bring you what you want if you pursue it. Like God gives you what you ask for if you have an emotional feeeling and you believe that you already have what you want."

"What do you mean?" Tatiana asked while taking a sip of coffee. "Is she the one who puts all these ideas in your head?"

"I don't think she does that."

"She doesn't?"

"No. She says the world brings you what you think about and believe as long as you have faith and ask for it in Jesus's name. You have to assume that you already have what you want."

"Do you believe that? You can ask in Jesus's name and if you believe, then it comes to you?"

"Jesus said that if you ask anything in his name then he will give it to you. The Old Testament says that the Lord is my shepherd and I shall not want. I think Jesus knew something that it has taken over 2,000 years to figure out."

"What are you talking about? This sounds like magic." Tatiana said. "I'm not a religious person, but please explain this to me."

"I think that if we accept Jesus as Lord and then ask anything in his name and believe, then we can have it."

"My, you are a changed person. I didn't know how deeply religious you are. That church has affected you."

"It's true," he said.

"Ok. I want a car," Tatiana said. "Where is it?"

"I think it takes more than that," Andre said.

"This is deep stuff. I don't go to church. I mean, I did as a kid. My parents took me to church, but I don't know much about the Catholics. I think it's time I paid a visit to St. Peter's and see what this is all about."

"You should talk to Sister Camille. She can explain it."

"I think you're right – with all of this anxiety and war that is still going on, people are ready to believe anything. They want their own Shangri-La. If all you have to do is think about things and they come, then we could have cured the Depression by our thoughts or ended World War II before 200,000 Americans died. It sounds like what Roosevelt used to say that we have nothing to fear but fear itself. All this belief that there is a Lost Horizon and a Shangri-La out there, has everyone believing the same thing you are saying."

"I'm feeling fine. I'm in my vortex," Andre said.

"Your what?" Tatiana asked looking astonished.

Oliver walked by. "What are you two talking about?"

"Andre is in his vortex. He's in another world at the same time that he in this one," Tatiana said. "Have you ever heard of such a thing?"

Oliver said nothing.

"He said the universe brings you anything that you ask."

"I have a few things I need right now," Oliver said and kept on going.

Back in her office, Tatiana perused through the Learner's Digest magazine from Andre and found the article about the lost gospel of Thomas. 'Surround yourself with your answer' the article read. She read through the article and found this verse that was translated:

> *All things that you ask straightly, directly from inside my name, you will be given. So far you have not done this. Ask without hidden motive and be surrounded by your answer. Be enveloped by what you desire that your gladness be full."*

"What does this mean?" she said to herself.

Then she pulled out files from her time in Paris covering the war and Andre's trial. There was a photo of Andre and Booker in 1930 when they were rescued after the fire. There was Sister Camille, Father Webster, Aunt Clara and George Thompson with Andre and Booker. The house, what was left of it, could be seen behind them.

She was curious about Andre having the gospel verse and wondered if it was connected to Sister Camille. "This might be a clue," she thought. Tatiana decided to go see the real Sister Camille. And once Tatiana put her thoughts to something, she would search until she found the truth.

Brandeesha walked in with a brown envelope. "This is for you." Tatiana opened the package. It was a draft of a short play. There was no return address. Someone had sent her an anonymous package. There was a note with the play: 'Check out the nuns.'

"How strange," she thought. "I was just thinking of them." She read through the script briefly.

Chapter 15

ANDRE STOPPED BY A LOCAL bookstore to find another copy of the Learner's Digest that Hans had given him. He read the article about the lost gospel of Thomas and was curious what Sister Camille might think of it.

"She and the other sisters are at the old house. That's where they go after the morning mass," said Father Sanders.

"I can't stay but would you give her this?"

"I will. What is it?"

"A copy of the Learner's Digest. It has a lost gospel that was found recently."

"Not that again," said Father Sanders. "They are always digging up old gospels. I heard about this one. If the apostle Thomas wrote a gospel then it would have been in the Bible. Even if it is for real there was a reason it was not included."

Father Sanders put the book down on his desk without opening it up.

"Are you coming to class today?"

"I wouldn't miss it," Andre said.

"I will drop off the magazine during my morning walk."

Father Sanders read the article after Andre left and then went on a walk with his dog to the old house. He had on a heavy overcoat, a hat and gloves. The walk was brisk.

"Come in here," Sister Camille said after he knocked. "It's cold out there."

Father Sanders handed her the magazine. "Sister Camille, this is for you."

"What is it?"

"The lost gospel of Thomas. Your friend Andre dropped this off for you."

"What is it?" asked Sister Laurie, walking in.

"Yes, what is this commotion?" asked Sister Aude. "What, pray tell, upsets my Sister from her hour of prayer?"

"Good afternoon, Sisters," said Father Sanders.

"Good afternoon, Father," said Sister Laurie.

"Good afternoon, Father," said Sister Aude.

"I'll let you read it for yourself. I don't think Father Webster will like it." Father Sanders turned around to leave.

"Why are you leaving?" asked Sister Aude.

"I think you might want to look at this without me," he said. "Sister Camille, I think you have found what you are looking for." He smiled and walked out, with the dog leaving first. The dog's toenails scratched the floor as they exited into the cold weather.

"What I'm looking for?" She pondered, opening the magazine.

"What did he mean by that?" asked Sister Laurie.

"Let's see," said Sister Camille.

"Let me read it," said Sister Laurie:

> *If they say to you, 'Where did you come from?' say to them, 'We came from the light, the place where the light came into being on its own accord and established itself and became manifest through their image. If they say to you, 'Is it you?' say, 'We are Its children, we are the elect of the living Father.' If they ask you, 'What is the sign of your Father in you?' say to them, 'It is movement and repose.'*

"We came from the light. I understand that," said Sister Laurie.

"We are from the light. God is light and we are its children," said Sister Camille.

"What does 'movement' and 'repose' mean?" asked Sister Aude.

"Movement is changing physical location. Repose means to lie at rest."

"That is a vibration," said Sister Camille. "God is the light and we came from God. At the subatomic level we are nothing but energy that is vibrating at a certain frequency. If we can match that frequency with what we desire then we can attain whatever we want. God brings us whatever we want but we have to understand his language to communicate directly with Him."

Sister Laurie continued: "Listen to this. Verse 106 says:

> *When you make the two – thought and emotion one – you will say to the mountain to move and the mountain will move.*

"And listen to this –

> *All things that you ask straightly, directly from inside my name, you will be given. So far you have not done this. Ask without hidden motive and be surrounded by your answer. Be enveloped by what you desire that your gladness be full."*

"That's it," said Sister Camille.

"What is?" asked Sister Laurie.

"Jesus is telling us to combine thoughts with emotion and to imagine that we already have what we're asking Jesus to grant us in our petitions. We are to surround ourselves with the answer that we want Jesus to grant."

Sister Laurie turned to Sister Aude. "Sister Aude, when you pray, do you imagine you already have what you are asking God to bring you?"

Sister Aude looked at her as if she had been caught in sin.

"Oh, Jesus, please forgive me, but I have done that. I have prayed that one day we will not have to work hard to make things, to toil in the soil; that one day we can ask God to give this to us and he will. But it doesn't happen. I've heard your talks, Sister Camille. I've even tried them – oh, Jesus, please forgive me for not trusting you – but sometimes I was so tired and wanted help that I asked Jesus to just let me say a word and bring us things, not even for me but for the poor, so that I would not have to work another day. I was so tired. Nothing happened. My prayers were not answered."

There was silence.

Sister Laurie went to comfort Sister Aude.

"This Depression was horrible. I wanted to say, 'Bring food to these people, bring money to these people,' but nothing happened. Do not trouble yourself, Sister Aude. Do you see what this is? This book is confirming what is already in the Bible. You have not done anything wrong. John 16:24 says:

> *Whatsoever ye ask the Father in my name, he will give it to you. Hitherto have ye asked nothing in my name. Ask and ye shall receive so that your joy may be full.*

"But why doesn't it work?" asked Sister Aude. "I've prayed many times to bring food to the poor. Why doesn't food show up after my prayer?"

No answer.

"It is saying to be surrounded as if your prayer has already been answered. Have the feeling as if it has already happened," said Sister Camille.

"But this book was not canonized," Sister Laurie said. "We don't know what was really meant. Sister Aude, when you pray, do you believe that your prayer has already been answered?"

"Of course not! If I believed it had already been answered, I would not be praying for it. How can I pray for something and believe that I already have it at the same time I am asking for it? I can't grasp that concept."

"It is easy. That is the purpose of your imagination," said Sister Camille. "Your imagination is a power that God has given us to change the world. We have to learn how to use it. Our thoughts are things. They are frequencies – vibrations. Our prayers are things sent out to the world. God answers prayers through matching our frequency – as ye sow, so shall ye reap. Jesus is telling us how to communicate with God. Then he gave us the ultimate answer that when we combine our thoughts and emotions and imagine that we already have what we are asking for, then we can do almost anything. That is a secret of the universe that has been hidden all these years."

"There has to be more to it than that," said Sister Laurie.

"Of course, there is. This presumes that we are living in a world of love, not anger but peace. St. Paul figured it out that love is the answer. Love is an emotion, a vibration. God is a vibration: movement and repose, as this lost book says. God is emotional and He speaks to our hearts. Women are emotional.

We can speak to God better than men. We know his language. That is why we have intuition. We already know because we are in touch with our feelings better than the male. Testosterone damages their emotions."

"Sister Camille!' said Sister Aude as they all laughed. "That was the first thing you said that I agree with."

"I didn't mean that," said Sister Camille.

Sister Aude and Sister Laurie looked at her.

She did mean it.

"I know what you're saying, but I have a hard time accepting this since it is coming from the Learner's Digest. This is not from the Vatican. We can be in trouble for promoting these ideas," said Sister Laurie.

"Don't be so obdurate, Sister Laurie," said Sister Camille.

"I'm not. You are shamefacedly telling us that we can make this world whatever we want by using our imagination. Like nothing is real, or whatever is real is in our imagination. Like Alabama in 1948 is not real. Like the whole world is a stage and we create our life from it."

"What are we doing here? What is our purpose?" asked Sister Aude, getting up from her seat.

"Our purpose is to find out our purpose," said Sister Camille. "It is not to accumulate wealth, money, or power. We can do these things if used properly in God's plan, but that is not why we are here."

Chapter 16

TATIANA DID NOT CALL SISTER Camille to ask for an interview. She was not sure whether she would agree. She would take he chances and go to the church unannounced and discover the church for herself. She did not call in advance. Tatiana knew it was easier to ask for forgiveness instead of permission. She was amazed at the majestic nature of the church from a distance and up close. A twenty-foot-tall Byzantine version of Jesus stood in the front of the church behind the altar. On each side were gold panels with statues of former popes. *Oh my gosh. I came too soon,* she thought to herself. *I forgot that Catholics go to church every day. I will attend Mass. Can I take communion?*

Tatiana did not kneel or make the sign of the cross. She attended the Mass and afterwards saw Sister Laurie as she was leaving.

"I'm here to see Sister Camille. Do you know where I can find her?"

"She just left," said Sister Laurie.

"I don't want to disturb her, but if she has a minute to talk, I would like to speak with her. I'm sure God will forgive her." Tatiana felt the tension from her awkward joke.

"Sorry," she said in a low voice as Sister Laurie left.

Sister Laurie soon returned with Sister Aude.

"Sister Camille left after Mass for the ranch home. I can take you, my dear. I'm Sister Aude."

"Sister Camille, are you here? You have a guest."

"Yes, my dear."

"This is the reporter from the newspaper. She wants to talk to you."

"Oh, yes. Are you here early for your presentation or am I in trouble?" asked Sister Camille.

"You are not in trouble," Tatiana said with a smile. "I was talking with Andre about you and the church the other day. He said that you and your church rescued him when he was young from the fire. I think he has an interesting human interest story."

Sister Camille and Tatiana walked into a study in the room next to the entryway and sat down. Tatiana pulled out her notepad and pen.

Starting at the beginning, she asked Sister Camille why she became a nun. Sister Camille said she was raised in the Catholic Church and wanted to be a nun all of her life.

"I was called by the Lord," she said.

"And what is your full name?" Tatiana asked.

"I don't reveal that."

"Where are you from?"

"I don't reveal that, either."

"Wow. Okay. How did you come to be with St. Peter's?"

"I was assigned here in 1929. I previously was at a convent in San Diego."

"What do you do?"

"We work with the community to bring help and assistance to the poor in the South and to bring them into the church, if they so desire. We do not make that a requirement. We help everyone."

"Is that how you met Andre Williams?"

"No. I met him after the fire at his home."

"Can you tell me about that?"

"That was such a tragic day. I can still smell the smoke."

"What happened?"

"We saw the fire as we were coming out of the old chapel. It was a horrible site. The two young boys were there and we took them in for a while, then their aunt took them back."

"Did you keep up with either of them after that?"

"Andre came to visit me years later when he was a teenager. We would visit often. I helped to educate him. I let him use the library, and sometimes he would play his guitar for me."

"Did he attend school here? That came out in the trial, you know."

"I considered him my private student but he wasn't enrolled here. He is now. All good things come to those who imagine their destiny."

"Imagine their destiny? Is that what you said? Andre says there is no imagination and that our dreams are reality."

"His dreams brought him here, I suppose. He imagined it, and that led him here years later. He believed he would be here and felt as if the universe brought him to us. I am so grateful to have known him and for God bringing him to us. I did not know the other young man."

"Booker," Tatiana said.

"Yes, Booker. He chose a different path."

"So, tell me more about this idea that the universe brings you what you want."

"Oh, it does."

"It does?"

"It does. Jesus brings you whatever you ask in his name," said Sister Camille. "You should read the Bible more. You should consider coming here to our church. We would love to have you."

"Next thing you know, you'll have me in the choir and leading a women's Bible class," Tatiana said.

"Oh, my goodness."

They laughed.

"I'm interested in what you're saying, but I'm not sure I understand what you are saying," Tatiana said. "Can you explain it?"

"Explain what?"

"That the world brings you what you ask for."

"Jesus brings you whatever you ask in his name."

"But that's not true."

"It is true. Our mind is seeking fuller expression and expansion which has never been achieved before."

"I'm lost. Translate, please."

"I have come to believe that we can create our own new conditions in life and that Jesus will give us whatever we ask in his name," said Sister Camille.

"I'm lost … again. This is way, way up there for me. I'm a Methodist. You nuns must be on some kind of higher spirituality," Tatiana said.

"This is my relationship with Jesus," said Sister Camille. "It took me years to understand it, and it expresses what I have been seeking. My desire is for peace of mind. As soon as we can control our minds then we will be given God-given energies."

"Are you saying that you can produce contentment in your own mind?"

"Of course. God brings us what we ask for."

"It is that simple?"

"Yes. You have to have contentment and remove all negativity. Be careful what you ask for. You might receive it."

"If I want all poverty to end in the world, why doesn't it happen? We ask Jesus to end poverty so why doesn't it end?" Tatiana asked. "Why did we experience a Depression these last twenty years if we could just instantaneously change that in our own mind? And why couldn't a billion prayers have done that so that no one went through the Depression?"

"Jesus does not work that way."

"But you just said that Jesus will give us whatever we want if we ask in his name, so why doesn't he eliminate poverty and the Depression right now, this second?"

"He will."

"Okay. I'm asking that he end all poverty in the world right now, in his name."

"God works in mysterious ways and will answer your prayers," Sister Camille said.

"You are NOT answering my question."

"Jesus will answer your prayers."

"I can't believe what I am hearing," Tatiana said. "This all sounds great and wonderful but nothing happens when I do what you are saying. Otherwise I would have had a lot of things by now in Jesus' name." She paused. "I need to ask you something, Sister."

"What is it?"

"Have you ever heard of the lost gospel of Thomas?"

"Yes, I heard that they found it and have translated it."

"Have you ever heard of the saying that you should 'surround yourself with the answer?'"

"I believe that your thoughts are things that leave you and go into the universe and attract to you what you desire, if you only believe. You have to have faith."

"You think that?" asked Tatiana.

"Yes, I do," said Sister Camille.

"If I want something badly enough then all I have to do is think about the solution to it and then the universe brings that to me? Why is there still poverty after a billion prayers to end it?"

"Poverty is being eliminated slowly. I believe that you can do and have whatever you wish in His name. We are all gods because we are a part of God. You have to believe it like it is already present. You will find that the universe is based on love. Love is the answer. But if you have negativity and fears, the world will bring that to you first instead of what you truly desire. If you can combine thought, feelings and emotion, you can move mountains."

"Move mountains, you say? Where did you read that?"

"What?"

"Moving mountains."

"That is in the Bible."

"Uh-huh," said Tatiana. "I appreciate talking with you."

"Do you know your way out?"

"I do. Thank you."

Tatiana stood up and said goodbye, and Sister Camille walked her to the door.

On her way down the stairs outside, Tatiana slipped and hit her head. Sister Laurie on the second floor happened to be looking out the window and saw the fall.

"Oh, Sister Aude, come with me," she said. "Sister Camille, the reporter Tatiana has fallen."

The nuns all rushed to Tatiana.

Stefan, a new teacher at St. Peter's Catholic School, was walking toward the home right as Tatiana fell. He ran to her and lifted her head up, while Sister Aude brought a washcloth to put on Tatiana's head.

Tatiana knew she was not hurt. She just wanted to rest for a few moments. Looking about in the commotion, Stefan saw Sister Aude. Their eyes met. They said nothing.

She's a nun, he thought. *What's the use?* But Aude looked back at him. She had never been in love.

"My gosh, I am so sorry," Tatiana said.

"You are just fine, my child," said Sister Camille.

"You really scared us," said Sister Aude.

"Let me bring some ice," Stefan said. "I think we need to chill down what is going on here."

Tatiana was awake and not hurt. It was a bump on the back of her head. She was not unconscious, just embarrassed.

"Do you think she's okay?" asked Stefan. "She seemed startled when I saw her, and I don't know what could be on her mind."

"I don't know, either," said Sister Aude.

"She felt something," said Stefan.

"She did. It hurt, I'm sure," said Sister Aude.

"I hope not badly," said Stefan.

"I will be fine," Tatiana said. She stood up and gathered her purse and notes.

Sister Camille said she would be glad to go with Tatiana to the newspaper or to home.

"That's not necessary," Tatiana said.

"I hope she is fine," said Sister Laurie.

"She will be," said Sister Camille. "How about you, Sister Aude, will you be fine after this?"

"What do you mean?" asked Sister Aude.

"I don't believe we've met. My name is Stefan. I teach at the school."

"I am Sister Aude."

"Can you believe she fell like that?" asked Stefan.

"It was an accident," said Sister Aude.

"Things happen by accident sometimes," said Stefan.

"I better be going," said Sister Aude as she walked off.

"And sometimes things are not accidents," said Stefan.

Sister Aude looked back at him.

Sister Camille stressed again that she could accompany Tatiana. "We hope you are fine. We can go with you to work."

"There is no need for that," Tatiana said.

Tatiana returned to the *Birmingham Defender* and told no one about her slip and fall. She wrote a story about St. Peter's that had the headline: "St. Peter's nun says we can have anything we want – just ask."

Chapter 17

THAT EVENING AFTER FINISHING HER story, Tatiana was lying in bed before going to sleep. "Oliver, what do you really know about Sister Camille and St. Peter's church? I mean, have you ever sat down and talked with Andre Williams for any length of time?"

"No."

"I used to think that a lot of Andre's behavior was due to the war. I didn't think he was over the war but now I have the impression that the nun at St. Peter's has a lot to do with the way he acts. She has been influencing him."

"What do you mean?" Oliver was shaving. He paused to rinse the razor in the sink.

"Have you ever listened to him talk? I mean, really listened to him?"

"No. I covered the court-martial and I found out about his past while investigating the story, just like you did. He was rescued by the church for a while and he wanted to go to school there with the rich white kids and dreamed up this fantasy that he went there and the white kids were poor and the black kids were rich."

"I don't think you really know him or understand him," Tatiana said. "You were looking at him like a soldier and not at his particular story."

"Nelms and I investigated his story. I called Ed and asked him to go look for the church Andre was talking about, and he did. That's why we brought him to the paper to help him move past that."

"That is one aspect of his story, but this nun that he's friends with, this Sister Camille, she is some kind of modern-day soothsayer. There's more to her story."

Oliver looked at Tatiana. "Like what?"

"She sounds like she speaks for all of St. Peter's – like she runs the whole thing. I have the feeling that she is the center of everything up there. You should have been in the interview with me and see how she says these things like they are so matter of fact."

"Like what kind of things?" Oliver continued to shave.

"The stuff she says. It is very powerful. I got nowhere with her. I couldn't even find out her real name. All she talks about is how the world brings you what you want if you ask for it in Jesus' name. You attract into your life what you think about, and you get what you want based on your emotions by believing that you already have what you want. This nun is telling people that, as if belief is all you need. If that were true, then why can't we eliminate poverty. If that were true there would have been no World War II. I'm completely mystified by her."

"There's more to it than just thinking about it," Oliver said. "You have to plan something and ask for it. It's part of the process. That's how life is. Someone thought about creating a car and now we have it, thanks to Henry Ford. She isn't saying anything new."

"I guess you're right, but it sounds mysterious when she says it. Then she wears that habit thing and it shrouds the whole conversation – like it is official and coming from the Vatican. These nuns are powerful in the Catholic Church. I think they really run that church.

"I suppose they can be."

"It's like she's saying there is some kind of big secret out there that is just now being discovered."

"I think there is real power in the mind and that is has been known about by sages for thousands of years. People ignore it." Oliver said.

"What have you imagined and then it happened?"

"I imagined being a foreign correspondent in Europe. I dreamed of it and then went after it. That's how it works."

"But she is saying that Jesus taught us that we can have anything we want if we ask for it in his name."

"He did say that," Oliver said.

"Oliver, you're not listening to me!"

"What did I do?" he asked, looking at her with shaving cream on his face and holding a razor in one hand.

"He couldn't have meant it the way it sounds. How come I never receive what I want?" Tatiana said. "I want a new car. In Jesus' name, I want a new car."

Tatiana got out of bed and walked to the window and opened it and looked out. "See, look out there – no car."

Oliver walked to the window. "There is the car right there. See it? *Voilà.*"

"Don't be silly." Tatiana walked back to the bed and pulled the covers over her. "I'm not talking to you."

"You are talking to me. You just said you were not talking to me but you are."

"You're not funny," she said.

"I am funny," he said.

"You are not funny. I'm not talking to you. I'm going to bed. This conversation is ended."

"Ended?" he said.

"And another thing she said. She said that we are all gods. Can you believe that? This nun said that. We are not all gods," Tatiana said.

"Jesus said that, too," Oliver said.

"Okay, that does it. You are suspended. You have to sleep downstairs in your own room."

"I am downstairs, and I am in my own room."

"Oliver! You are not listening to anything I say. You're taking her side!"

"I'm sorry. I'm no biblical scholar, but that is in the Old Testament. That is in the book of Psalms and Jesus said it. It is in the New Testament. You are a journalist. Do your own research."

"You are no help. You are defending everything she says."

"No, I'm not. I'm just being honest."

"Yes, but honesty is a weapon. We practice it every day at the newspaper," Tatiana said.

"You are right," Oliver said, putting his razor back on his face to continue shaving.

"I think that Sister Camille is key to Andre's story. Particularly the wild tale he told on the witness stand during his court-martial."

"What story?"

"About how he thought that the nuns were black when they were white. That was a real clue to his behavior. I still haven't gotten over that story. That was the biggest whopper of a story I have ever heard. How do you recover from that?"

"He was delusional," said Oliver.

"You can't be delusional on the witness stand. That is perjury."

"He was in some deep state of mind back then."

"Don't say that. I hate that," Tatiana said.

"Say what?"

"You said 'Deep State.' I hate that term. There is no Deep State. Now Andre is talking about it and says his source at the FBI is confirming it."

"So, there is a Deep State. *The Deep State ...*" Oliver said in a low tone.

"Don't say that! That is weird. There is no Deep State in this house. Okay? I'm changing the subject.

"Ok with me."

"I think Andre would make an interesting human interest story for the paper. Maybe I can segue that into a story about Sister Camille and the other nuns and what they have been stirring up here in Alabama by planting a big church in Protestant land. I think they are trying to make a statement."

"What statement is that?"

"I don't know yet."

"Let's talk about something else," Oliver said. He walked over to the bed and got in bed next to Tatiana. He embraced her.

"Don't do that. I'm mad at you. When I'm mad at you, you don't get to do that. You are punished."

"I am punished?" Oliver asked while stifling a laugh. He knew all of Tatiana's games.

He moved his hand down her nightgown. "What is that?" he said.

"Don't touch that," she said.

"I can touch that." He touched a slight amount of fat on her belly.

"That is my private fat. Like your private war. That is my private fat."

"Are you sure that is fat?"

"Of course, it is.

"You don't have much of it. You're too thin. I think you need some meat on your bones. I can still remember you coming into Café La Coup in Paris in your military uniform. This slim, elegant, fashionable lady in her brown military uniform with white gloves. You were so beautiful."

"Yes. We had that long conversation that went on forever. That was exhilarating to be in Paris during the war. How romantic, and then you bring up my belly fat. I'm going to sleep."

"It's 9 o'clock," Oliver said.

"I'm tired. Can't you see that I'm tired?"

Tatiana opened up her book to read.

"What are you reading?"

"*The Sun Also Rises.*"

"I've read that," Oliver said.

"Are you reading your books?"

"Not yet," he said.

"I need to read to go to sleep," Tatiana said.

Nothing was said for a few minutes.

"Are you a nice girl?" Oliver asked.

Tatiana grimaced. "I'm always a nice girl. I'm tired. Can't you see I'm tired and that I am reading a book to fall asleep?"

"At 9 o'clock? Do you know where your parents are?"

"That reminds me. I called my parents and they want to come to see us."

"Are you ready for the show?"

"When you talk, you keep me awake. I read a book to fall asleep, but now that you mention it, I can't believe I'm saddled with that play. I said I was honored to be Joan of Arc, and then that pathetic Brandeesha said she would burn me at the stake or light the match. No telling what kind of bomb she is going to throw in the newsroom tomorrow."

Oliver kissed Tatiana.

"Ouch," Tatiana said.

"Ouch what?"

"The bump on my head from the church. I fell and bumped my head at St. Peter's after interviewing the famous nun."

"What? Why did you fall at the church?"

"I don't know. I fell, and then I was sort of like resting. I was so tired I played like I was really out for a few moments. I guess I liked being the center of attention. I was embarrassed, and it did not change my story."

Oliver looked at her.

"Just like Andre," she said. "He did the same thing. He fell and dreamed a wild story about interviewing President Andrew Johnson and a war between the Yankees and the modern-day Ku Klux Klan."

"The same thing is happening to you," Oliver said. "You read *A Connecticut Yankee in King Arthur's Court*, didn't you?"

"Yes."

"Then you fell when you went to visit the church. You were affected by that Sister Camille, and now your thoughts are bringing you what you think about."

"Okay, that's it. I'm not talking to you any longer."

Tatiana was fully relaxed and had no idea the firestorm she would start after writing her story about Sister Camille.

"Are you ready for your presentation tomorrow?" Oliver asked.

"Yes," she said. "I can do that from my sleep."

Chapter 18

THE NEXT MORNING AFTER READING the paper, Father Webster was appalled at Tatiana's story and called Sister Camille to his office. "This article says you are promoting some kind of prosperity religion. Nuns take a vow of poverty and do not preach sermons. I know you didn't mean what you said, but we simply can't have this kind of innuendo running in the newspaper. It is not biblical."

"I know, Father. I don't know why she wrote that."

"Approval of an interview goes through me. You can't just sit down with reporters. You have no idea of their true motivation. You can't trust what they are going to write. Some come with an agenda and are seeking facts to justify that agenda. You really have to be careful what you say to them. They are selling a product just like everyone else. The only person you need to talk to and tell the truth is our Lord."

"I know, Father. I don't know what came over me. Will you forgive me?"

"All sins are forgiven at confession to those who truly repent," said Father Webster. "Even the pope goes to confession."

Silence.

"I think you are confusing Jesus' words that he will do anything you ask in his name with what is being written about in the last thirty years by these New Age thinkers and is being referred to as prosperity preaching. It is putting ideas in people's heads."

"Yes, Father."

"Have you ever heard of Wallace Wattles?"

"No."

"He was one of those New Age thinkers in the '20s who wrote a book called *The Science of Getting Rich*. Totally self-absorbed information about thinking only for yourself and to go where the money is. You will receive money because money is just a vibration down to its core like everything else. Or if we do things in a certain way then we will receive money. If we all lived our lives like that, then there would be no one helping the poor. Many people are sick and old and don't have enough money to do anything to earn money to meet their needs, much less lie down and imagine having money and then it is to come to you in some unforeseen way down the road. The answer is prayer. Wattles was eventually excommunicated from the Methodist Church, yet his book continues to sell and every ten years or so someone discovers it and thinks he found the secret to the universe. Believe me, you have to do quite a lot to be excommunicated from the Methodist Church."

Sister Camille said nothing.

"How did you come up with this law of attraction anyway?" Father Webster asked.

"I didn't come up with it. The reporter is the one who drew that conclusion."

"Father Sanders says he dropped off an article from the Learner's Digest about the Gospel of Thomas to you and the other nuns. Where did it come from?"

"Father Sanders said that Andre Williams dropped it off."

"Why did he do that?"

"I don't know."

"Did you say anything about that to the reporter?"

"No."

"Thank goodness. It would be devastating if that reporter had found out about that."

"In what way?"

"I read the translation of some of the verses. Some people are taking that gospel as saying that all you have to do is think about the answer to your problem and then the universe brings it to you. If that were true then there would be no need for a relationship with Jesus. There is a reason that book was not canonized. This reporter could accuse you of promoting a gospel that was not canonized. I must forbid you from speaking again publicly on this subject, and do not talk to that reporter again. Or to any reporter for that matter."

"Yes, Father."

Chapter 19

Students and guests filled the lecture hall at St. Peter's Catholic School. On stage a pull down screen could show images from a new projector.

"I'm glad that you could attend this part of our regular lecture series," Father Webster said as a welcome. "This week is African American studies, and our first speaker, Oliver Smith from the *Birmingham Defender*, will talk about his time as as a combat journalist during World War II and the contributions of the African American soldier."

Oliver was confident. He had lived his speech.

He began: "Let me first point out that while I will talk about World War II, African Americans have fought in every major conflict in which the United States has been involved. The 54th Massachusetts Volunteer Infantry during the American Civil War, the 9th and 10th Cavalry regiments during the Indian wars and the Spanish American War, and the 369th Infantry Regiment during World War II established outstanding records."[10]

He was just warming up.

"Let me switch gears for a second. After the Civil War the U.S. placed federal troops in the southern states to protect the former slaves and to preserve their rights under the Constitution after the amendments were passed to abolish slavery and provide equal protection, due process and voting rights. Then when the federal government removed the troops, the states began enacting

Jim Crow laws to infringe on the rights of blacks to vote. There was violence throughout the South when blacks began to vote and were being elected. People didn't know if they were voting for white or black people so they campaigned as "white" or "black" candidates – sometimes called "White League" or "Black Leagues" as in the case in Louisiana. There was election fraud against blacks voting. There were killings, lynchings and massacres. In one southern state there was an actual coup of the governor and President Ulysses S. Grant sent in federal troops to restore the governor. All the gains were being reversed by state laws designed to separate the races. Racism was rampant in the South with the rise of the Ku Klux Klan and the slaughter of African Americans. Then the United States Supreme Court permanently damaged the country with its *Plessy v Ferguson* case that held state segregation laws were not unconstitutional. That decision could arguably be the most damaging judicial opinion in the history of this country. We are living under legalized segregation and White Supremecy."

The room was stunned with silence.

Oliver felt the pain of the South and the pain of the war he had endured. Seeing the old photographs brought the war back to him like it had just happened. While emphasizing the contributions of the black soldier during World War II he downplayed the fact that the services were segregated. He did not complain because he had been chosen to report on the war in Europe.

Then he resumed. "There were lynchings in the South of blacks who did nothing wrong. I guess I'm moving away from my topic. The U.S. Army was the first military branch to take on racism and to stop the discrimination against the black soldier. World War II could not be won without the use of more Americans, and more Americans meant more black Americans.

"The purpose of my presentation today is to show that things began to change. The black soldier was necessary to fight in the war. Racism still existed during the service – Jim Crow was alive and well in the Army – but there were attempts to slow it down. Where higher commanding officers demanded it stop, then it stopped, but where there was no leadership, Jim Crow survived. By the end of the war there was an integrated black and white fighting unit that fought in Germany in 1945. A total of 708 African Americans were killed in combat during World War II.[11] Andre Williams, who is here … where are you, Andre?"

"Here."

"He fought with that unit. He should talk to you sometime," Oliver said.

"Where did the black fighting soldier serve?" asked Father Sanders.

"I'm glad you asked that, and feel free to interrupt me," Oliver said. "Okay, Andre, show the first slide. I'm going in chronological order. The Tuskegee Airmen, have you heard of them?"

Many in the audience said yes.

"They were trained in Alabama and were sent to Africa where they flew missions over Sicily, Italy and Germany. Here is a photo of them. This photo is Ollie Stewart, a journalist with the *Baltimore Afro-American* who covered the European campaign."[12]

Silence in the room.

"I boarded a British ship and we traveled to Morocco. We thought Hitler was going to engage the United States in the Mediterranean Sea, but he never attacked. The U.S. was leasing its military ships to the British and was testing to see if Hitler would attack a U.S. ship, as that would have provoked the U.S. into the war."

"What did you do when you were there?" asked a student. Oliver said he traveled throughout North Africa looking for the black soldier so he could send dispatches back to the newspaper.

He continued. "Another fighting force that I will mention briefly were the Buffalo Soldiers – 400 black soldiers were sent to fight in Italy during World War II. They engaged the Germans as they were retreating from Italy. I followed them there, as did my colleague Cub, whom you will hear from in a minute. Then we went to Normandy to cover D-Day."

"Did you go ashore?" asked Father Webster.

"Yes, once it was clear. Cub and I were there. Cub covered the 320th Barrage Balloon Battalion. Cub is going to cover the 320th in his presentation so I won't go there. We traveled with a convoy to Paris. The Germans were leaving Paris and decided not to destroy it. Later the 761st Tank Battalion, which consisted of trained black soldiers at Camp Worth in Texas, were sent to travel from Normandy and fought all the way to Germany under the command of General Patton."

"Tell me what were the black combat fighting units during World War II?" one student asked.

"There were the Tuskegee Airmen fighting from North Africa, the Buffalo Soldiers who fought from Italy, the 320th Barrage Balloon Battalion who installed barrage balloons on Omaha and Utah beaches on D-Day, and the 761st Tank Battalion that drove through France to Germany. The black soldier fought on all fronts."

"Were there black generals?" asked a student.

"One. Brig. Gen. Benjamin Davis, Sr. who served in the European theater."

"Andre, put up the next slide." Oliver took a pointer and pointed to the map like an intelligence officer briefing a squadron. "This is a slide of Europe. I will show you how the war in Europe was won. The Allies fought in Africa, to Sicily, Italy and then invaded France at Normandy and then invaded from the south of France, and by that time Germany was surrounded on all sides. The Russians marched from the east until all sides reached Berlin, and then Berlin was taken and divided in half."

Oliver enjoyed the presentation, and he had much more material. The audience was receptive, and everything just clicked.

"That was really good," Brandeesha said.

"Thank you," he said.

"Nice job, Oliver," Cub said.

"This was worth it," Nelms said.

"How do you like our church, Mr. Nelms?" asked Sister Camille.

"Nice. I haven't been here in a while," he said.

"You should come back," said Sister Laurie.

"Who is this?" asked Mr. Nelms.

"I'm Sister Laurie," she said.

"You're the ones who rescued Andre years ago?"

"We are," said Sister Camille.

"That was really great, Oliver," Tatiana said. "I hope I can do the same."

"You will," he said. "Break a leg."

Chapter 20

"FOLLOWING MR. SMITH IS MR. Leroy Miller, a reporter with the *Birmingham Defender* who also covered World War II. He will talk about his days as a combat journalist. Mr. Miller attends my journalism classes, and I'm happy he can be here today."

"Thank you, Father Sanders. I need your class. So, I'm talking to you about my days as a journalist. Let's see, I covered the black soldier being trained in the United States and then I went to Italy in 1943 to cover the Buffalo Soldiers before going to France for the Invasion of Normandy."

"What are the Buffalo Soldiers?" asked a student.

"They were a black fighting force that dates back to the Civil War. My job was just like Oliver's – find the black soldier and learn his story and report it back home. The black newspapers could not access the Associated Press wire reports, so the black newspaper was sometimes the only available resource for black families to learn about the contribution by the black soldier during the war."

"How were the African American soldiers treated?" another student asked.

"When the war started the American military had a long history of discrimination. Segregation was officially sanctioned, and the word 'colored' still appeared in the name of all-black units. As the war unfolded there were manpower shortages, and in 1944 more black soldiers were sent to the front lines. Before the invasion of France, the number of black soldiers had risen to 700,000, but most were stationed in the United States; by December 1944, more than two-thirds were overseas."

"Was there discrimination against the black soldier?" asked another student.

"Yes. One soldier I followed enlisted in Los Angeles and was sent to Fort Benning, Georgia, for training. He was placed with about thirty recruits and was accompanied by a white lieutenant who did not know about Jim Crow. The train stopped in El Paso, New Orleans, and Birmingham. In Birmingham he took the white and black recruits to the Hotel Bankhead, where all of them sat together while the Negro waiter stared at them while they ate with the white recruits."[13]

"Did anything happen?"

"Nothing. The recruits left and saw white guys in the street about to start trouble. The newspapers reported the event. It turned out that Bull Connor learned of the incident and sent his boys, but nothing happened. I followed Oliver Smith through Normandy. We met up in London in 1944 before the invasion. We were briefed by the military. We wore military uniforms and were given honorary ranks."[14]

"How was the military then?"

"In Britain it was good. The Negro American soldier was treated like royalty. The Brits were astounded that the Americans imported Jim Crow to England and wanted to enforce it over there. The Brits were caught in the middle, not wanting to go along with the practices of Americans, but they needed the Americans in the war. There were fights in clubs many times but not on the part of the Brits. The Brits welcomed Negro American soldiers and were fascinated by them. In fact, the Negro soldier was paid more than the British soldier. Negro American GIs did not know what it was like to be treated so well when their country did not, and they knew they would be going back home to a country that did not appreciate them."[15]

There was silence in the room.

"I will move on," Cub said. "You heard Oliver mention the Tuskegee Airmen, the Buffalo Soldiers and the 761st Tank Battalion that fought on all fronts. But by far the most dangerous of all missions during the war was assigned to a black battalion that had no prior military experience."

"What was that?" asked a student.

"It was the 320th Barrage Balloon Battalion. They were sent directly into war on D-Day and were trained under fire. Theirs was arguably the most difficult military assignment during the entire war and goes for the most part unnoticed. It was handed to a group of men with no prior combat experience.[16] Maybe someone will write a book about this unit.[17] Andre, show the first slide."

The slide showed a large barrage balloon.

"That is a photo of one of the balloons. We called them 'silver sausages.' The 320th Barrage Balloon Battalion was an African American battalion in the Army Air Corps and was composed of 621 men whose job it was to raise hydrogen-filled balloons to protect the infantry coming ashore on the invasion of Normandy. Their first assignment was Utah and Omaha beaches on June 6, 1944, the most dangerous day of the war. These balloons flew at around 200 feet. One of the batteries was sent to Cherbourg, and the three-remaining stayed at Omaha and Utah until October 1944. This battalion served 140 days in France."[18]

Cub continued: "D-Day did not go as planned. Infantry companies were pulled off course and Omaha beach would be a killing field until the troops finally broke through the German pillboxes and they were completely wiped out. Only when conditions were clear could the U.S. soldiers begin to raise the balloons. I observed the battalion space the balloons from two hundred to 2,000 feet apart. The balloons were tethered by an almost invisible steel cable with small bombs attached. The wire was lethal and could sheer off a wing. The balloons forced German planes to fly higher."[19]

"What were the balloons supposed to do?" asked a student.

"The primary aim of the barrage balloon pattern is to keep the enemy planes above the barrage or around it, so that the planes could be shot down by the Allies' automatic weapons. My information shows that by nightfall June 6, 1944, some 57,500 Americans and 75,200 British and Canadian troops had landed on five invasion beaches. There was enemy fire all day. Twelve barrage balloons were raised but claimed by the enemy. In the evening twenty more balloons were raised over Omaha beach and thirteen over Utah beach. The Germans rushed three hundred planes to France and launched additional attacks. Over 1,000 German planes were on attack and nearly six hundred were lost."[20]

"The men of the beach dreaded the nighttime visits they called 'Bed Check Charlie.' Among the important men who fought was Corporal William Garfield Dabney, from Roanoke, Virginia, who was a member of the Barrage Battalion. He enlisted in the U.S. Army in 1942 when he was 17 and before he graduated from high school. He persuaded his grandmother to let him enlist and volunteered for special services, which he thought would have him loading artillery weapons. At least one hundred forty-three balloons floated 2,000 feet above the Normandy beaches. President Eisenhower cited the unit for conducting its mission with courage and determination and for being an important element of the air defense team."[21]

"What did they do after October 1944?" asked a student.

"They went to England and then back to Georgia for training to serve in the Pacific theater. They didn't use barrage balloons at Pearl Harbor. Some say that had they used them, there would not have been a Pearl Harbor. They made it to Hawaii and then the war ended."[22]

Going through all of the wartime conditions, Cub realized the effect the war had on him. A tear came from eyes as he recalled his days in Normandy. The photos brought back the memories of the war as if he were still there. It had only been a few years since the war was over. The war was still with him. He had not moved on; he had just moved.

Chapter 21

———— ⁂ ————

THE CROWD FOR TATIANA WAS much larger because they wanted to hear from the first black female journalist to cover World War II.

"I guess they saved the best for last." Laughter. "I became interested in being a foreign correspondent when my father showed me a picture of some women foreign correspondents. They were all white women, and he thought I could be the first African American combat journalist. I grew up in the newspaper so I knew the business but I had no training. So, my father sent me on an assignment to cover a day in the life of Eleanor Roosevelt and then the opening of the Pentagon. I went to London, England, to prepare for the invasion of France. While in London I covered the 6888th Central Postal Battalion that was in Birmingham.

"While we were in London, we knew there was going to be an invasion into France but we did not know when. Then I became sick and was hospitalized and could not make the trip. Later I traveled through France through Rouen and reported on the Canadian Army. Many people do not realize the extent of the contribution of the Canadian military personnel who served during World War II. Over 1.1 million Canadians served in the Canadian Army, Royal Canadian Navy, and Royal Canadian Air Force. They served in Italy, Europe and the North Atlantic."

Tatiana said more than 44,000 Canadians died and 54,000 were wounded. "I wasn't in Europe at the time, but in August

1942 the Canadians landed nearly 5,000 soldiers of the Second Canadian Division along with 1,000 British commandos on the coast of France in Operation Jubilee, called the Dieppe Raid, Dieppe being a German-occupied port in northern France. Of the 6,086 men who made it ashore, 3,623 were either killed, wounded or captured. This raid showed that it was going to be awhile before the Allies could invade Normandy. The 3rd Canadian Division landed on June beach during the Battle of Normandy."[23]

"How do you decide what to report on?" asked one student.

"I was looking for the contribution of African American women to the war effort. I was suppposed to go ashore with Oliver and Cub but then I injured my arm in London and had to stay there until I recovered and found a way to travel to France. In London I interviewed the first African American majors in the Army, Major Charity Adams and Major Harriet West Waddy. In Paris I covered Charles de Gaulle. I reported on Andre's trial.

"Let's not get into that," Andre injected.

"I'm not going to discuss the trial but to point out how reporters disagree over some stories. Oliver and I disagreed over that. To him it was obvious that Andre was suffering from some kind of wartime condition that affects soldiers, but as journalists we cannot let ourselves become affected by what we report. If we did, then we would not be able to report the news objectively."

Listening to her, Andre thought that Tatiana was wrong. Many journalists experienced the same shell shock that the soldiers experienced. All of a sudden Tatiana began to feel dizzy. She fainted. Oliver and Cub rushed to catch her but couldn't get there in time. Her head hit the floor with a noticeable and painful sound.

"Call for an ambulance!" Oliver said.

PART B:
THE DREAM

Tatiana was admitted to the hospital for observation. The attending physician decided to keep her overnight. She relaxed in her bed. In her mind she was fine, but she couldn't understand why she fainted. Two fainting spells so closely together could not be overlooked, but she knew she was not in serious trouble. The brown envelope with the Griddle Iron script arrived mysteriously to her room and was on the tray table beside her bed. She assumed Betty had delivered it to her read. She opened up the package and within the package was a second smaller envelope.

The play proposed a scenario that did not exist in real life. The federal government had been taken over by a sinister force called the Deep State that had also taken over the State Department, the Department of Justice, the Federal Bureau of Investigation, the new Central Intelligence Agency as well as the main stream media in New York and Washington.

The media was divided into separate forces called the horizontal media and the vertical media who oppposed each other. The Soviet Union had been taken over by an evil force named Zoros, who had embedded agents in the U.S. government. The embedded agents were called "The Deep State." Their job was to control the United States through a hidden network of spies who reported to Zoros. The Deep State proposed to take over each U.S. state, one by one, until the entire country was conquered. Alabama would be first state to fall because it had elected politicians that the Deep State opposed. Alabama was a called an "orange state."

The Deep State approved of the other U.S. states that were called "green states." Alabama had to go because it was too orange. To take over Alabama, Zoros ordered an "open door" policy to allow immigrants to walk over the border, while legal immigrants from other part of the world would have to wait years before entry or citizenship was permitted. Zoros planned to flood Alabama with communists from the Soviet Union who were atheists and fascists who opposed free speech or free religion.

"Someone is sending me a message. Brandeesha could not come up with this," she said to herself.

She went to sleep. Sister Camille appeared. Next to her was a soft ball of white light.

"What is that?" asked Tatiana.

"That is God," Sister Camille said. "At least a representation of him to us as best our minds can comprehend in our limited capability. We can't even comprehend what God is. God is all around us. God is within us. Touch the ball."

The white light circled Tatiana and she touched it.

"He wants to join with his creation. He is a creator. You are a creator. We are all co-creators. He knows your every move, every thought; always has and always will. Once you learn to have faith and join with the Creator, then all is possible. Just ask anything in the name of Jesus and it is yours. To reach that, you have to believe and have faith."

Sister Camille disappeared. Then she reappeared.

"My child, I will reveal to you the secret of the universe."

Tatiana could see herself leave the hospital, and she and Sister Camille appeared together in a black fog with miniscule golden rays stretching back and forth at a rapid speed and in opposite directions.

"Was that white ball God?" asked Tatiana.

"Yes, the best that can be represented to us. The entire universe is God and consists of nothing but energy. Nothing else. It can neither be destroyed nor created."

"Where are we in this?"

"We are here. If we go down far enough, we are nothing but vibrations. This is God. We are all gods. That was what Jesus was telling us. When he said that we could have anything we want if we ask in his name and believe, no one believed him."

"What is the past?"

"The past is right there. Just rearrange the energy and it falls into place. The past never leaves us. We can go back and forth because energy is rearranged. There is no past. There is no future because when the future comes, it is now. The past, present, and future are nothing but energy rearranged at the sub-atomic level."

"This is so beyond me," Tatiana said.

"It is real."

"Why do nuns and priests pray?"

"To speak to God," said Sister Camille. "Our prayers are energy being released. Thoughts and prayers are things."

"Why are some of the rays going in the opposite direction?"

"Those are negative energy. The others are positive energy. Here there are no mistakes. If you took a piece of paper and painted white on one half and black on the other half, what is the difference? Which side is the mistake? Neither. They are just different energy forms. There are no real mistakes because all mistakes can be corrected by rearranging the energy. There is just positive and negative energy. If you are positive, then you attract the positive energy. If you are negative, then you attract negative energy."

"So, what do we do with our life?"

"We are here to find our purpose. We are always here. We will never go away," said Sister Camille. "We receive what we want and ask for in Jesus' name when he is ready for us to receive it. All we have to do is think about what we want and the energy rearranges itself, and then ask for it in His name and believe that you already have what you wish for with the energy and feeling that you have it. It is that emotional energy that connects to God. Jesus will bring it to you. That is true."

"I don't believe it," Tatiana said.

"Someday mankind will be able to harness this energy in his mind and be strong enough to do the things he wants. We live in different worlds at the same time, and once we learn how to merge these worlds with our internal energy then we can do anything we desire. We will be able to transfigure ourselves and move mountains."

"What?"

"Jesus showed us the way when he was here but we did not understand. That is why he talked in parables."

"Are you for real?" asked Tatiana.

"Of course, I'm for real," said Sister Camille. "I'm here."

Tatiana woke up.

The world and everyone in her dream would change.

Chapter 23

ANDRE CALLED HANS TO SEE if he could meet with him again. He wanted to continue his investigation of the Deep State.

"May I speak with Mr. McClannahan?" he asked.

"Who?" asked the operator. "Does he work here?"

"Yes."

There was a long wait before McClannahan answered.

"I can't talk here," he said. "Meet me at the garage across from that café we went to the other day."

"Fritz Café?"

"Yes, that one."

"What time?"

"4:40 p.m."

Andre was there on time. Soon McClannahan appeared wearing a pair of jeans and a blue work shirt and a T-shirt underneath. He looked around suspiciously to make sure no one was there.

"I'm undercover. I don't have that much time," said Hans as he adjusted his shirt.

A small magazine dropped out of his back pocket.

"Sorry," he said as he picked it up.

"Is that the Learner's Digest you gave me?"

"Yes, did you read the article about the lost gospel?"

"Yes," said Andre.

"Read it again and see what was left out of your Bible."

"Are you religious?"

"I'm interested in other world religions."

"What can you tell me today?" ask Andre.

Hans said nothing and then moved behind a concrete pillar in the garage.

"Where did the name 'Deep State' come from?" asked Andre.

"Who knows ... maybe deeply imbedded Russian spies in the government."

"Who is Zoros?"

"He's a billionaire who spends his money around the world trying to either overthrow governments or to change the political leadership.He infiltrates a political party and then has his candidates elected."

"Did he set up the Deep State?"

"Probably. He runs it. No one has ever seen him. Zoros controls the Soviet Union and now he is trying to control the U.S. He has a tougher problem because the U.S. has states and he can't control and he hates that. In some of the states the people have guns and weapons and actually carry them around to enforce the Second Amendment."

"The Second Amendment? What is that?" Andre asked.

"It's a big deal now," said Hans.

"Keep talking. What is the Deep State's interest in Alabama? Why start here?"

"There aren't enough resources in the world to feed everyone. He's shifting people around the world by mass migration. The number one reason for mass migration is that the host country will accept the migrants. But if there are not enough resources then the immigrants will go to war to take over the resources."

"What does Alabama have to do with this?"

"Alabama is the the most orange of all the states in the U.S. Zoros doesn't like that."

"What is an 'orange state'?"

"The people in orange states are hard core on the rule of law, the presumption of innocence, are for less immigration, less government spending, more religion in schools, less taxes, pro-life, pro-gun, and pro-family. The are not into the idea that there are more than two sexes or they are non-binary. Marriage is between a man and woman. A real woman."

"What do you mean?"

"You don't want to know. That part is too difficult to discuss. You wouldn't believe what is going on if I told you."

"Ok. Then what are the 'green states,'" asked Andre.

"The people in green states want more social spending, they want 'green energy,' that is electric cars, the end of the gas vehicles. They want free medical care for all, free college education, all student loans cancelled, higher taxes on the wealthy. They want religious, conservative thought or speech censored. They want to turn Alabama green by opening the border and fill it with immigrants who will vote for green candidates. They want the immigrants to be able to vote without proof of identification at the voting booth. They green states are protected by the media who promote only the green state agenda. The list is endless. Do you want me to go on?"

"No. Are these states Republicans or Democrats?"

"Those parties no longer exist. Zoros ordered those terms discontinued in the media. From now on there is either orange or green – sometimes brown."

"I have to start investigating this story," Andre said.

"You would be laughed out of the newsroom if you ran with this based on what I tell you. I can't be a source."

"What else does the Deep State do?"

"They control the news media in Washington and New York. Deep state political operatives have infiltrated the media and work to promote the Deep State agenda. Be careful who you talk to. Trust no one. One more thing. I will give this for free. Look up the name John Brown, the new head of the DJB, and Director John Bongino, the new director of the GCJ."

"What is the DJB and the GCJ?"

"Shew," said Hans putting his finger to his mouth. "Don't say those words. Those are top secret code words. Never to be repeated again."

"Ok. Who are these people?"

"They are two key Deep State heroes. They were instrumental in clearing Jill Rodderman, who was running against Card. She had engaged in wrongdoing while setting up an elaborate conspiracy to take down Card by claiming that the Soviet Union was assisting Card in his reelection. Imagine that. She used a classic diversionary tactic during a campaign and Brown and Bongino ran with it, knowing that it was false. Your courts even helped Bongino secure a wiretap on Card and his aides."

"Who is the man named Card?"

"Don't say that. He is your soon to be Governor."

"What's the other person's name?"

"Rodderman."

"Never heard of her," Andre said.

"You haven't learned your lines yet," said Hans.

"How do you know this?"

"It's coming out in a secret grand jury in Washington, where it was discovered that a lot of names were queried in a top-secret database by the DJB so that phones could be wiretapped. A Navy Admiral figured out what was going on and told Card to watch out. Card moved his offices after that. Bongino was paying visits to Card to purportedly interview him but he was actually spying on him. Then his aide, Paul Strozinski, arranged to have two spies try to entrap one of his aides, Michael Flynt and get him indicted. It worked. The fake dossier was created by a British spy working for MI-6.

"If grand jury testimony is secret, then how do you know about it?"

"I just do. I've got to go. My wife needs me at home."

Chapter 24

ANDRE NEXT MET HANS IN the bathroom of the basement floor of the public library after it opened at 9:30 a.m. He had researched the names of John Brown and John Bongino. Homeless men come to the library to use the bathroom and to wash up. Hans told Andre to go into a stall at 9 am and tap his foot one time. If a tap came back, it would be Hans.

Andre went into the stall and sat down. He tapped his foot. Another foot tapped in response.

"I have a wide stance," said Hans. "Did you find out about Brown?"

"Yes, impressive résumé," Andre said in a whisper.

"What about Bongino?"

"He's impressive, too."

"You didn't do your homework," Hans said. "My, what a pity. What kind of reporter are you? I don't need their résumés. I have their résumés. It is what is not on his résumé that you need to know. You know what happens to journalists when they don't do their homework? They get played. Don't trust anyone in your business. Know your sources. Get your facts. Have more than one source."

"Is this a game?" Andre asked.

"How about this," Hans said, taking a puff on his cigarette. The smoke filled the bathroom. "Did you figure out how Bongino was able to have two highly paid positions, one with a defense contractor and one with a wealthy financier?"

"No."

"He's a marsh creature. The financier was a Rodderman supporter. Bongino's job was to protect Rodderman when she got in trouble because he wanted to keep his job."

"You mean the GCJ is not a politically independent agency?"

Hans laughed as a puff of smoke came out of his mouth. Then he coughed. "Are you kidding? It's packed with Deep State agents."

"I didn't find that."

"Of course, you didn't find that. None of that is in the media. The media is Deep State and it doesn't report on itself."

"How about this: The GCJ and the newly created DJB leak information to the media when they want to bring down a target. So does the EPK. They use the media to influence the narrative and to investigate things for them, and when the target gets a guilty conscience and wants to cooperate and they can't get the target on the underlying crime, then they go after them for lying to the GCJ."

There was a pause. "The leaks put pressure on criminal targets to talk to the GCJ. EPK charges a defendant with numerous possible crimes and leaks to the media to put pressure on the defendant and to influence the public. If the GCJ finds no crime, then they charge the target with lying to the GCJ. They call this a "process crime." It only takes one GCJ agent to testify that someone lied. Then you go to jail. So the point is never speak to, or agree to cooperate with the U.S. justice department."

"Sounds like a setup," Andre said.

"It is and it works. You have to have a lawyer to deal with your justice system here. There's a two-tiered justice system going on with your government now."

"No one in my paper will believe that."

"Of course, they won't. They are Deep State."

"My paper is not Deep State, whatever that is."

Silence.

"I'm still listening," Andre said.

"One famous lady was sent to jail when she didn't testify at her own trial. They didn't get her on the crime they were investigating her for, but they got her for lying to the GCJ during the course of their investigation. That was Bongino's claim to fame. He brought down a famous woman and had her put in jail, not because of the crime, but because she did not tell the truth during the investigation. In other words, she waived her Fifth Amendment rights when she talked to Bongino and his group. Bongino brags about it all the time."

Andre was in a state of disbelief. This didn't sound like the America that he grew up in, even one with segregation. The door to the bathroom opened. They stopped talking. A homeless man walked in and saw that both stalls were occupied. He bent down and looked up into the stall and saw Andre. Then he stood up back up. Andre was frozen. How embarrassing, he thought. The homeless man walked out.

Andre left the stall and went to the door of the restroom and put the rubber stopper to prevent anyone else was walking in.

"Check out a firm called Nexus," Hans said. "They are a company that performs 'research' on political candidates. They are Deep State and provide false stories about opposition candidates. The Washington and New York media run with it all the time. The MI-6 agent is Christoper Irons. He and a man with Nexus called Glenn Simpleton wrote what is referred to as the 'dirty dossier' on your Governor Card. Then they handed it over to Bongino and the Deep State media agents who ran with it. Soon the public believed that your Governor Card was colluding with the Russians. Directors Brown and Bongino knew it was false and promoted the story to their Deep State media darlings. John Clapton, Director of MJ also gave it to the press. Two senators gave it to Director Bongino who ran with. When Rodderman got herself into deep trouble, Bongino decided to exonerate her before investigating her. He wanted to keep his job."

"How did all of this craziness begin?"

Zoros ordered the horizontal newspapers to stop covering the corruption of Deep State candidates or green politicians. Only focus on removing orange politicians from office. When that happened the vertical media sprang up, which Zoros did not expect. The vertical media is at war against Deep State heroes, Bongino, Brown, Clapton, Strozinski, Simpleton, Irons, and Zoros. Zoros will eventually shut down the vertical media and silence any opposition to the horizontal media and the Deep State. Before long you will be the only one left, kid. It is up to you."

"Doesn't that violate journalistic standards for newspapers to be aligned with one particular party?"

Hans smiled. "You are so naïve. You have a lot to learn. Newspapers have always been aligned with political parties. But it is different now. With all of the other forms of media springing up the mainstream media will never control the narrative. Zoros is creating a network of media organizations that will take over the world. It will be the only way to access information. If you don't agree with them then you will be punished and removed from the platform. They call it "Big Tech." They are not bound by the First Amendment or anything. You won't be able to sue them for slander either. Their platforms will permit all kinds of slander and false accusations, except for positions and viewpoints that Big Tech agrees with. Snot nose kids who call themselves "Fact Checkers" will be telling you what you can say and can't say."

"How do you know all of this?"

"I know. Believe me, I know."

"I'm learning something new," said Andre, who'd been hurriedly taking notes now for almost an hour.

"I have to work late tonight on a case. My wife is going to be mad at me for leaving her with the kids in the evening. She wants me there to take care of the kids to give her a break. I wish other husbands would do that."

Hans walked out, then Andre.

"It's about time!" said half a dozen homeless men standing outside the bathroom.

Chapter 25

ANDRE LEFT ST. PETERS AND went to see Tatiana at the hospital. He brought flowers that he picked at the church.

"Here are some flowers I found for you."

"Oh, thank you. I'm just here for observation."

"Where's Mr. Smith?"

"He went to the business office to sign papers. So how is your friend? How is your Deep State story coming? I can't believe I said that."

"It's coming along."

"Don't be pulled into the Deep State line," Tatiana said. "Andre, all new journalists get that joke pulled on them after they start reporting."

"I hope this is not a joke."

Andre walked over to the side of the bed of Tatiana and noticed her books and the brown envelope. "What's this?"

"Something I got in the mail at work."

Andre looked it. "I received the same thing. So did everybody."

"What is yours about?"

"I know how you hate the term, but the play is about the Deep State and Zoros's plan to take over the world."

"That is so stupid. Is this Betty's play? I would like to say that this has Brandeesha written all over it, but I doubt she could come up with something as intricate as this script," said Tatiana.

Andre said nothing.

Tatiana switched the subject.

"Andre, I meant to tell you that before my presentation I spoke to your friend Sister Camille.

"You did? What did she say?"

"She says the same thing you do – stuff like the universe brings you what you want or you attract things into your life through your thoughts and emotions. She sounds like you. Did that come from the lost book of Thomas that was written about in that article you gave me?"

"No. I've been talking to Sister Camille most of my life."

"Do you believe all that stuff she is saying?"

"You mean about the universe bringing you what you want? I think it makes sense."

"In what way?"

"Jesus said to ask and you shall receive. I'm figuring out something about the universe and how it works. Thoughts are things that change your reality."

"Thoughts are things, you say?"

"Yes. Be careful what think about and especially what you read because it can bring it into existence."

"Listen to what you are saying," said Tatiana.

"It's true. I read a book about President Andrew Johnson and then I had this dream and he was in it."

"You read a book about Andrew Johnson and you had a dream about him. He did not come into existence. You are confusing dreams with reality."

"Our imagination is evolving and our minds are becoming more powerful. We have this immense power in our imagination. Our brains are really just a small version of the endless universe up there. We are now able to bring the real world and our imagination together. We are able to merge the two."

"You need to listen to yourself. That does not mean that your dream was real and that you somehow merged that dream into reality. There is no record of Andrew Johnson meeting you. So, your dream is not true. That is the difference between a dream and reality. One is not true."

"Thoughts and dreams are reality," Andre said. "That's because that event took place in an alternate reality."

"Oh come now, Andre. You are not listening to what I'm saying. The dream could not be true or real because President Andrew Johnson was not really there with you. There is no record of you two meeting."

"Not in our history books there isn't."

"I want to laugh. Your hypothesis does not make sense. Your dreams are something else but they are not reality and they are not true. Oh, my head hurts," Tatiana said.

"I'm sorry. Do you need to call the nurse?" asked Andre.

"No. Go on. You were saying?"

"Have you ever had a bad dream and cried out?"

"Yes."

"Your heart beats faster and you were afraid?"

"Yes."

"Was your heartbeat real?"

"Yes."

"So, you believed the dream and your body reacted. It was a real event. Your subconscious cannot tell the difference between reality and a dream."

"But who is to say what is real and unreal? Who defines what is reality and what is a dream?" asked Tatiana.

"A third-party perspective I suppose," Oliver said, walking into the room. "Are you in some kind of Deep State?"

"Don't say that; that is weird. You know I hate that," Tatiana said. "Are you coming to take me home?"

"Yes This is too deep a state for me."

"Oliver!" said Tatiana.

"Young Andre is suggesting that man is evolving," Tatiana said. "He says that power is in our mind, that dreams are real, like they are some kind of preview towards the future, I suppose."

"It's true," Andre said. "Our dreams may be the first steps toward stepping into that third world. Our mind is evolving and getting stronger. Soon we will be able to …"

"Stop that, Andre. That is enough," Tatiana said.

"The doctor says to stay here and tomorrow so they can do some tests. One test is not available until tomorrow," Oliver said.

"Oh, Oliver, I can't stay here. I have a job to do, and I'm not going to come this far just to write in a hospital bed!"

"Where have I heard that before?"

A doctor walked in.

"Good luck with your story, Andre," Tatiana said.

Andre smiled and left.

"Hello, Mrs. Phillips, I'm Dr. LaSalle. I heard about the fall at the school. Not knowing the origin of it, I would like to keep you here overnight to figure out if there is anything going on that we need to know about."

"Thank you, Doctor," Oliver said. "Is there anything serious?"

"I doubt it. We need to run some tests tomorrow just to make sure and one cannot be run until tomorrow afternoon."

"Tomorrow afternoon? I want to go now," Tatiana said.

"You will go soon," the doctor said and then left.

After Dr. LaSalle left, Oliver opened a paper bag. "Just so you won't get bored, I brought your books. How are you going to read all of these in two weeks?"

"I'm a fast reader. I skim the paragraphs on the first read. The second read is where I understand what is going on."

Tatiana changed the subject.

"Oliver, can you go home and check on the chickens? You don't have to stay here tonight. I'll be fine."

"Are you sure?"

"Of course. You have the whole house to yourself. Are you going to run through the house screaming having the place to yourself?"

"Not at all," Oliver said. "You know I need you at home with me."

Oliver kissed Tatiana and then he left.

Tatiana looked around and saw the brown bag of books. She opened the bag to find *The Sun Also Rises, Tales of the South Pacific, A Farewell to Arms, For Whom the Bell Tolls, Lost Horizon,* and *Joan of Arc.*

She opened *The Sun Also Rises.* In a few hours she was almost finished. Then she fell asleep.

Chapter 26

THE NEW, IMPROVED AND MYSTERIOUS Griddle Iron script was being played out in Tatiana's imagination. The play did not make fun of Governor James Folsom, President Harry Truman or Republican presidential candidate Thomas Dewey. The play was called *Fake News* and would make fun of the media – a fake media that did not exist.

In the play, the *Birmingham Defender* was part of the "horizontal news media" and the *Font News* was a new television station that was part of the "vertical news media." Tatiana and Oliver wrote a column together frequently attacking the fictional Alabama governor named Ronald Card. Tatiana assumed that this was a way to make fun of Governor Folsom without using his real name.

"I want to play the commentator with the *Font News*," Brandeesha said.

"Fine with me," said Betty.

"We can't attack the real Governor Folsom," said Betty. "That wouldn't be nice. He is good for the state. He's cleaning out the Capitol."

"Is making fun of a real person, off limits?" Betty asked.

"Yes. This script says that the horizontal news media is controlled by an outside influence by the name of Zoros," asked Brandeesha.

"What happens to the vertical media?" asked Betty.

"It doesn't say."

"Someone is to take on Zoros and kill the Deep State and return the media to real journalism by purging the political operatives masquerading as journalists." Betty stopped and then asked: "Does this really happen? Do political operatives infiltrate the media and pose as journalists?"

No one in the cast responded.

"In this play, Zoros and the Deep State order the their candidate, Jill Rodderman, to win in her primary. Her opponent in the other political party is named Ronald Card," said Brandeesha.

"The Deep State controls the GCJ. Is that the FBI? The GCJ clears Rodderman of criminal charges and then sets out to frame Card based on a counter-diversionary tactic created by Rodderman to try to divert attention from her legal troubles. The GCJ and the horizontal press run with it knowing that the story is false."

"So, we have Tatiana and Oliver, being part of the horizontal media, attacking Governor Card on a daily basis," said Brandeesha. "I will attack both of the them at the *Font News*. I can't wait to attack Miss Tatiana the Great, the lady who interviewed Eleanor Roosevelt. Whoopi!"

"In the play, Rodderman is upset over her loss to Card and she calls his supporters the 'Basket of Deplorables.' That's mean. Would someone really say that in real life?" asked Betty.

"No way. This is 1948. No one would ever say that about an opponent's supporters," said Brandeesha.

"But what if they really are like that? Like, what if they try to overthrow the governement or start an insurrection?"

"If they did that, then they would be deplorables," said Brandeesha.

"Tatiana, the play says that someone is to hold up a bloody, decapitated head of Ronald Card," said Brandeesha.

"No, we are not doing that. That is sick," said Betty.

Brandeesha continued. "Here is Zoros' Master Plan. He wants refugees to immigrate from the Soviet Union into Alabama and to be given immediate citizenship and sent to Birmingham, which will become a sanctuary city. Birmingham elects its first communist mayor, who wants to stop all citizens from carrying knives. This is enough to neutralize the Basket of Deplorables."

"Card cannot handle all of the immigrants coming to Alabama, so he starts sending them to Chicago and Washington, D.C. that are called sanctuary cities. But then when they start coming, then they cry foul and ask for the National Guard to be called out."

"This play is complicated. I mean, what is a sanctuary city? Isn't a sanctuary in a church? And Birmingham electing a communist mayor? I don't see that happening and I don't think you can take the knives away from the people in this state. This guy doesn't sound like he is from Birmingham. He sounds British."

"It says that Card wants five billion dollars to build a wall for border security."

"That would never happen."

"Look at this line: 'I would rather run against Crooked Rodderman than Billie Saunders and that will happen because the books are cooked against Billie!'"

"Why does he call her Crooked Rodderman? That's mean. Brandeesha, this bothers me. No candidate would ever call the other candidate by that name, would they? I mean 'Crooked Rodderman' sounds mean."

"No. They would never say that."

"It says that she worked at the State Department and would meet with foreign officials and after their meeting with her they would donate to her charity. They call that 'pay for play.' It says that they government permitted the sale of plutonium to the Soviet Union, and then after the sale was approved, then the Soviet Union donated millions of dollars to her charitable foundation that was set up in Canada, so that the U.S. could not investigate it. Then her husband made millions off of speeches to the Soviets. Are these the Deep State characters?"

"Remember, that none of this is real and would not happen. That is why the script is called "Fake News.""

"Okay," said Betty. "I just want to be sure."

"It's a play, Brandeesha. "President Truman would never let this happen.""

"We have to do something to let these Deep State people redeem themselves. I will figure out how they can be redeemed at the end, if that works for you," Betty said.

"Okay. As long as we don't offend anyone."

"All of this is going on in Washington, D.C. It has nothing to do with Alabama," Betty said. "Why is this play being sent to us if this has to do with Washington and not Alabama?"

"Keep reading. The play leads to Alabama. It says that the federal judge who issued the search warrant based on the dirty dossier was in Alabama."

"Do you know a federal judge in Birmingham?" Betty asked.

"No. I don't know any judges. Just the one who ruined my custody case. That was a state judge," Brandeesha said.

Brandeesha did not realize that Judge John Thomas, who presided in her modification of custody, was now a federal judge in Birmingham. Brandeesha was represented by Jesse Weinstein in that case, the same lawyer who defended Andre in his trial.

The script, with some assistance from Brandeesha, created the final scenario: The Deep State, controlled by Zoros, had taken over the horizontal media and had deposed the new governor of Alabama, Ronald Card. Zoro's plan was to take over the vertical media and to eliminate all religion in the country by a mass migration of atheist communists who would invade the country through Alabama.

The Deep State would end freedom of speech, freedom of the press, freedom of peaceably assemble and to petition the Government for a redress of grievances in favor of the presumption of guilt, abandonment of the rule of law and search and destroy. The culture as we knew it would be canceled. There would be diversity of skin, but no diversity of thought.

"Let's make Andre the hero who figures all of this out at his newspaper and he saves he world," said Brandeesha.

"You are mean to Tatiana in this script. You need to make her the heroine. She can save the world from the Deep State and Zoros."

"She's reading *Joan of Arc*. She can be Joan of Arc. She can save Governor Card from the Deep State."

"See, that was not so hard."

"Except I want her burned at the stake at the end."

"Brandeesha!" said Betty.

Chapter 27

"I KNOW THE LAST REHEARSALS have been difficult," Betty said.

"We have had to live together and grow together. At times I was worried we were not going to be able to put on this play. I would cry. John would cry. We would cry together. We would not cry together. I was looking for an answer and I found no answer. I prayed for an answer and there was no answer. I prayed again and there was no answer again and I prayed and I received an answer."

"Praise God," Brandeesha said.

"Yes, it's true," said Betty. "I am happy to report that there is an answer to our dilemma. Brandeesha has come up with a storyline for the Griddle Iron Show."

The cast clapped.

"Great. I can't wait," Tatiana said.

"Brandeesha, would you tell the cast the storyline?"

"I decided that we won't be able to make fun of what is going on right now in the government because there will be too many people opposing that on either side – too many unhappy attendees – so I came up with a scenario that could never happen in real life so no one can get mad over who we make un of," Brandeesha said.

"What is it?" asked Tatiana.

"Alabama is being overrun by communists fleeing Europe after World War II, as ordered by the Deep State."

"There is no Deep State," said Tatiana.

"I know. This is a play, Tatiana." Brandeesha continued: "There are so many atheist communists coming into the state that they are threatening our way of life and they want to impose their lack of religion in Alabama. They will take over all of the churches, synagogues and mosques. The governor is trying to stop the mass migration by building a wall along the border of Alabama and Louisiana to keep them from coming through New Orleans unless they follow a legal process for entry."

"Build that wall! Build that wall!" said John.

"This is already horrible," Tatiana said.

"*Je suis desole*," said John.

"Soon the Deep State has overthrown the governor and taken over Alabama. Governor Card is out of power. The Deep State is run by Zoros."

"Stop right there," said Tatiana. "This isn't a play that you wrote Brandeesha. This is the script that was sent to me. Did you write that? Did everyone get the same script?"

Everyone acknowledged receiving the script.

"Ok. I didn't write it. I thought you sent it to me Tatiana, since you wanted to have the lead in the play," Brandeesha said.

"I didn't write it. It was sent to me too. Obviously, someone is trying to influence us with this play. Will the real author of the play stand up? Who wants to go with this?" asked Tatiana.

"We've changed it. It's not the same script," said Brandeesha.

"What have you changed?"

"I knew you were reading *Joan of Arc,* so we created the script so that you will rescue Governor Card and restore him to power, only to be burned at the stake. I mean, your character, Joan of Arc, is burned at the stake. Not you, of course," Brandeesha said.

"That is such a mean thing to say," Tatiana said.

"I'm sorry you were offended. I didn't mean it."

"What are some of the skits?" asked Tatiana.

"We created *Exonerate Prior to Investigate*, where the GCJ and EPK exonerate the character Jill Rodderman for mishandling of classified information before investigating her. She knew the Deep State would protect her, and then the Deep State with help from characters named Bongino, Brown, Clapton, and a Russian named Strozinski, begin to frame Governor Card, the fictional governor of Alabama, for collusion with the Soviets when there is no evidence of collusion with the Soviets. The Deep State hates Card for defeating Rodderman. They ordered her to be governor, but the Basket of Deplorable stopped the Deep State. No one stops Zoros. He's mad now."

"That would not happen" said Oliver standing before the group looking at the script.

"I know. It could never happen. That's why we can do it in a play. Who can complain about something that is fake news?"

"Makes sense," said Barbara.

"The next skit is *Insurance Policy*."

"And what might that be about, Brandeesha?" asked Tatiana. "I can hardly wait."

"That is the character Paul Strozinski's backup plan. If Rodderman wasn't elected, then the Miller investigation was set to go after Card to impeach him by claiming he colluded with Zoros and the Deep State."

"Who is Miller?" Oliver asked.

"He is some kind of Soviet-style prosecutor who goes after everyone connected to Card and leaves Rodderman and her mob alone," Brandeesha said.

"Sounds like a two-tiered justice system," Oliver said. "That doesn't happen."

"That's *Fake News* for you," said Brandeesha.

"This is really getting complicated and serious. Griddle Iron is supposed to be funny. No one in the audience will understand what this play means. I read some of the script. Isn't the Deep State the one who is behind Rodderman to win?" Tatiana asked.

"Yes," said Brandeesha.

"So why would Card collude with Zoros if he controls the Deep State and the Deep State is behind Rodderman?"

"Don't ask me. I'm just going along with the script," said Brandeesha.

"Now I didn't read the script closely, but tell me again who is the character John Miller?" Oliver asked.

"He was appointed by a Deep State hero John Silverstein, who wants to tape record everyone he meets. He's with the EPK and he ordered Miller to go after Card if he were elected governor and to ignore crimes by Crooked Rodderman and her gang," said Brandeesha.

"That's awful. There is no way that could happen. I agree with Oliver. This script is trying to say that there is a two-tiered justice system that clears some politicians deliberately and goes after politicians that it hates. Our government does not do that kind of thing," Tatiana said.

"Yes, they do," Brandeesha said. "I mean, no they don't."

"Any more skits?" asked Barbara.

"Yes … *Dirty Dossier* … *Coup D'état* … *My Turn*."

"What is *Dirty Dossier*?" asked Roger.

"The *Dirty Dossier* was written by Glenn Simpleton, who owns Nexus. Nexus is a political campaign organization that looks for dirt on candidates. Simpleton wrote an article ten years ago about lobbying in Russia, and then he changed the names in the document to put in the fictional character Governor Card and his aide. He gave the dirty dossier to Christopher Irons, a British spy with MI-6, who then peddled it back to the GCJ. Irons never went to Russia to do his research and all of it was false. Director Bongino, who hates Card, and wants everyone to vote Democratic, attached it to a federal wiretap application he verified that the dossier was true. He didn't know that Simpleton actually wrote it and laundered it through Iron to circulate it back into the intelligence community. Somehow Director John Brown with the DJB got a copy of it and leaked it to the press. His aide Director Clapton of the PMJ leaked it to the press as well. Then a Democratic U.S. Senator named Blade sent a letter to Director Bongino asking him to investigate the dirty dossier. Someone gave him a copy. A U.S. Senator named John McElhaney, who hates Card, gave a copy of it to Director Bongino, who already had a copy of it," said Brandeesha.

"This entire scenario sounds like insubordination to me. Someone wants to bring someone down. Why?" said Oliver.

"Hatred, is my guess," said Roger.

No one said anything.

Brandeesha picked up after the lapse. "The script says that Bongino is to operate from a higher honor – like he is above the law. Whoever plays him needs to know that," Brandeesha said.

"Roger, you play Bongino. You are at least six feet two inches."

"Six feet three," said Roger.

"Tall enough," said Brandeesha.

"The script says that Bongino is six feet eight," said Barbara.

"I don't know anyone that tall. He needs to play basketball," said Roger.

"Ok, let's get serious. What is Nexus?" asked Tatiana.

"Some organization that works for Rodderman and who supplied the dirty dossier to a British spy who then gave it to the GCJ ..."

"Stop, stop, stop, I'm totally lost by this script as I'm sure everyone else will be lost as well and it is quite obvious that this is a biased play that is attacking one side. We have no idea what the other side is about," said Tatiana.

"This whole play is extremely complicated and it is the most preposterous thing I have ever heard. I'm not sure anyone watching this will think it is funny, " said Oliver.

"That's the point. It is funny because it could never possibly happen. Don't you get it? If we made fun of Truman or Dewey, we would be making everyone mad, so by using this script that has a fake scenario – one that could never exist – then no one is harmed by the play."

No response.

Tatiana piped up trying to bridge a gap: "I see what you're doing with this script. You are saying that none of us can make fun of what is going on right now in Alabama, such as Truman not being on the ballot. We are so politically opposed to each other that we can no longer have a civil conversation about anything. I'm good with that, but this play seems biased itself, as if it is guilty of the conduct that it is complaining about."

"The point is that if we can't talk about current issues because everyone on both sides gets offended and they go Deep State on you, then we have to to find a way to talk again."

"I finally get it. For once in your life Brandeesha, you make sense," Tatiana said.

"Yay!" Brandeesha said. "To the Basket of Deplorables!"

"Now she makes sense," Tatiana said.

"If you say so," said Oliver.

The entire cast began to clap. For the first time the cast achieved unanimity.

"Now I finally agree with you," Tatiana said.

"The title of the Griddle Iron will be *Fake News*," Brandeesha said.

They all congratulated themselves.

"Yes!" said Betty.

Chapter 28

As the fictional play began to merge with reality, Tatiana began to question the legitimacy of the election of Alabama Governor Ronald Card. Not being legitimately elected, there was no reason to accept any of his proposals or actions.

Every evening Brandeesha bought the evening edition of the *Birmingham Defender* and read what Tatiana and Oliver had written about Governor Card. Then at 9 o'clock in the evening on her own newscast of the *Font News*, Brandeesha would look straight into the camera and attack Tatiana and Oliver. "Congratulations, Oliver and Tatiana. Liberal Oliver at the *Birmingham Defender* and his wife, Tatiana Phillips, the most blatantly biased news reporters on this planet," she began. "Tatiana and Oliver, yes, the married couple at the infamous *Birmingham Defender*, have done it again."

Then she put up screen snippets of their most highly charged accusations, condemned Tatiana and demanded her resignation. She held up Tatiana's column and had the camera zoom in on her picture to show her face on the screen. Then she would say: "Look at that! It is abuse just to look at that." Card supporters were outraged and rallied behind Brandeesha and enjoyed her attacks on Tatiana.

Each night Brandeesha continued her attacks: "The *Birmingham Defender* continues their usual nasty coverage with their most absurd and emotionally unhinged coverage, calling the governor a 'schmuck.' Yes, the 'Kleenex Queen' with the *Birmingham Defender* continues with her pathetic daily emotional routine. She can just get up and write what comes to her mind. Imagine that. Just vomit all over the front page, and by the way, Tatiana, if you're listening, the facelift is obvious. Just listen to another one of Tatiana's columns:

> "Look at him being a schmuck, thinking he can invite people to the governor's mansion and wowing them and that's how he operates. I know this firsthand. The governor gives you something and then you are going to give him a break. How pathetic is that?

"Journalism is dead in America. Then listen to this: 'This governor is rotten and for the record, we are nervous. Wow – the Kleenex Queen is 'nervous.' I would like to see her fight in the military in combat and defend her country for once," Brandeesha said, railing at Tatiana.

Tatiana was powerless to respond to the attacks by Brandeesha. She could handle an attack by a politician but an attack by a rival journalist was unreal. Governor Card began to rail against Tatiana as being dumb and that the only reason she had a job was because her father was a famous newspaper publisher in Chicago. Card figured out that bashing the media was popular with the public. Media figures were becoming fodder at his rallies. He had the horizontal news media placed in separate areas marked for them and were told not to come outside of their designated areas while Brandeesha, as a member of the *Font News*, was given a seat on the stage by Governor Card and allowed to speak to the crowd. Card would point out the media and then the crowd began to yell at them: "Lock them up." Then Card would say, "Why don't they turn the camera and show how many people are here? Look at them, the crooked media!"

The crowds roared: "We are the Deplorables my friend, and we will keep on fighting to the end!"

Chapter 29

THE *FONT NEWS* WAS DAMAGING the *Birmingham Defender* financially and Nelms knew it. Why read the paper if the news is on the television, free of charge, he thought. When was the last time you bought something based on a newspaper ad? This was serious business, because the newspaper depended on advertising for revenue. Nelms was considering selling the paper to Tatiana's father. Nelms met with the accountant for the paper to figure out what to do.

"Revenue is down. The company needs a new printer."

"A new printer?"

"Yes."

"What is the paper's break-even point?"

"Let's see, the fixed costs are $200,000. That's two cents per sheet of paper. If you sold the paper for ten cents that is eight cents."

"How do you calculate the fixed cost?" Nelms asked.

"Seller price minus variable cost. You could pay for the printer in two years at the present sales."

"Find out the critical path to a new printer and discontinue the old one while we stay in operation."

"Do you have other sources of revenue?" asked the accountant.

"No."

"How do propose to grow your newspaper?"

"You don't grow a newspaper."

"What?"

"You expand it or develop it. You grow crops, you don't grow a business."

"Oh."

That was Nelms at his best.

"To answer your question, I need a vision, a plan and the atmosphere to make it happen," Nelms said. "With the *Font News* attacking us, we need to understand our viewers better. When we do a survey, we usually ask what is the quality of the service -- like if the paper is delivered and inexpensively. I think the readers need to evaluate our writers. Our news and opinion writers."

"They will never stand for that," Oliver said, walking in.

"Why not, Oliver? We evaluate teachers, judges, lawyers, restaurants. Why not inquire what they think about some of our writers?"

"We print the truth," Oliver said. "There's no need to evaluate the truth."

"Yeah, but something else is happening out there."

"Like what?"

"Are we printing the truth or our opinion? Something is going on out there. We can print the truth but spin it to make it sound sensational when it is not; like there is trouble when there isn't trouble, but issues, or spin chaos when there were only valid disagreements?" Nelms said.

"What are you saying? That we're not printing the truth?"

"We are printing the truth," Nelms said and paused.. "But that's not enough. We need a new printer and we need new sales. We need more revenue. How do we do that?"

"What are you wanting to deliver?" asked the accountant.

"A newspaper," Nelms said.

"Can people buy it?"

"Yes, they can."

"What's missing?" Oliver asked. "Why are sales down?"

The accountant had a quick response:"sales are down because people aren't buying the paper. If they buy the paper, it is because they believe in and need the service, they have the financial resources, and they believe in the person selling it. If we have all three of these qualities then the exchange is irresistible. That is just a law in business. What's missing is that the public no longer believes in what we are delivering and they found another outlet to deliver what they want."

"How do you know that?" Oliver asked the accountant.

"I read the paper. I read other papers. I watch the news. The public is not yearning for us to tell them what the press is telling them. They have their own opinions. Right now, the papers have it backwards. News is editorial. Editorials are news."

"What are you trying to tell us?" asked Nelms.

"To sell your paper you need to be transparent."

"How do we do that?" asked Oliver.

"Don't hire political operatives to provide the news. They have hidden agendas. Disclose the journalist's party affiliation, political contributions, and who they voted for in the last political election in your newspaper. Then the reader will know where the writer is coming from."

"The media will never do that," said Oliver.

"Place the press under the same transparent scrutiny as politicians. Then employ journalists who represent both sides of the people and the issues."

"What?" said Nelms in disbelief.

"I guarantee that their reporting will change when the spotlight falls back on them. This is a win-win. You can sell to everyone when you do that. There is no need for a horizontal-wing paper or a vertical-wing paper. You can have both in the same paper and sell to everyone."

Nelms and Oliver looked at him and said nothing.

Chapter 30

TATIANA WOKE UP IN THE hospital and saw an intravenous injection in her arm to hydrate her. Oliver was sitting in a chair next to her bed.

"We're still checking you in," he said.

"Oliver, do we write a column together?"

"Hardly. I could never see us doing that," he said and gave her a kiss. "Are you feeling better?"

"Yes. Oliver, where is the governor?"

"Probably in the governor's mansion."

"Who is the governor?"

"What is this about? You know who the governor is."

"Oliver, this is important. What is his name?"

"For a minute there I thought it was Ronald Card."

"Have you been reading the Griddle Iron skit?"

"Of course. How silly of me. All this Deep State stuff and Brandeesha working at the *Font News*."

"It's ridiculous, but it is only a play," said Oliver.

"One more question. Are the communists trying to invade Alabama to turn the state blue?"

"If you keep asking questions like that, the doctor will keep you here another night."

Tatiana smiled. "I know. I was just checking."

"So, what is going on with you?" Oliver asked.

"I had a dream where the Griddle Iron play was more than a play. It was becoming real."

"What does that mean?" asked Oliver.

"I'm thinking that…. I'm thinking that I have to be careful what I think about and what I read. It seems like it is really happening."

"You visualize when you are awake. You dream when you are asleep."

Tatiana reached over and picked up the script to the Griddle Iron show.

"Oliver, who sent us this script? This could not possibly have been from Brandeesha or Betty. Don't get me wrong, but they could have never written anything as fantastic as this."

"I don't know."

"It uses the term "Deep State" throughout the entire play. Roy Otwell floated the Deep State conspiracy when he was here and this script arrives later. Is he the one behind it? It makes sense. He is a journalist. He could have written it."

"That is a possibility," Oliver said.

"Now Andre is investigating a similar story. I hate the term 'Deep State' because once you hear it you can't get it out of your head."

"One good thing is that when you are dreaming, you are having good sleep and you are in a deep state of mind," Oliver said.

"Don't say that. It only reinforces that 'Deep State' stuff."

"I won't do that."

"Oliver, I dreamed that my father passed away and it made me upset. I'm calling him right now and inviting my parents down right now."

"You said they were already coming down."

"Yes. I want to confirm that. So, what is going on with the paper?"

"Nothing," Oliver said. "Just Truman and Dewey for me."

Chapter 31

TATIANA SETTLED BACK INTO BED and closed her eyes. She imagined herself at the newspaper, ready for work after her presentation at St. Peter's. She was training her mind. She began to realize that there are two kinds of minds: a trained mind and an untrained mind. The difference is that the trained mind can focus on one thought for a long period of time to the exclusion of hundreds of other thoughts circulating in the brain at the same time. This was how prayer and meditation were accomplished. The more practice then the better the mind. She could control her mind through focusing seriously on a subject.

"I heard your Army buddy was here," she said to Andre. "Did you ask him about what happened to Booker? I mean, did you ask him if he shot Booker?"

"You are back on the job. You get right to it."

"Did you ask him?"

"I talked to him about whether he picked up another weapon where Booker was shot, and he said he did. I'm sure it was his rifle that shot Booker and not my rifle."

"That is good news, sort of. It means that you did not shoot Booker, and that must be a great relief to you."

"It will be."

"Okay." Tatiana walked away but an hour later returned with a pen and note pad and coffee in her hand. "Andre, let's talk about something important; nothing about the Deep State. Tell me about your mother."

Andre laughed.

"I don't remember much," he said. "I remember we went to church on Sunday. Every Sunday she had something cooking in the stove to wake us up. All five of us had to sit together on the first row at the church. She always put money in the offering. My father directed the choir and we watched him. We had to watch him. There was nothing else we could do but sit in our seats. I remember my brother Ben getting up and leaving once on an Easter because the last song took so long, he couldn't stand sitting there any longer. He got in trouble for that."

"Can you tell me about the fire at your home?"

"I remember being in the rooms where everyone else was and then looking out the window. My older brother was on his horse and he was motioning for me to come outside. It was my turn to go out and help graze the horses. We would usually take them up the street where there was good grass. I didn't want to go. It was hot that day. I remember we had an electric fan that turned off for no reason just a few minutes before I left. I went out and got on the horse and looked at the roof and saw smoke coming from the shingles. We were all downstairs. When I went outside and got on the horse, I saw smoke coming from the roof. I said, 'Franklin, look!' He jumped off his horse and went in the side door yelling, 'Everyone get out of the house! The house is on fire! My sister said she was taking a bath at the time and had to get out in a hurry."

"Your aunt started the fire?"

"That's what we think. She used matches to light the birthday cake in the attic and we think those matches may have started the fire. Then for years she put the blame on Booker and me. She is a strange aunt. The story goes that that Booker's uncle took both me and Booker away from her when we were young for some reason and he raised us after that. She never got over that."

Chapter 32

⸙

"NICE NEW PAINTED NEWSROOM," OLIVER said.

The entire newsroom was refurbished and everyone had new typewriters, new desks, new everything. All of the reporters were dressed well per Nelms' wishes. The staff came to Nelms' office for the regular Monday morning meeting.

"How's Tatiana?" he asked.

"She's fine. Nothing serious," Oliver said. "She is in the hospital for observation. It shouldn't be long."

"That's good," Nelms said. "Have you heard about the immigrants flowing over the border from Louisiana?"

"They're coming in droves. Almost two million this year, the most ever. The federal government refuses to control the border. Mostly in Texas, Arizona. Then they are sent here. The Texas and Florida governors are then sending them to Washington, D.C., New York, Amy's Vineyard where the elite of the elite green voters live. These are the so called "sanctuary cities." When fifty immigrants arrived at Amy's Vineyard the rich green people freaked out and demanded that the military intervene and after twenty-four hours they were deported to a military base. The green voters want open borders but want the orange states to take care of the immigrants."

"Why aren't they going through the normal immigration process, like through Ellis Island," Nelms asked.

"There's a theory," Oliver said.

"I'm listening."

"It's so fantastic that I don't think you'll believe it. Young Andre here has been investigating it. He has a source."

"Tell me," Nelms said.

"The immigrants coming to Alabama have one thing in common: They are communists fleeing the Soviet Union."

"Do you blame them?" Nelms said.

"No. My source tells me that the immigrants are flooding Alabama intentionally to change the voting pattern of the state," Andre said.

"How do you know this?" asked Nelms.

"My source. I can't say who he is," Andre said.

"I respect that. What does he say?"

"He says that what is going on is a mass migration ordered by the Deep State, an organization run by someone named Zoros. The Russian state is run by Aleksandr Putaineue, who reports to the Deep State and Zoros. He wants the immigrants to be able to vote in the next election without having identification. It is considered racist to do that."

"To ask them to identify who they are when they vote – whether they are American citizens and are entitled to vote is racist?" Nelms asked.

"It is now," Andre said.

"For what reason? Why is there a mass migration?"

"To take over the United States."

Nelms laughed at this.

"My source says there are communists in the federal government," Andre said.

"Are you referring to the House Un-American Activities Committee? I never really believed there were communists in the government or in Hollywood," Nelms said.

"My source says there are. He says there is a Soviet spy named Alger Hiss who worked in the State Department. He says that Whittaker Chambers, who was a communist party member, identified Alger Hiss as a spy. People believe that the Soviets are infiltrating the U.S. government to form some kind of invisible political influence. Congressman Richard Nixon on that committee is going to prove that he is a spy."

"That committee is a witch hunt," Nelms said.

"Mr. Nelms, have you ever heard of the Deep State?" asked Andre.

"That's a joke."

"My source says Zoros has already taken control of some news organizations."

Nelms laughed. "Zoros, you say? And what is Zoros's plan?"

"To flood the states with millions of communist immigrants and place them strategically so that they will tilt the voting pattern to vote for more socialistic reforms and turn the states into a voting block that will govern all of the states. The U.S. will slowly become communist. Alabama is an orange state."

"Orange state?" asked Nelms. "What do you mean by orange state?"

"It's a term that the Deep State uses to define each of the states. The orange states are the most religious and conservative states that believe in less taxes and less government. They are pro gun rights."

"What is the purpose of this so called 'Deep State'"?

"The Deep State wants all states to be green, meaning more socialistic, more solar energy, the elimination of fossil fuels, less free speech, they also believe in a woman's right to abort a baby up to the point of birth."

"I see. What happens if you have a state that is neither orange nor green?" asked Nelms.

"That is called a brown state," Oliver said.

They all laughed.

"I know those sounds funny, but it isn't," said Andre. "I'm still investigating it so don't take this word for word. My source says that the GCJ, EPK, DJB, and PMJ are already part of the Deep State."

"And what is the GCJ, EPK, DJB, and PMY?" asked Nelms.

"They are secret government agencies," said Andre.

Oliver smiled. Nelms didn't know what to say.

Andre continued. "My source says that there is a two-tiered justice system run by Deep State operatives at the GCJ and the EPK who target politicians they don't agree with. They exonerate before investigate and take down politicians that they don't agree with."

"Ok, I've heard everything now. Andre, check out your source. He's playing you."

Chapter 33

OLIVER WAS WORKING LATE AT the newspaper. Cub went home but decided to go back to work. He saw Oliver working late.

"Hello, Cub, what are you doing here this late?"

"I have some stories to send out. Oliver, I want to go to South Africa."

"Haven't been there. I went to South America. One of my first articles made me $650."

"If I paid our expenses would you go?"

"Why do you want to go to South Africa?"

"All my life I wanted to make a trip like that."

"Are you trying to get away or get away from yourself?"

"No," Cub said.

"Did you and Brandeesha break up?"

"No."

"You can't get away from yourself by going to another country. Let's go get a drink."

They walked down the streets of Birmingham and could hear the jazz sound of a saxophone playing. People were still on the street, walking, talking, sitting at outdoor tables, drinking, enjoying the outside. The bars and restaurants were open until 4 a.m.

"This is a good bar, lots of liquor," Cub said.

They walked in and ordered a drink at the bar.

"I want an absinthe," Oliver said.

"Same as he's having," Cub said. The bartender nodded and went to make the drinks.

"What is an absinthe?" Cub asked.

"It's a green spirit made from wormwood, green anise, and sweet fennel. It was created by a Swiss physician in the mid-19th century. They say it makes the heart grow stronger, but studies show that the wormwood mixed with alcohol does not make the heart grow fonder."

"Man, you are some crazy dude."

The bartender brought the drinks.

"Okay, so here's for making the heart grow stronger," Cub said, taking the drink.

"Is it good?" Oliver asked.

"Not sure about good, but better than what we made in the hills," Cub said. "My father could make the whiskey so strong he could use it to run his car."

"I bet he did."

"Do you know that in ten years we might be dead? I still want to go to South Africa."

"Stay here. There's nothing wrong with Birmingham," Oliver said.

"I'm sick of Birmingham," Cub said.

"I have to get back to the paper and send off a story by the wire," Oliver said.

"Just like the war," Cub said.

"Yes, just like the war."

Oliver and Cub went back to the paper. Cub went to sleep on the couch in the lobby. He had nothing to do and didn't want to go home.

Oliver woke him up.

"Was I asleep?"

"You snored. Let's go to the Café Birmingham."

On the way over, through the streets of downtown Birmingham, Cub looked around and said, "Oliver, what are we doing?"

"I don't know," Oliver said. "I don't send stories by wire and I don't need an aperitif and I don't drink absinthe. This is not Birmingham."

"Something strange is going on," Cub said.

"I know what it is," Oliver said.

"What is it?"

"It's Tatiana."

"What about her?"

"This is just a dream of hers, and we shouldn't be in it."

"I'm not following you."

"This is not real," Oliver said.

"How can that be?" Cub asked.

"I don't know."

"What is causing this?"

"Ever since Tatiana went to the church to interview the nun, Sister Camille, things changed. The nun put some idea in her mind that the universe brings you want you want or think about. Like there is a big secret out there that no one knows about. They call it the attraction law; the world is nothing but energy waves at its core."

"Man, do you realize what you're saying?"

"I know how ridiculous it sounds. We could not be in her dreams but she must believe what the nun is saying, and it's working."

"She really is a wonder woman," Cub said. "What is causing this?"

"Remember Book Call?"

"Yes. So what?"

"Did you pick any books?"

"Yes, *Grilling in Alabama*. I haven't grilled anything yet and I'm sure not dreaming about grilling."

"You see, you haven't read it, so nothing is happening to you."

"I know what this is. This is a scene out of *The Sun Also Rises*. She is reading that book and we are in her dream."

Cub stopped. "She's placing us in her dream in place of the real characters in the book? How is that possible?"

"It's not possible. This is just a dream."

"How do we get out of here?" Cub asked.

"We wake her up." Oliver said. "I have to leave."

"If you don't, we're going to be tired in the morning," Cub said to Oliver as he began to run down the sidewalk to the hospital. Oliver went to the hospital and Tatiana was asleep. Sure enough, *The Sun Also Rises* was open on her bed.

Thank goodness she didn't finish it. I could have been stuck in this dream all night, Oliver thought.

He put the book on the desk by her bed and left.

Oliver went back downtown and decided to stop in Le Gabriel. He sat at one of the tables outside on the sidewalk.

Then he saw Tatiana walking by or someone who looked like her. She came over to his table.

"What do you want to drink?" Oliver asked.

She didn't recognize Oliver.

"Ricard," she said, sitting down.

"я Я журналист (I am a journalist)," Tatiana said in Russian. "A Ricard," she said to the waiter in English.

"That's not good for young reporters," Oliver said. "Do you like Birmingham?"

"I don't know. I don't know this town," Tatiana said.

"Do you want to go somewhere else?" Oliver asked.

"Yes. Are you going to buy me dinner?"

Oliver hailed a horse-drawn cab and it took them to another bar that was open.

"Are you sick?" asked Tatiana.

"Yes."

"How did you get sick?"

"From the war. What's your name?"

"Tatiana. Tatiana the Great."

Oliver laughed. "Tatiana the Great. Cool. Have you been talking to Brandeesha?"

"I would never talk to her."

"Is Tatiana a Russian name?"

"Yes."

"I detest the Russians," Oliver said.

"я тоже ("Me, too). They are influencing this country. I want all communists out of the country."

"Let's stop here," Oliver said.

They went into the restaurant. At the table were Nelms, Cub, Brandeesha, John, and Betty.

"Oliver!" Nelms said, raising a glass of champagne.

"That's a friend calling me," Oliver said.

"My, my, what have we here? I do believe I am seeing a woman of the night," Brandeesha said, referring to Tatiana.

"That's Tatiana. She's a swell girl," Cub said.

"Are you going to ask me to dance?" Brandeesha asked Oliver.

"No," Oliver said.

"He's mad about me," Brandeesha said of Oliver.

"Don't be a damned fool," Oliver said.

"Oh, darling," Brandeesha said, stroking Oliver's head.

Tatiana looked on and said nothing.

Then a white nightclub entertainer with two white women came on stage. A waiter came with a bottle of champagne.

"What have we here?" asked Nelms as the entertainers came to the stage. "Who is that white dude?"

"We are going to do a tune or two from my most orchestral work." The singer waited for a response. One person whistled.

"See? Orchestral and obscure."

The audience laughed.

"And a one ... "

The music began on the sound of one. The singer motioned to stop.

"We rehearsed that so well ..."

Laughter from the audience.

He started over.

"And a one ... "

The music started again as he said the words.

"It doesn't start on one," said the singer. Then he laughed awkwardly and said, "And a one ... two, uh ... one ... two, three ... " and the music began. The orchestra, which included strings and horns, played an introduction and then the singer began to sing:

Hello, it's me ...

"I thought you were going home. Remember what we talked about?" Cub said as the singing continued.

"Yes, but I found Tatiana," Oliver said. "She doesn't recognize me."

"What?" Cub asked. "Are we still in a dream?"

"Yes. Have you ever heard of music like that before?"

Cub turned around to listen. "What did they say that white boy's name is?"

"Something like Runt or Runderen," Brandeesha said.

"Never heard of him but that white boy can sing," Nelms said.

Seeing you …

Brandeesha popped the cork off a champagne bottle and the champagne went over everyone. They laughed and moved away from the champagne.

"It went pop," she said.

"That's what this sounds like – pop," Cub said. "I'm going to call that pop music."

Then the singer told the audience to sing the words: "Sing the words."

"This generation of kids is going to hell," Nelms said.

The audience began singing the words.

Think of me

"Let's see where this takes us," Oliver said.

"I'm fine with this. I hope I can get up in the morning and go to work. I'm going to be really tired. Go, Tatiana!" Cub said, lifting a glass of champagne.

"I need another," Brandeesha said.

"And another," Nelms said.

"Another," Oliver said.

"Who are your friends?" Tatiana asked Oliver.

"Don't you know? Just journalists," he said, looking at her. She didn't recognize any of them.

"Who is the skinny girl sponging off everyone at the table?" Tatiana said, referring to Brandeesha.

"She works at the newspaper … don't you know?"

"I would never know her."

"I guess you wouldn't," Oliver said, smiling to himself and enjoying whatever he was in – either reality or dream, or Tatiana's dream.

The singer ended his song with the last words "Thinks of me... Think of me..." and said: "You only get one of those in a lifetime."

Oliver and Tatiana continued talking and then Tatiana left the table and went to the bar to talk to other men.

Oliver left, and on his way out he gave the head waiter twenty dollars and said: "If she asks about me, then give her this twenty-dollar bill. If she doesn't, then you can have it."

"I think you will lose your money," said the waiter.

Oliver left the restaurant around 10 p.m. after the first song from the band. He decided to check into a local hotel instead of going home. He went to his room and sat on the edge of the bed. He pulled an envelope from his coat pocket. He forgot to open it up. It was an invitation from his mother for a surprise dinner party with Tatiana's parents. They were coming to see them. Maryellen wrote that she hoped Tatiana was pregnant and that they could announce the news that evening. Oliver smiled. It would be up to Tatiana to do that if that were the case. A few minutes later the concierge rang his room.

"Excuse me, Mr. Smith, but there is some kind of woman here at the front desk asking for you."

"Send her up," Oliver said.

When Tatiana arrived, she said: "Oliver, it was a silly thing that I did."

"What?"

"Leaving you like that. Let's go back."

They exited the hotel. "I'm checking out," Oliver said.

"I will have to charge you for the night," said the concierge.

They went back to the club and the band was still playing. Nelms had left, and Brandeesha and Cub were at the table. Cub walked over to them. "I thought you left," he said.

"I did but I came back," Oliver said.

"I can see that. How have you been?" Cub said, introducing himself to Tatiana. Tatiana didn't respond.

Oliver and Tatiana went to another table and sat down.

"He brought me to Birmingham," Tatiana said to Oliver. "He offered me two thousand to go to Montgomery. I told him I knew too many people in Montgomery."

"You mean Cub?" Oliver asked.

"Yes. He owns a number of clubs in Alabama. Some kind of syndicate."

Oliver laughed to himself and looked at Tatiana. Cub was really Shorty Miller who had been a shoe shine man and a war journalist.

"Don't look at me like that. He knows I'm with you tonight."

Then the singer and his band and singers returned to the stage for another song. The introduction began and he sang:

It was late last night …

"I have to go," Tatiana said.

"So soon?" Oliver asked.

"Cub is driving me out for breakfast in the morning. Do you want to go?"

"I have to be up early in the morning," Oliver said.

Oliver walked her to the door of the club, and then a horse-drawn carriage came by and stopped. He kissed her. "Take her to the hospital," he told the cab driver.

"Goodbye, darling. I will see you at the hospital," Oliver said as Tatiana stepped inside the carriage.

Tatiana looked out the window and said: "No reason to be an ass."

Chapter 34

Oliver went to the hospital to sleep on a couch in Tatiana's room. In the morning, the noise of nurses and breakfast carts and commotion filled the room.

"Hello, it's me. I've thought about us for a long, long time," he said, looking at Tatiana as she opened her eyes.

"Can we go?" she asked.

"I don't know. Tatiana, I was up all night. I couldn't go to sleep. Would you happen to know why?"

"Not a clue. I slept. I was in deep sleep. You wouldn't believe what I dreamed last night."

"Try me."

"I dreamed that I met you and Cub and Nelms at a bar. I met you at a café and we went to a club in a horse-drawn cab. That was very strange for Birmingham."

"What were you reading last night?"

"*The Sun Also Rises*."

"Don't you see?"

"What?"

"You dreamed about what you were reading. But what's different about your dream is that you are bringing us into it. I felt like I was there with you. Tatiana, you are a '*Wonder Woman*' and whatever you are doing could be dangerous, really, for other people."

"You couldn't be there. It was my dream."

"I was there. So was Cub, Brandeesha, and Nelms."

"No. They couldn't have been," said Tatiana.

"I know that, but I was there."

"Brandeesha was her usual pathetic self. She called me a woman of the night."

"That was funny, and the limousine, too. Nice touch there. This law of vibrations you are talking about, there is something to it."

"Yes. It is like I saw the light."

"You saw the light? What is the light?"

"The light represents God."

"This is deep for me," said Oliver.

"Yes, me, too. I was in a deep state."

"A deep state?"

"Oh, that stupid phrase again. Stop saying that to me. A deep state of sleep is what I mean."

"Do you believe that the world brings us what we think about?" asked Oliver.

"After last night I'm beginning to," Tatiana said. "Sometimes I think that these dreams are real. You can't tell what is reality and what is a dream."

"You're not serious?"

"Some say that the difference between a dream and reality is truth. Reality is true. Dreams are not true. Like there are two worlds. Your right hand is reality and your left hand is a dream."

"Interesting."

"Dreams are escapes, a longing to be somewhere else. There are no borders or limits."

"And what is reality?" Oliver asked.

"Reality is cold. There are no heroes. Just people who are torn or torn down. All heroes are stripped bare until they are a myth."

"Wow, this is deep."

"But in a dream, heroes awake."

"Which do you prefer? Reality or a dream?" asked a curious Oliver.

"That is a hard one. Reality is authentic and sometimes it is desirable because it is reality and is the truth. But a dream begins at the edge of the desired world where truth becomes uncertain after that. In a dream anyone can do anything."

"Spoken like a poet. It will be interesting to see what happens when man can merge the two." There was a pause and then Oliver said: "What has come over you?"

"It's that nun. It has to be. She came to visit me."

"When?"

"Last night. As soon as I get out of here, I'm going to expose her for the fraud that she is," Tatiana said. "Nuns are to be quiet and peaceful. She is promoting some type of thinking that the universe brings you what you think or ask for. That is not religion. That is a false religion. Oh Oliver, there is something strangely odd going on in this world."

"She and that church rescued Andre, so I would hate for you to do something harmful to them."

"Oh, so we pass on legitimate stories now?"

"Yes, when they could do great harm."

"That's for the public to decide. We have an obligation to tell the truth. That nun is saying the universe brings you what you ask for, like there is some kind of 'law of attraction' out there."

"Didn't Jesus say ask anything in his name and he will bring it to you?"

"Now that is unfair. You are siding with her."

"No, I'm not. That is right out of the Bible. It's just that for the last 2,000 years no one understood what it meant."

"That is exactly what she says. She has gotten to you," Tatiana said.

"No, she hasn't. I haven't even talked to her. What you are describing is in the Bible, but I just don't remember it being taught in the same way. Christ said to ask anything in his name and he will give it to us if we believe. It is that simple. We are all 'gods.' Don't you see what is going on? We are made of God; that means God is within us. So, when we dream or visualize, then that imagination really is the God power given to us. We can turn our dreams into reality. All we have to do is believe and ask for it in Jesus' name."

"Why, I never," Tatiana said. "Oliver, you don't sound like yourself. I never imagined you as ..."

"As what?"

"As religious. I'm not religious. I mean, we go to church sometimes. We pray. I pray. Nothing happens. Jesus doesn't talk to me. I quite frankly wish he did so I could experience what everyone else is experiencing. Everyone else talks to God but not me. They tell me about how they pray to Jesus and they have this relationship with him. I think they call that 'mental illness.'" [24]

"I wouldn't repeat that."

"Why?"

"Because a lot of readers are religious and would be offended." Then Oliver looked at the table besides Tatiana's bed.

"What is this?" Oliver asked looking at the brown envelope on the desk next to her hospital bed.

"That? It's the Griddle Iron script."

"Oh yes. I threw mine away. Nothing like fake news in a fake script. The question is who sent all of the scripts?"

Tatiana said nothing.

Chapter 35

TATIANA'S POWER BEGAN TO AFFECT others. She saw Sister Camille as someone determined to help the poor and homeless around the church in a different way than anyone could have imagined. The nun spoke to an employment agency and asked that it send homeless people with no jobs to St. Peter's. She wanted to see if there was a way to help them.

"What are you planning to do?" asked Sister Laurie.

"I want to know if poverty is a state of mind," said Sister Camille. "Mankind is proving the power of conscious thought, feelings, and belief. The entire universe runs on the concept of belief. Belief is a power, an emotion, a vibration. Love is a power, an emotion. Love is the answer."

The room was filled with the most penniless and homeless you could imagine. Tatiana arrived late. She looked in, and Sister Camille, Sister Laurie and Sister Aude were at the front of the room. The only available seat was on the third row, where no one was seated. Tatiana walked to the front, grinning like the cat that had eaten the canary.

"Sorry," she said awkwardly as she sat down.

"You don't need to apologize," said Sister Camille.

There was chatter in the back. Around forty people, white and black, began to enter and filled in the seats.

"Welcome," said Sister Camille.

"Welcome to our church," said Sister Laurie. "Thank you for coming. Come and take a seat and listen to Sister Camille."

"We're glad that you are here. It is good to be co-creators," said Sister Camille.

No one said anything.

"I suppose you are wondering why you were asked to come here."

"Yeah, I've heard about what you have been saying to the people," said a homeless man. "Offering anything you want if you just ask for it, then, bang, there it is."

"That's not what we're saying," said Sister Camille. "We would like to introduce a new concept. You are the creator of your own reality. I am calling on you to expand and to add to your reality of the greater source. God through Jesus Christ. Your life is a reflection of your thoughts, feelings and emotions. We want you to create a new reality and when you can combine all three of these you can move mountains."

"Yeah," said another man. "I want to know if this is just hocus-pocus."

Laughter.

"There is no reason to complain of injustices or why you do not have what you want. You can have what you want by asking Jesus and believing," said Sister Camille.

"If that's true, then why did we go through that Depression?"

"We didn't have to," said Sister Camille.

"Right. You're a snake oil vendor."

Gasps in the room.

"How about me? I can't walk," said a blind lady in a wheelchair. It was the same lady in Mountain Springs whom Andre would see growing up.

"Jesus healed many like you just because they believed," Sister Camille said. "There is no reason to talk about things that make you feel bad or are not good."

"This is b.s."

"You don't have to be here and have the food and housing if you don't want it. If you want to leave you can leave now."

No one left.

"Why did no one leave?" asked Sister Camille. "Because you held out for the chance. The chance that we are correct. That is belief forming. What if you truly believed that you could have whatever you want and the world brings it to you?"

No response.

"If you want to be part of this, you have to do everything that I say. If you cannot do that, then you need to leave now. We cannot have anyone in this group who doubts this program and does not believe. Is everyone ready, or do you need to leave?"

No one responded.

Tatiana was grimacing while taking notes. She was going to expose Sister Camille. She wrote down in her notes: Snake oil vendor *par excellence*, a total fraud.

Sister Camille began. "Let me read this verse to you in the Bible. It is John 15:1-8 where Jesus said to his disciples:

> *I am the true vine, and my Father is the vine grower.*
>
> *He takes away every branch in me that does not bear fruit, and everyone that does he prunes so that it bears more fruit. You are already pruned because of the word that I spoke to you. Remain in me, as I remain in you. Just as a branch cannot bear fruit on its own*

unless it remains on the vine, so neither can you unless you remain in me. I am the vine, you are the branches.

Whoever remains in me and I in him will bear much fruit, because without me you can do nothing.

Anyone who does not remain in me will be thrown out like a branch and wither; people will gather them and throw them into a fire and they will be burned.

If you remain in me and my words remain in you, ask for whatever you want and it will be done for you.

By this is my Father glorified, that you bear much fruit and become my disciples.

"Now I want to tell you something that I have known and come to realize through the teachings of Jesus. There is a golden thread that runs through all of his teachings that makes them work for those who sincerely accept and apply them."

"And what is that?" asked a man.

"Belief."

The group groaned.

"We've heard that," said one of the homeless men.

"I thought we were going to have dinner here," said another man.

Laughter.

"Believe this," said another. He put his hand under his armpit and pulled it down. It made a disgusting sound that jolted the room.

Everyone reacted.

"Oh, my God," said Sister Aude. Sister Laurie and Sister Aude looked nervously at each other, not sure what to do.

"Sister Camille, this is not working out. I think we should leave," said Sister Laurie.

"You got nothing that we don't know," said another man.

"Belief can work miracles. There is power in believing what Jesus said," Sister Camille continued.

"And what did Jesus say?" said another.

"He said that to those who have, more will be given, and to those who have none more will be taken away."

"That's just great. I have nothing, so nothing else can be taken from me," said the old blind lady in the wheelchair.

"Yeah," said one.

"Yeah, we got nothing. That's why we came."

"I have three babies to feed and no money, no home, no husband," said a lady with her children. One was an infant who started to cry.

"If you have God in your heart, then God will deliver more to you. If you do not, then more will be taken away and will be given to others who believe. What he is saying is that you create your own world based on what you believe. What do you believe now?" asked Sister Camille to the first homeless man.

"I think: Where is my next meal?"

"That is what I mean. You don't know where it is, so you think you don't have it, so you have nothing. Now I want all of you to believe that you will all have meals three times a day for the next two weeks. Now do you believe it?"

"Yes," said one.

"If you don't believe it, then you can leave right now."

The room became quiet. No one left.

"Do you all believe it?"

"Yes," said another.

"We are all in agreement?"

"Yes," said another.

"That is good. All of you will have free housing for the time being at the campus until you can move on. You will have three meals, new clothes, a place to sleep. All of you will be given a spa treatment, haircuts, manicures, pedicures – including the men."

Laughter.

"That wasn't supposed to be funny," said Sister Camille.

"A pedicure?" asked one homeless man.

There were groans in the room.

"If you want to be part of this you will all participate. You will be given new clothes. All of you. Are we in agreement?"

Wow, Tatiana thought to herself.

"So now I want to go around the room and ask each one of you what you truly want in your life. Then I will ask that you believe that you will receive it," Sister Camille said. "Sit and meditate for it, and when you believe that you will receive it, raise your hand, and go over to the corner where you will be measured. You will have a fine dinner tonight before retiring to your rooms. Tell me when you believe."

"I believe right now," said one of the men immediately.

"What do you want?" she asked.

"A good-paying job," he said.

"That is too general. I want you to tell me the exact job."

"A stockbroker."

"Where?"

"At one of the places downtown."

"Do you have any training?"

"No."

"So why would they hire you if you have no training?"

"I don't know. You didn't ask me that."

"So, what does it take to be a stockbroker?"

"An education."

"Where do you get that?"

"At school, I guess."

"Where is a school?"

"I have no money for school."

"Do you believe that you can have an education if you want it?"

"Yes."

"Then you have come to the right place. You are going to St. Peter's College starting tomorrow."

Sister Camille went on to tell each person in the room that his or her condition of poverty was a state of mind. She said that they could decide their future in their own mind by bringing their imagination into the real world. This was a difficult concept for many of them.

"You imagine it, dream it, and believe in it. You need to live in the world that you imagine for yourselves as if you already have it. Surround yourself with your answer."

The group slowly left the room.

Tatiana couldn't help going up to Sister Camille and asking, "Do you think Father Webster will like what you are doing here?"

"What do you mean?" asked Sister Camille.

"Oh, come on," Tatiana said. "Throwing all these ideas around in their head. Giving them false hope. Practicing white magic. You know you could really harm them by raising their expectations unrealistically like this. Some of them are disabled and cannot walk."

"How did Jesus heal the sick?" Sister Camille snapped back at her. "St. Peter, St. Paul ... they all healed."

Chapter 36

"I DON'T KNOW, OLIVER," SAID the young nurse being played by Tatiana, in her dreams. Tatiana was thin, sexy, and beautiful in her Navy uniform. Her dream was quite a change from the real Army uniform she wore in Europe during World War II. Instead of traveling with the Canadian Army through Rouen to Paris, Tatiana was in the Solomon Islands in 1942 where the Navy was building an airfield on Norfolk Island shortly before the Battle of the Coral Sea.

James Michener's *Tales of the South Pacific*, being Tatiana's next book, involved a white nurse, Nellie Forbush from Arkansas, who was attracted to Emile De Becque, an older Frenchman who had left Marseille, France, twenty-six years earlier after killing a man. In French Polynesia, De Becque had built a fortune and was free of the law.

De Beque was being played by Oliver who was seeking to convince Tatiana to remain with him on the island along with his children. Tatiana was not aware that Oliver had children. She was totally surprised by his revelation. Oliver tended to drop bombs in Tatiana's lap with new revelations just as things seemed to going so swell between them. After dinner one night he dropped eight bombs in her lap. Why not? It was World War II and bombs were being dropped on the islands. Tatiana was used to bombs in war, but not in love.

Oliver played his fictional character well. He wanted to be a foreign correspondent and remaining in Paris after the war like another World War II journalist, Ollie Stewart, an African American who had done just that. But Oliver went home to his where his parents lived and they wanted Oliver to be married and to have a family. In Tatiana's dream, Oliver was now an expatriate of France living in French Polynesia with his children and he would find the right mother for them.

Tatiana and Oliver had a wonderful dinner together with champagne, appetizers, white wine, fish, shrimp, and lobster that Oliver and his workers had caught. Anyone dining at Oliver's home would be impressed by the finest of cuisine.

"Tatiana, je voudrais que vous rencontriez ma famille," Oliver said in a French voice.

"I can conjugate a few verbs. I see that you used the formal 'vous' for me. I thought we knew each other well by now."

"We do."

"I didn't know you had a family."

"These are mine," he said. Oliver had all eight of his children come into a living room area after dinner to meet Tatiana. Then they left.

"Where is their mother?"

"There are four mothers."

"You have eight children by four mothers?"

"Yes. I lived as I could. I have no regrets."

"Where are their mothers?"

"I have no idea where they are now."

Tatiana said nothing in response.

"I am older than you. We can have children. I can arrange for you to travel to Australia where they can be born and to return here, and when I die you can take them back to America, if you like. I have money."

"Let me see. You have eight children from four different women who were not your wives because you didn't marry them. You are older than me and we can have children. Then as a bonus, I can travel to Australia where they can be born. Then I can return here to be with you. Then, when you die, I can afford to take them back to America? Is that your offer?"

"Yes, Tatiana," Oliver said in a soft French tone. He walked up and sat next to her and placed his hand on hers.

"Well Oliver, I am so impressed. I have never had an offer like that before," Tatiana said.

"Then you will stay? I can teach you French."

"Now their mothers were …?"

"Tonkinese, Filipino, Japanese …"

"And you loved their mothers?"

"Of course, Tatiana. I loved all of their mothers."

"Is this the part where I'm supposed to become racist and angry because you had children with a Tonkinese, Filipino, Japanese, and whoever else?"

"Yes, you are supposed to be upset," Oliver said.

"Let's see, on this island in French Polynesia the Tonkinese are some of the most beautiful women in the world – and you being the Frenchman that you are; you are supposed to live by the standards of the Catholic Church. Are you to remain celibate on this island until you find that one person to marry after an enchanted evening? Is this the part where I run out and go back to the hospital?"

"Yes," Oliver said. "I know it is silly by today's standards, but this is how the book reads and you know how you cannot deviate from the book."

Tatiana left in her two-door jeep and drove down the mountain. At the hospital she was approached by the Catholic nuns Sister Laurie and Sister Aude. Tatiana was crying.

"You were visiting the Frenchman again, weren't you?" asked Sister Laurie. "You would leave a life in Arkansas for a life here and you might not return again."

"But he is rich, and the mountains …," Tatiana said. "It is nothing like Little Rock. But I can't get over his …"

"His what?" asked Sister Aude.

"It's nothing."

"Love is universal. It is here in Polynesia as well. Try not to judge him too harshly. Solomon had over a thousand wives," said Sister Laurie.

"I'm not going back to him!" said Tatiana.

"Love will enable you to move mountains," said Sister Aude. "A man or woman can move a mountain by moving the smallest pebble."

"Go to your Frenchman," said Sister Laurie.

Tatiana woke up in the hospital.

"Oliver, I know you want children. You told me you did."

"What? I didn't say anything."

"You didn't have to. I think you want a lot of kids. I bet you want eight children. Don't you?"

"I haven't thought that far."

"You could at least be subtle about it and not spring that on me so suddenly. If it weren't for me you would be traveling all over the world having kids with all the women in the South Pacific. I bet you would like to have a thousand wives, wouldn't you"?"

"What is going on with you? Where did that come from?" "How much longer do I have to stay in the hospital? I think you are keeping here on purpose."

"Not much longer I hope. Maybe I should remove all of your reading material."

"I'm taking a shower."

"A shower?" Oliver asked.

"I'm going to wash that man right out of my hair."

Chapter 37

TATIANA TOOK A SHOWER AND then got back in bed.

"You know, Oliver, I think I have a skit for the Griddle Iron Show that Betty will like about one of the books."

"She will like it as long as it has to do with Broadway."

"You know I really don't need to be here. I'm not sick, and I'm wasting my time reading when I can be working."

"It won't be much longer."

"I need to go home. This hospital is making me dream. Maybe it's the medication."

"What kind of dreams?"

"All kinds. The state has been taken over by the Deep State. There's a lady named Jill Rodderman, whom I have never heard of, and the nun that Andre goes to see a lot is trying to cure homelessness through some kind of mind trickery. It is all ridiculous."

"That is the Griddle Iron script," Oliver said. "Except for the nun. That part is new. Where did that come from?"

"I feel like I am experimenting with newfound powers. I have to be careful what I think or read," Tatiana said. "I have to filter. If I think about something, it comes. So, if I am thinking about something that I really hate, then it comes. If there are things I want, then they come, too. I'm okay with the good stuff coming but not the bad stuff."

"So, don't think about it."

"It's not that simple. You can't just not think about something."

"Don't you see? You just hit on the answer. The key is to be in control of your own thoughts and to place things you don't want to talk about outside of your mind. That's all you have to do."

"This is all due to Sister Camille. She is a sorcerer. My life was perfect until she came along. She is the one who disrupted all of it. What is that Catholic Church doing up there in Protestant land?"

"She isn't disrupting your life."

"Yes, she is."

"Okay, so what is happening? Let's go to the heart of it and find a solution."

"Oliver, I've learned that there is no past and no future. There is only now. When you break the universe down to the smallest components, everything is a vibration. Thoughts are vibrations, so if we think something, we change our life, so there really could be multiple lives that we lead out there."

"Where are you getting all of this?"

"It happened after my visit to St. Peter's. That nun. She is something else. If you wondered why Andre was saying those ridiculous things during his trial about the white nuns and the black priests – that has to be tied to his delusional thinking of the world bringing to us what we think about. Watch what he says and talks about. It is all about getting what you want by focusing on it."

"But that is how you get what you want. You focus on it. There is nothing wrong with that. That is how the universe works."

"Oliver what if I told you that man is evolving. After a million years on Earth, the mind is developing new powers. We can't travel in outer space because there is no atmosphere, but what if I said you can travel within this universe through other dimensions by using your thoughts and imagination?"

"I would say you could get a job with the National Advisory Committee for Aeronautics."

"You're silly. Listen to me. Our minds are developing powers that enable us to do things by thinking about them. In other words, if we wanted to build a building, a lot of people would have to put the building together with bricks and mortar and labor. Now we can project thoughts toward the universe and can build the building in our own mind and the atomic particles will come together for us so we don't have to manually do anything. That is the future of mankind."

"That is way out there. Man has been dreaming of doing that for centuries. Are you some kind of wonder woman?"

"Yes, I'm Tatiana the Great," Tatiana said with a devilish smile.

"That's what Brandeesha calls you."

"I know."

"It's just your reading. You are being influenced by the books you're reading, which is good because if you are dreaming it, then you are experiencing it and then you can really get to know a subject."

"Did you know that Mark Twain wrote a book about Joan of Arc?" Tatiana said.

"I did. Is that what you are reading now? He wrote that anonymously in installments in a magazine and it was later released as a book."

"Tom Sawyer and Huckleberry Finn meet Joan of Arc," Tatiana said.

"Remember our date in Paris during the war?"

"Yes."

"You mentioned Joan of Arc on that date. Where she was burned at the stake in Rouen, France, must have affected you.

That's why you picked that book over the others. You were attracted to it. The law of attraction does work."

"Maybe you're right."

"All these experiences are influencing you, and you're having dreams. They might make an interesting book. You should write them down and try to make some kind of story about them. Your own kind of private war, like Tatiana's War."

"This is so silly. I'm going to sleep."

"Okay. Don't get burned at the stake during your dream."

"If I get burned at the stake, you will be the first to know. In fact, you can rescue me, Lancelot."

"That was Camelot. Joan of Arc didn't get rescued, but I will do that."

"Please do."

Chapter 38

A t work Oliver answered the buzzer on his desk.

"Mr. Smith, Mr. Nelms needs to see you and Mr. Miller in his office," Brandeesha said.

"Thank you."

Oliver went to Nelms' office. Cub was walking in. "I wonder what this is about?" Cub asked.

"Have a seat," Nelms said. "How is Tatiana?"

"She's doing fine," Oliver said while taking a chair.

"Good. Anyone want coffee?"

"Not me," Cub said.

"Me, neither," Oliver said.

"I don't know how to say this, but let me ask you: What did each of you do last night?"

"I slept at the hospital," Oliver said.

"Okay. Did anyone have a dream recently?"

No one said anything.

"No one is willing to answer?" asked Nelms. "I see."

There was a pause.

"I did," Cub said.

"What was it?"

"This won't get me in trouble at work will it?"

"No."

"This was my dream. I was at a bar with you and Brandeesha, then here comes Oliver and Tatiana. Then some singer, maybe it was jazz, although I've never heard anything like that in my life. He had trouble getting the orchestra to start off on time."

"Interesting dream," Nelms said. Then Nelms turned to Oliver. "Tell me about your dreams."

No one said anything.

Then Oliver spoke up. "I had the same dream."

"You did?" asked Nelms. "I thought I was crazy. This sounds fantastic, but how could we all have the same dream?"

"I don't know but I think I might be able to explain it," Oliver said. "Ever since Tatiana went out to see the nun at St. Peter's, she has been having dreams. She says that the universe brings you what you think about or ask for. Your imagination is a god-like force within you that enables you to bring what you dream into reality. She said that thoughts are things sent out to the universe."

"I knew it. I knew she believed me," Cub said.

"Knew what?" asked Nelms.

"She really is a wonder woman," Cub said.

"She's no wonder woman," Brandeesha said, walking into Nelms' office. "Mr. Nelms, this a delivery ticket you need to sign." Nelms signed it and Brandeesha left. On her way out she said, "We know who she is … she's Tatiana the Great!"

The room seemed to shake after she said that.

"Right," Oliver said.

"Brandeesha, would you close the door after you leave?" asked Nelms.

The door slammed. No one said anything.

"Her dreams are so strong that she's putting us in her dreams and somehow we are feeling her thoughts like we are right there in her dream with her; like there are different worlds out there being merged," Oliver said. "Have you ever heard of that?"

"I haven't," Nelms said. "There is a fine line between a rational and irrational person. There was something peculiar about last night. Did anyone know who was singing at the bar?"

No one did.

"What was a long haird white boy doing singing at a black club? His music was not from today. I've never heard music like that," Nelms said. "I think this dream or fantasy, for lack of a term, is in different time periods. Tatiana is not creating two worlds, she's mixing different worlds together, combining the future and the past. I'm just glad it's not real."

Oliver said he did some research. "There is this theory called astral projection where you can leave your body and go into another world. It is mentioned in the second book of Corinthians by St. Paul, who said he knew a man in Christ who experienced the third world."

"That's in the Bible?" asked Nelms.

"It is," Oliver said.

"You Catholics know the Bible."

"I'm not Catholic, Ed."

"Right," Nelms said. "Anything else?"

"Tatiana says that man is on the verge of discovering imagination and the ability to make thoughts into action and that when you merge the two, you have great powers."

"Like telekinesis?"

"Yes, I think so. It is the ability to make things move through thoughts. Like the new television. She said someone imagined the television and then created it. She says eventually we will be able to create physical things with our mind power. That is the future of man."

"Won't that be something," Cub said.

"She says there are other dimensions out there and that is how people will travel through space some day," Oliver said. "To do anything now you have to imagine it, believe in it and, this is the kicker, don't laugh …"

Oliver stopped to think for a second and wondered if Tatiana might be suffering from "shell shock" or "battle fatigue" during her time covering the war. Could this explain what was going on with her? Tatiana was sensitive to the suffering of others and she along with Oliver and Cub witnessed much of traumatic experiences during the war. Maybe the speeches they gave at the church triggered those emotions again. Could journalists suffer from the same pressures of war?

"I'm not laughing," Nelms said.

"You have to believe that you already have what it is that you're asking for."

Cub started laughing.

"Don't laugh Cub. Tatiana says we live in a multidimensional world that changes based on our observation of it. What is in our brain is a smaller version of what is up there in space, in the universe. Our brains are really a part of God that is investigating the universe for him through each of us. We are god-like creatures who really have immense power but don't know how to tap into it. Once we learn how to merge our imagination with our emotions, then we can move mountains. Jesus said that if we ask anything in his name, it will be given to us. The universe is nothing but a relationship with God that vibrates at a certain frequency where love is the universal emotion and then our observation of the universe changes it."

"So, what is the bottom line? What is the secret of the universe?" asked Cub.

"Love," said Oliver.

PART C:
THE WAR

Chapter 39

THE WAR BETWEEN THE HORIZONTAL and vertical media in Alabama began as outlined in the script delivered to members of the Griddle Iron show. Andre continued his investigation into the Deep State. At his next meeting with Hans, in a parking garage, Hans had on a brown shirt, brown pants, a black belt and big steel-toed shoes.

"Long day. I'm working undercover as a janitor. You have to be willing to do anything in this job. It has to be done cleanly so people appreciate you. They respect working with you if you do it neatly and don't disturb anyone, particularly in the morning."

"My people tell me that the Deep State doesn't exist," Andre said. "They say this is a joke that is played on cub reporters. Is that true?"

"You are so naïve. The mainstream media is part of the Deep State," Hans said as he swept the floor of the garage.

"What? It couldn't be."

Hans stopped sweeping. "Don't kid yourself. The Morning News and the Herald have been taken over by the Deep State. Zoros controls them. Moscow even reports to Zoros. The Russian president, Aleksandr Putaineue, reports to Zoros. Zoros ordered Putaineue to attack Ukarine. The communists are are in our government and in Hollywood. That is why Richard Nixon, the congressman from California and the actor Ronald Reagan with the Screen Actors Guild in Hollywood are working to rout out the communists. Those guys are going to be rewarded someday for what they are doing. One day they will become president of the United States. I know."

"I don't believe it," Andre said as he started to leave.

"Don't walk off," said Hans. "Ask yourself, man, think. Why are the papers either horizontal or vertical? I mean, why can't they all be like they used to be – neutral and reporting the news straight up – with no attempt at influencing the public?

"I don't know."

"Think about it. Someone is coming. Just act normal." Hans began to sweep again. He walked over to the man and they talked. Andre couldn't hear them, but it sounded like Hans was stuttering. Maybe he was playing an undercover character. The man patted him on the shoulder and walked away. Hans came back and had no stutter.

"We were talking about why papers are either horizontal or vertical and are no longer neutral?"

"Yes," Andre said.

"First of all, they have no code of ethics. If a lawyer does something wrong you can take action against them with the bar association. There is no recourse against a biased journalist or newspaper. Second, you are with the press, so how could you possibly understand the common man? It is obvious."

"I'm still listening."

"The media has been infiltrated. The horizontals have been taken over by Zoros. The verticals have been taken over by what they call the 'Basket of Deplorables' who are anti-government. They hate Zoros and think he is trying to dominate the world and is part of a worldwide conspiracy."

"Is this all that you have?"

"Plenty, and it's more than that. Zoros is bent on destroying religion in the country. The Catholic Church, then the Protestants, then Islam, until there is no more religion. They are taking over all the churches, synagogues, and mosques. The Deep State will control the government and the religion in your country."

"How will they take over the church?"

"That's easy. First by planting false stories that there is some kind of quote 'law of attraction', unquote, that the universe is some vibrational magnet that has nothing to do with Jesus or God. If we all report to some magnet out there, then why is there a need for Jesus? Why doesn't Jesus stop that?"

"What is it that they actually say?" Andre asked.

"They say the universe brings you what you ask for and then you are to have some emotional feeling like you have what you want. So the vibrational forces bring it to you. If that were true, then why do you need God? That is the Deep State's plot to rid the world of religion."

"I have heard that what you think about comes into your life," Andre said.

"You've heard it? There are some people out there promoting the belief that you can turn on your mind to access any talent or skill you want. You become a superhero in your imagination. Then you will become stronger by exercising your mind. Your imagination takes over and becomes the dominant personality and the true reality merges the two worlds together. Your imagination becomes reality."

"I've heard that," Andre said.

"That's just false."

Andre was taken aback.

"Ok … how do you know if someone is Deep State?"

"Their hair turns white after conversion," said Hans.

"That's funny – the Deep State makes your hair turn white."

"Just a joke. One sign is that a person refuses to negotiate or compromise. It's their way or the highway. There is no middle ground. The only way to win is to forcibly win by having the votes to vote them down. Get rid of the sixty vote cloture rule in the Senate and go nuclear on everything. Nuke 'em just like your people did three years ago."

"What do they do?"

"The EPK and GCJ have become weaponized to take down the politicial opposition. Their agents talk about exoneration before investigation; they hand out immunity with nothing in return. They entrap people. They prosecute them for lying when they haven't violated the law. They call it a 'process crime.' They use false affidavits, false stories. The courts don't hold the government accountable. Logic doesn't work. Check it out."

Andre wrote down what Hans was saying.

"What is your job? You and Ellis?"

"Ellis is working to rid the country of the Klan. I'm working to rid the government of the Deep State."

"What specifically do you do?"

"I watch the shows on television. When hatred jumps out, then I report the measurements on a daily basis. Hate is a strong emotion. I watch that emotion here, on this planet. Hate can send you back light years."

"Any other stories you can tell?"

"Yes, some people are convinced that we are being invaded from outer space."

"What do you mean?"

"Didn't you hear about the Roswell incident last year?"

"No."

"That was a UFO sighting in Roswell, New Mexico. After that, people have been reporting seeing flying saucers and being taken into outer space. We checked it out. It was an experimental military balloon designed to monitor nuclear testing in Russia that fell to the ground, and now the public thinks little green men from outer space were taken to Carswell Air Force Base in Fort Worth and are being held in some underground facility. This kind of reporting is difficult to stop. Just when we try to stop that reporting then another comes along and then it is reported."

"Like what?"

"Did you hear about the Mantell incident?"

"No."

"An Air Force pilot, Captain Thomas Mantell, an Air National Guardsman, crashed his F-51 Mustang fighter pursuing an unidentified flying object. UFO is what they called it. Before he crashed his plane, they reported that he was chasing a UFO. All he was chasing was a skyhook balloon sent up to collect weather data. It looks eerie in the sky. Now people think the whole country has been invaded by Martians. We have to shut that kind of talk down."

"Do you have anything else?"

"No. I have to buy a toy for one of my kids."

Andre watched Hans leave. Then Hans turned around and said: "I can meet tomorrow."

Chapter 40

To STOP THE FIRST WAVE of the mass migration into Alabama as commanded by Zoros, Governor Card ordered all the Alabama National Guard men and women into service, including any former military personnel who served during World War II. They would serve to stop the invasion across the Louisiana border and from the Gulf Coast.

New Orleans was being taken over by the flow of migrants. Four million migrants had come across the border because the Deep State ordered it. That was the magic number to turn Texas and Alabama green. No identification would be required for these new immigrants who were not eligible to vote, but for Zoros ordering that they be eligible to vote. To ask for an identification card from them was racist.

"We will have border security and we will have a country. We have no choice," Card would rail at his rallies.

Alabama was in its own world, isolated from the rest of the country, and would have to defend itself until the United States military could respond. The Deep State had launched its attack on the governor who went into hiding at an undisclosed location, surrounded by aides.

Card issued press releases attacking the press. One day he had enough of Tatiana and Oliver over their coverage, calling her a low IQ, talking about how she was bleeding from a facelift after visiting the governor's mansion, and characterizing the *Birmingham Defender* as fake news.

Oliver and Tatiana were stunned by the attack on them. They were scheduled to be on vacation but returned to work to address the governor's charge.

Tatiana said: "If he goes low, we go high."

"I'm okay," Oliver said. "Alabama is not okay."

All around the newspaper, the reporters had sympathy for the way Tatiana and Oliver were being treated by the governor.

"He was unprepared when he came to office. It's personal now with Tatiana," Oliver said.

"My parents, God bless them, if they could see the attacks on us, they would ask what is the world about," Tatiana said.

"We are going to go on vacation after this," Oliver said.

"We have a really big problem with the guy in the governor's mansion," Tatiana said. "He's not the guy we knew before. He is not well. He's mentally ill."

Leaving the newspaper in their car, Tatiana said, "Oliver, I'm so ashamed. Someone wrote a letter to the editor that we should be fired."

"That was Brandeesha. I read it."

"I know. I didn't want to mention her name. Even she thinks we should be fired. She is a Deplorable. How can she identify with them? They are insurrectionists and want to overthrow the government."

"We have to have a different kind of reporting to take on what is going on now," Oliver said.

Chapter 41

BIRMINGHAM BECAME A SANCTUARY CITY filled with thousands of homeless immigrants walking the streets with no place to live and without adequate facilities, leaving many on the streets and the state incapable of meeting their needs due to being unprepared for the mass migration. The governors of Texas and Florida began to send the mass migrants to the sanctuary cities in green states, like Illinois, New York and including Washington, D.C. to the home of the vice-president, who said that the border to the U.S. was secure, despite 4 million migrants coming across the border in one year.

When the governor of Texas arranged to send fifty Venezeulans transported to Florida, the governor of Florida arranged to have them transported to Amy's Vineyard, home of the wealthiest island resort in the United States, that had over 100,000 open hotel rooms that could be used to house the migrants. While the cameras roled the wealthiest and elite green voters appeared to welcome the migrants. But in less than twenty-four hours later, the governor of Massachusetts, had them deported to a military base. "We don't have the infrastructure for them," said one of the wealthiest residents of the resort island. Zoros was outraged over the political stunt by the orange state governors and called the actions of the governors as human trafficking or kidnapping. Zoros ordered the Deep State media to attack the governors in the press and for local sheriff's to find a way to prosecute the governors.

The horizontal media pointed out that the Deep State operatives with the federal government were transporting migrants in the middle of the night across the U.S. without notice to the local communities. Zoros ordered the vertical media not to cover the federal government movement of migrants, but only focus on the political stunts of the orange state politicians.

Birmingham elected its first communist mayor, who took a soft view on Americans who had left the country to fight in war zones for forces radicalized by Zoros and then return home, bringing their radicalization with them. Crime was rampant in the city because the immigrants had no jobs, and in order to provide they had to steal.

A suicide bomber blew himself up in Birmingham, killing seven people. The new communist mayor announced that Birmingham was open to anyone who wanted to come to America. He ordered all knives banned in Birmingham: "No excuses. There is never a reason to carry a knife. Anyone who does will be caught and will feel the full force of the law."[25]

Brandeesha railed at the mayor of Birmingham during an on-camera interview. "What could be a bigger priority than people coming back from and being allowed to enter this state for the purpose of killing the people from Alabama? Why isn't that your number one priority? Why are these people allowed to come back in the first place, and then the mayor doesn't appear to know where they are, no disrespect to you."[26]

The mayor tried to respond: "This is one of the questions obviously that the police ..." but Brandeesha interrupted him before he could finish. "How do you not know where they are?" she asked again.[27]

"I can't follow 400 people."[28]

"Why can't you?"[29]

"We need resources for the police, and experts."[30]

"Why can't you instruct the police right now and say every one of those people who have come back from a war zone who are in Birmingham, you want them followed."[31]

"The Birmingham Police Department has been reduced."[32]

Brandeesha raged at the mayor that evening on the news, and she continued her attacks on Tatiana and Oliver: "This blatantly biased liberal attack machine of the *Birmingham Defender* shouldn't be throwing stones from its incredibly fragile glass house where they have some of the most vile and disgusting articles written."[33] Then she continued to rail at Tatiana, holding up one of her articles in the newspaper and reading from it: "Then the Kleenex Queen writes:

> He looks like a goon. Look at him, he's mauling him like an idiot. What an embarrassment to Alabama. This man is lying to you. You've got to stop putting his wife on television. This is politics porn. He's totally unprepared for the job of being governor. This is not funny. This is really bad." [34]

Brandesha looked directly into the camera and said: "What exactly is the purpose of the *Birmingham Defender*? It is fake news, a propaganda machine with its poor liberal whining, sniffling, lugubrious Kleenex Queen who is 'nervous.' The Kleenex Queen at the pathetic and blatantly biased *Birmingham Defender* is desperate because no one is listening to them or buying what they say. She has Card Derangement Syndrome and are bringing it to a new level."

Tatiana woke up from her sleep and went to the bathroom. She looked in the mirror and saw herself as Tatiana the Great.

"Cub, I can't believe you showed me that comic book. Now I am dreaming about it." Then she got back in bed.

Chapter 42

"Did you buy a toy for your kids?" Andre asked Hans.

"Yes. Two. One likes to gets on my lap. I bring out a book and start to read and she gets back down. Then she gets a book and gets back up on my lap for me to read her book, and then I start to read and she gets back down. She can't sit still for a minute."

"My wife and I talk about kids sometime," Andre said.

"You should try it. It will stabilize you. You know you have to get up and go to work and bring in a paycheck."

"Why did you want to meet so soon? Anything new?"

"I guess you heard that someone gave Jill Rodderman a Russian hat and she said, 'If you can't lick 'em, join 'em. Isn't that funny? She started the Russian hoax and then continues to perpetuate it."

"I heard about it."

"Rodderman is Deep State. So is Bongino. That's why he exonerated her before interviewing her. Bongino handled her investigation himself and kept it in his office in D.C. and limited it to just a few people. Then he gave immunity to her staff. He knew that the other offices of the GCJ would investigate her properly and would convene a Grand Jury who would have indicted her. Zoros ordered Bongino to exonerate her so he complied. Then he and Rodderman set out to frame Card. Bongino threw the case against her deliberately. Bongino hates Card and calls him a mob boss."

"Ok. What do you know about John Miller?"

"We think he is Deep State. He has Deep State tendencies. He says he is not Deep State. He hates being linked with the other Deep State characters. He is always saying 'I am not Deep State.'"

"What if he is not Deep State?" Andre asked.

"We will see if he follows the normal protocol of the ECJ. He's running the collusion investigation that Rodderman and Bongino launched. As long as Card is in power, Miller wants to stay in power to try to find a way to impeach him. He is generally well thought of, but we are investigating him closely because he approved of the Plutonium One sale to the Soviets and that is the part can't quite figure out yet. It doesn't sound like Miller to do that, so there has to be more to it than what we know."

"Why did they sell plutonium to the Soviets?"

"That is top secret. Bongino and Miller approved of the sale of twenty percent of the United States' plutonium to the Soviet Union."

"Why would the U.S. sell plutonium to the Soviet Union?"

"I have no idea, but it is my job to investigate the whereabouts of all nuclear material. An explosion from that kind of material can penetrate light years into the universe beyond what you can imagine. You know that a ripple in the water turns into a tidal wave when it reaches the other side of the world. Imagine what a nuclear bomb is like when that power reaches the other side of the universe. I mean, it's like nothing you can imagine."

"Why doesn't someone do something?"

"Welcome to the marsh is all I can say. The Deep State can do whatever it wants. What can anyone do? Tell Richard Nixon? Rodderman hates Nixon. She said if Nixon ever became president, she would do whatever she could to impeach him."

"Someone has to be told that this is going on."

"Your people need a special prosecutor to investigate the special prosecutor."

"It's hard for me to believe that this is really going on?" Andre said.

"Only you can get the story out there because none of the other newspapers will touch it. I'm telling you that the Deep State decided it cannot live with your Governor Card being the governor."

"What can it do?"

"They are always saying - 'Get Card.' They will go after everyone around Card and criminalize everything they do. It is classic Soviet-style tactics. They paint a crime on their target and find a way to bring them down. Show me the man and I will show you the crime. This special prosecutor in your country is like a Soviet-style inquisitor who can prosecute people for crimes that are not crimes, get them to plead to crimes that are not crimes, and then prosecute them for lying if they can't prosecute them on the underlying charge."

"My editor is going to have a hard time believing this."

"You really are new to politics and the media," said Hans. "Welcome to the marsh."

Andre was amazed Hans had so much information he could not get anywhere else.

"Do you have your kids by yourself tonight?"

"No. We are all home together. That is one thing about this job is that I have regular hours. I can get here at 7 a.m. and leave by 3 p.m. on the dot."

Chapter 43

JESSE WEINSTEIN AND JOHN THOMAS, both with continuing reserve obligations after serving during World War II, were recalled back into the service to fight the war in Alabama.

They were assigned to the Rule of Law Task Force, which operated in a secure compound on the outskirts of Birmingham. By this time Birmingham was surrounded by a concrete wall and was safe from communist insurgents who began shooting missiles indiscriminately into the city. They had a launch pad that they would pull out of a garage and launch a missile into the city. The missile could land anywhere; thus the name "indiscriminate" since there was no specific target in mind.

The Rule of Law Task Force was created to assist the local Alabama judges to prosecute crimes through the local Alabama courts, many of which had been taken over by the communists, who imposed communist law and were reluctant to prosecute their own. There was now a two-tiered justice system where resident Alabamans were held accountable under Alabama law as it existed but the communists, insurgents, and terrorists were criminalized and held accountable according to the customs of the local tribes.

The U.S. military was not sure of the loyalty of all of the Alabama judges, as many had gone to the side of the communists. A compound was created where the judges could rule without fear of assassination if they were to rule against a terrorist. The military used the intelligence sources of the federal government to investigate crimes to bring cases to justice.

Jesse Weinstein assumed command of the Rule of Law Task Force for six months before John Thomas could leave his job and arrive as its director. Weinstein earned the trust of the members while running the task force, but when Thomas arrived, he resented Weinstein's control of the organization and the loyalty of the military.

Weinstein and Thomas shared the same office space: one long room with two desks at one end and a long desk where all the junior and senior officers met each morning to brief the two men. Weinstein took control of the meetings and sat at the head of the table while Thomas sat on the other side of the table, befuddled and unsure how to wrestle control of the task force from his subordinate without angering the crew who had been serving quite well under Weinstein. Thomas knew it would be difficult, but slowly he would exert himself and wait for Weinstein to rotate out when his orders would end and he would be sent to another location.

Over time Thomas kicked Weinstein out of the conference room, taking it for himself entirely, leaving the group to find another place to meet. This left a large number of officers having to squeeze into a small office while Thomas had the entire office to himself. That was Thomas' way of showing Weinstein who was in charge.

For six months the war raged into Birmingham with frequent missile attacks from homes around the city bombarding the U.S. Embassy to drive out the Americans. From the mountains of Quary Valley, Aleksandr Putaineue was in hiding and was directing the attacks to take Birmingham while the U.S. military tried to locate him in the countryside.

Chapter 44

———— ❧ ————

Brandeesha decided to appear on a new talk show of women called *The Spam*, featuring none other than Tatiana as a guest host. Tatiana was looking forward to taking on Brandeesha on television. Tatiana began the program by accusing Governor Card as a child abuser and attacked his wife, Janette. "She doesn't care. She is planning Christmas in July. These are child abusers. They are murdering the children of America."[35]

Brandeesha interrupted, "You say he is murdering the children of America? You know what is horrible? When we have sanctuary cities."[36]

Tatiana responded, "When Card tells people of the U.S. to beat the hell out of people at his rallies! Think about that!"[37]

Tatiana walked off the set.

Brandeesha got up to follow her, but Tatiana cursed Brandeesha on her way out.[38] She would have none of Brandeesha. That evening Brandeesha appeared as a guest on a nationally syndicated show hosted by Laura Ingersoll, a known conservative commentator who followed Brandeesha's show. Ingersoll asked Brandeesha: "Tell us, just how horrible was it having to go on *The Spam*? I know it must have been abuse to even do that. All power to you, girl, for having the courage to go on that show."

"It was horrible. It was the worst thing you could imagine. I've never been treated so horribly by those people with their Card

Derangement Syndrome. I was thrown off the set." Brandeesha began to cry as she described the experience.

"Tatiana Phillips, Mrs. Tatiana Phillips, the Kleenex Queen as we know her …"

"Here take a Kleenex," said Ingersoll.

"Thank you. She pulled the plug and walked off but it didn't end there. And I think the sad part about all of this is that, you know … I said in the first segment, we need to start talking to each other. We need to start having a conversation. I said that two minutes before. I felt like today was a microcosm of what is happening in America."

"You are right about that."

"The horizontals suffer from Card Derangement Syndrome. Tatiana shuts you down; doesn't allow you to talk. She asks me a question, then yells at me, yells about Governor Card and when I try to answer she continues to yell and it didn't end there. What happened was that the segment was over. I left the stage, starting to go downstairs, and I saw her and had to walk by her, and Tatiana said, 'I fought for civil rights and victims my whole life,' something like that, and then she started cursing me."[39]

"What did she say?"

"She said – well, I can't repeat it. I was stunned. I mean, I am a guest at that horizontal program and this is how they treat their vertical guests. They believe in free speech as long as you agree with their speech. They claim they are for free speech but only so long as you agree with them. They have to have their safe rooms, their counseling, their free education, free everything, they are so afraid that the snow is going to fall on them. They are for open borders, the rule of law applying only to the orange states, and they favor illegal immigration over Americans. Imagine that – they favor the Russian immigrants over Americans."

"You should get a Purple Heart for going on that show," said Ingersoll. "It's abuse just to watch it."

Brandeesha nodded her head as she continued to cry.

"There you have it," said Ingersoll. "This is just another example of how vile and disgusting and despicable horizontal new media can be with their Card Derangement Syndrome and their criminalization of politics. They go after Card and give a free pass to Rodderman. They do not believe in the rule of law, the presumption of innocence, search and destroy. They believe that women should be believed and men should shut up. Why wasn't Rodderman indicted? That is the Deep State for you"

"Lock her up! Lock her up! Lock her up!" the audience began to yell.

Then Ingersoll went to her next guest.

"Tonight, I have Raymond Royale the Washington, D.C., commentator who covers the Vatican and Catholic stories. Thank you for being here, Raymond."

"Well, thank you," he said.

"Tell us, Raymond, what do you have for us this week on our weekly installment of 'View and Unviewed'?"

"This week is really interesting. In a small city in Mountain Springs, Alabama, there is a very large presence that is spawned by a St. Peter's Catholic Church, which includes a school. It's in what is typically Protestant country in the South. It is quite unusual as during the 1930s during the height of the Depression it raised money to build this very nice and elegant complex and over the years has developed a large worldwide audience through its use of the new television audience. There are Franciscan priests who hold daily services on television, and they're taking their message across the world."

"That's good," said Ingersoll.

"Yes, but combine that with a local newspaper called the *Birmingham Defender* with two reporters named Tatiana and Oliver Smith, a married couple who have a daily column that attacks the governor of that state."

"What happened there?"

"Tatiana Smith had an impromptu interview with one of the nuns, apparently unannounced. She didn't go through the priest or the diocese for that. The nun didn't even think to ask because the reporter came to where she was staying unannounced. It was one of those typical 'ask for forgiveness instead of permission' moments, I believe, and the nun, without realizing who she was really talking to, began to answer her questions. Her name is Sister Camille."

"So, what happened?"

"Three of these nuns, Sister Camille, Sister Laurie, and Sister Aude, saw how few resources there were to feed the poor so they put on a program to see if some of the people could take charge of their own life based on changing how they think about themselves."

"That is a good thing, isn't it?"

"Yes, but they were dealing with the *Birmingham Defender*, a well-known horizontal newspaper. You know it went south after that, if you can excuse the pun."

Ingersoll laughed.

"What did they do this time?" she asked, laughing. "I heard that the newspaper began attacking the church and these poor nuns. Just how low can the horizontals go?"

"Apparently not low enough," said Royale.

"I know," said Ingersoll. "The former Democratic U.S. Attorney has been running around the country saying 'when they go low, we kick 'em.' That's part of their mob mentality.

They're even sending in people to attack vertical news journalists at their own homes. Just look at the mob violence at the recent Kavanich hearing for the U.S. Supreme Court. One U.S. Senator jokingly referred to it as the first intergalactic convention called to confirm a Supreme Court justice."

They laughed.

"During the interview, the nun told the reporter that we can all have what we want if we ask in Jesus' name," said Royale.

"What's wrong with that?" asked Ingersoll. "It's right out of the Bible."

"Yes, but some of the horizontals, not all, I might add, have made fun of religion on the air. One such horizontal television personality said that any kind of relationship with God is called mental illness. They took what she said out of context and said that the nun was promoting some kind of prosperity religion based on what has been referred to as the 'Law of Attraction.' That's not what she was doing. I talked to her and she said that was not what she was trying to convey. She had no intention of suggesting that. It was truly a misunderstanding."

"What else do you know of these reporters?"

"Tatiana Smith is the daughter of a well-known publisher of a newspaper in Chicago. She covered World War II in Europe. I give her credit for that but suddenly the reports go that she changed and no one knows why. One of the nuns said that after she fell and hit her head after one of her talks at the church and she has never been the same. They've tried reaching out to her but she appears to be in another world."

"What specifically has she been doing?" asked Ingersoll who was an attorney prior to becoming a talk show host.

"For one, she and her husband at the church have been attacking the governor in that state on a daily basis."

"That is Governor Ronald Card?"

"Yes. He defeated Jill Rodderman in the race for Alabama governor, who survived a bruising Democratic primary some say was rigged in her favor to exclude her primary opponent named Billie Saunders from winning, no matter how many votes he received through the use of what they call super-delegates."

"What is a super-delegate?"

"It is a member of the legislature. They receive a vote. It is a way for the establishment Democrats to keep their own in power and to prevent the people from duly electing a primary candidate based on popular vote in their primary."

"Sounds like this Jill Rodderman has trouble accepting a vote by the people and prefers to be elected by her super-delegates."

"It appears so."

"When Card unexpectedly defeated Rodderman for the governorship of Alabama, Rodderman has been retaliating since then."

"The vertical and horizontal media have become unhinged in that state by calling each other names. The verticals say that the horizontals suffer from 'Card Derangement Syndrome.' They are resorting to calling each other names. I'm told that the media outlets down there are putting on a play, its called the Griddle Iron Play, where the media really goes after each other and contends that there is some sort of 'Deep State' in existence that is controlling our federal government and the media. It is quite a sinister plot being proposed in the play."

"Sounds interesting. I might want to see it," said Ingersoll. "Now what is 'Card Derangement Syndrome'?"

"The verticals say that about the horizontals – that they oppose anything their governor wants to do simply because he is the governor and was not legitimately elected. They wanted

Rodderman to be governor so they can't compromise on anything. It goes both ways. The horizontals will call the verticals racists and the like."

"That's sad. Really sad."

"All we can do is hope and pray that someone intervenes. Perhaps a miracle. They need someone who will lead the battle and take charge and restore the rule of law in Alabama and leave that governor alone and quit harassing him. I call it 'gubernatorial harassment.' If their chosen candidate had won, she very likely could have been indicted for actions had she been investigated by a credible investigation. She literally got off scot-free while others with lesser conduct were prosecuted and went to prison."

"This is a time when we need some type of modern-day Joan of Arc to restore the rule of law in that state and in this country," said Ingersoll.

Tatiana and Oliver were watching the show from the television at the *Birmingham Defender*. Tatiana was outraged. "Joan of Arc, she says? That lady is pathetic."

"Leave it alone Tatiana," Oliver said.

"Those two are so disgusting," Tatiana said. "I can't believe they let them go on television and talk like that. Who watches that? I can't even watch it. I tell you – no one should ever watch the *Font News*. I can't believe Brandeesha went on that national show and started crying. She puts on this poor 'little old me, come help me.' I swear I'm going to burn her at the stake!"

Chapter 45

"OKAY, LET'S TRY TO HOLD it together at rehearsal," Betty said. "We have come so far and have accomplished so much. I am excited. John is excited. I cried. John cried."

"I cried," said John, raising his fist into the air.

"He's a wimp," Cub said.

"Okay, Cub, be nice to John. Sit down, John."

"Yes," said John.

"Now let's get back to it. Tonight Tatiana, let's rehearse your song, *My Turn*. I want the horizontal media at stage left and the vertical media at stage right - see how funny that is, stage right, stage left …"

Groans from the cast.

"Well, *excusez moi!*" said Betty. "We had such a good practice last time. John thought it was funny. Oh John, I love you."

John said nothing.

"Okay, Tatiana sings and when she gets to the part where she is protected by the Deep State then all of you Deep State characters – we will have you dressed like devils – you will come out and surround her."

"Where did you get the devil idea?" asked Tatiana.

"In the script, Card and Rodderman debate and he says that someone made a deal with the devil. Isn't that funny?" said Brandeesha, smiling devilishly.

No one thought that was funny.

"Okay, Tatiana, let's go through your song."

"Ok. I'm not much of a singer."

Tatiana began to sing:

> *This is my turn.*
> *Everybody loves me …*
> *I don't know what 'c' means.*
> *That's far too classified for me*
> *I have no plan, but it is my turn.*
> *We don't need another man.*
> *We need a woman.*

Disgust from the cast.

"Very good. Very good indeed. I'm impressed," said Betty.

"That's pathetic," Tatiana said. "If we are going to portray her that way, we have to make fun of this Card character in the same way. This play is so titled. It is obvious that a Deplorable wrote it. We have to be fair and balanced."

"You don't do that in your pathetic fake news one-sided newspaper," said Brandeesha.

Tatiana looked at her.

"Okay, please continue," said Betty.

Tatiana sang the second verse:

> *This is my turn …*
> *The world is waiting for me.*
> *Bongino said that no reasonable prosecutor would*
> *prosecute me …*

Tatiana stopped. "Betty, these lines are sexist, misogynist and racist; they are terrible. I won't sing this part. I can't make fun of even if it is a fictional character like this. Women should not make fun of other women. We are supposed to make fun of men. These are garbage lines written by none other than Brandeesha."

"Yea!" Brandeesha said, raising her fist in the air. "To the Deplorables!"

"Betty and Brandeesha, this play is a garbage document. It is quite obvious that you two put this together to favor one side over the other one. The horizontals are portrayed as evil people while the verticals are portrayed as victims. You make fun of the Rodderman character but you don't make fun of the Card character. This is not right. I'm not singing anything from the *Font News*, and that is just like them to make fun of the Rodderman character. They have no right to portray her that way. This is mean. I say no, no, no," Tatiana said.

"That's nothing compared to what you do on a daily basis with your pathetic foul mouth Card Derangement Syndrome. And, by the way, the facelift is obvious!" yelled Brandeesha.

Silence.

The cast was coming apart again.

"This is not mean, and yes, you're right, Tatiana, if we're going to make fun of Rodderman, we have to make fun of Card," said Betty, trying to pick up the conversation.

"How come the only time the *Birmingham Defender* wants to be fair and balanced is during Griddle Iron play?" asked Brandeesha.

No one said anything.

"This is not mean. It is sarcastic. Politicians expect that. Everyone knows this is a parody. Let's all take a deep breath and give each other a hug," said Betty.

No takers. Some people began to leave.

"Let's skip this skit for now," said Betty. "Let's do *Deep State, Exonerate Before Investigate*, and Brandeesha why don't you, instead of Tatiana, do the song in *I Never Sent Nor Received* … and … and Cub, be ready to sing 'Dirty Dossier,' and we need someone to sing in the skit, *Witch Hunt*."

"I don't sing, I grill," Cub said.

"I'm not playing Jill Rodderman," Brandeesha said.

"That will make it funnier, if you play her," said Betty.

"All right," Brandeesha said.

"Cub, why don't we put a grill on stage and you can play the part of British spy Christopher Irons and talk with a British accent and sing how you cooked up the dirty dossier along with Glenn Simpleton," said Betty.

"Now that is starting to make sense," Cub said.

"Put this in the script. DJB Director John Brown gives the dirty dossier to the *Morning News* and *The Herald*," Andre said.

"Will the government officials will get mad at us if we make fund of them this way?" Oliver asked.

"No one could get mad because it's just a play."

"Okay, let's move on," Brandeesha said. "Cub, after you grill up the dirty dossier you give it to Strozinski and Scheetz. Then you take the dossier and grill it again and give the same document to someone else to represent circular reporting."

"That is so pathetic. Betty, would you kick Brandeesha out of this play? What if the president of the *New York Tines* or the *Washington Post* called to ask why we are making fun of them? This play is unprofessional. We are supposed to make fun of politicians and current events, but not the media. Brandeesha is a deplorable. She is using the Griddle Iron play to float her crazy, right wing lunatic ideas that the federal government and the news media report to the Deep State."

"Right. I agree with that," said Roger.

"She's right about that," said Barbara.

"Come on, Oliver, let's go home," Tatiana said to Oliver.

"Let's just give each other a hug and re-group," said Betty.

There were no takers.

"We have one more rehearsal before the play begins. We will be ready. Let's go home now and think about what we're trying to do," Betty said.

They all walked out. All the work that had been performed to bring the verticals and horizontals together was lost.

Chapter 46

AFTER CARD MADE HIS ANNOUNCEMENT that the National Guard was being recalled to fight against the communist invasion of Alabama, reporters were given the chance to be embedded with the troops. Cub was embedded with the Hostage Committee run by Brigadier General Sengleton at the U.S. Embassy in downtown Birmingham. Oliver and Nelms volunteered to drive ambulances for the Red Cross in Mobile. Tatiana and Brandeesha were assigned to the Rule of Law Task Force outside Birmingham. They were in the same bunk room, called a "hooch." Tatiana was a combat journalist again just like in World War II. This was a new experience for Brandeesha who was a secretary for Nelms. Now she was a combat journalist.

"I can't believe I'm bunking with you. Of all people," Brandeesha said, walking in the room and putting her military gear on the floor.

"I was a journalist during the war. I can show you how it's done," Tatiana said.

"Just don't bring your Card Derangement Syndrome into this room," Brandeesha said.

It was quiet. Tatiana lay on the top bunk staring at the ceiling. "Can you believe what we're going through?" she asked.

"What are you talking about?" Brandeesha said.

"The communists have taken over Alabama. The governor is ousted from power. The churches are taken over by the Russians.

The federal government is powerless to act. Now we are fighting together. The verticals and the horizontals. Women in combat. Someone has to save Alabama. Where is God right now?"

"Probably doing what he has to do."

"Everyone I know says they talk to Jesus or God. When you pray, do you hear anything?"

"Yes. Jesus talks to me. Most everyone I associate with has a relationship with Jesus," Brandeesha said.

"Most of my friends tell me that if Jesus talks to me, then I have mental illness," Tatiana said.

"Spoken like a typical horizontal. I told you to leave your Card Derangement Syndrome and your fake news outside the door. I can't believe I have to share a room with you. You need to apologize."

"Why do you hate me, Brandeesha?"

"I don't hate you."

"Yes, you do. You call me Tatiana the Great."

"You are Tatiana the Great. The lady who interviewed Eleanor Roosevelt and showed up late. Whoopee."

"Stop it," Tatiana said. "You hate me."

"*You* hate *me*! I'm a proud member of the Basket of Deplorables," Brandeesha said.

"Rodderman didn't mean to say that about Card supporters. She regretted it," Tatiana said. "But it was true. They are deplorable. They could storm the capitol if they wanted to and wouldn't think anything about it."

"She did mean it, and she regretted it after she saw all the backlash and saw her poll numbers. You hate Card. All you do is attack him every day. You have Card Derangement Syndrome. Then you make fun of anyone religious. I think you are an atheist."

Tatiana was taken aback. She waited to respond. "I don't think that at all. We need to be able to have a conversation."

"I saw what you did on *The Spam*."

"I apologized for that," Tatiana said.

"No, you didn't! You never apologize!"

"Are you angry at me, Brandeesha?"

"Yes. See, you don't listen. You don't have a clue."

"What are you talking about?"

There was no trust. Everything Tatiana said to Brandeesha was rejected.

Tatiana turned on a small light over her bunk and began to read Mark Twain's novel *Joan of Arc*.

"What are you doing?" Brandeesha said. "Turn that light off. I can see it through the bed bunk."

"It's just my book from book call."

"What is it?"

"*Joan of Arc*," Tatiana said.

"Do you need a match? What else are you reading?"

"*A Farewell to Arms, For Whom the Bell Tolls, Lost Horizon*."

"You are lost," Brandeesha said. "We have a war going on and all you want to do is read."

Tatiana said nothing.

Tatiana went to sleep and visualized the Griddle Iron Show where she and Brandeesha are in a scene debating whether Jesus existed. Tatiana wanted to be able to have a relationship with Jesus but it would not happen. She was secretly jealous of those who could communicate with the Son of God.

Chapter 47

"How is it going with Hans?" Andre asked Lanny while at lunch. "Are you surviving the war?"

"As best I can," Lanny said. "The bombings are routine now. Whenever I hear 'duck and cover' I go straight to the concrete shelter. No problem. Just wait and then, BOOM, the bomb hits. They never land near me."

"Me, too," Andre said.

"Lanny, if the government wanted to take out someone, how do they do it?"

"One way is through a counter-intelligence operation on an American citizen that they suspect of being involved in some kind of foreign influence."

"Wouldn't that be part of their job?"

"Yes, if it was legitimate.:

"So that's done all the time?"

"Yes. That's their business."

"Suppose that someone wanted to bring down an opponent in a political race," Andre said. "Would the government spy on them based on a document given to them by a private company that was conducting opposition research?"

"That's way above me."

"Just what is your job?"

"The Klan. I'm here to take down the Klan."

"What does Hans do?"

"That's something I can't talk about."

"You don't know if the government would secure a search warrant on a political candidate based on opposition research?"

"Not a chance. Any decent court would be able to figure that out, by just a few questions."

"The story that Hans is telling me is really sinister. He says that the director of the GCJ used a document given to him by a British spy, who got it from a company by the name of Nexus. It was from an article published ten years earlier in the newspaper about lobbying. They updated it by changing the names."

"Sounds like a garbage document," Lanny said.

"He said that government agents were checking names in a database and listening in on their conversations. They call that 'unmasking.' He said a Navy Admiral figured out what was going on and told Governor Card and so he vacated his offices."

"Sounds like some nut-ball conspiracy theory. I wouldn't report that story. You could get into real trouble."

"What about the judge who approved the search warrant? Would he need to know it was phony opposition research?"

"He would need to know."

"So, what if it was done?"

"What was done?"

"Secure a warrant to listen in on conversations based on false political campaign research."

"And the judge did not know about it?" Lanny said. "You would have one important story, I imagine."

Chapter 48

AFTER VISITING WITH THE TROOPS, Tatiana and Brandeesha went to talk with Judge John Thomas, now Captain John Thomas and Captain Jesse Weinstein in their offices to begin reporting from the front.

"How will we defeat the communists? They're taking over the entire state. If they're not defeated, then they will be able to take over the entire United States," Tatiana said.

"That is their plan," said Jesse Weinstein.

"How are they doing it?" asked Brandeesha.

"First by establishing their own churches in every town and city."

"Are communists also atheists?" Brandeesha asked.

"Yes. They have developed it into a religion – a religion of atheism – in a manner of speaking," said Weinstein. "Now they want to impose atheism on all of us. They have their own meeting places in former churches that are the perfect warehouse for indoctrination of terrorists."

"Where are they getting their money?" asked Brandeesha.

"From us," said Weinstein.

"What is their mission?" asked Tatiana.

"First, they move into a peaceful neighborhood and take over the churches, synagogues, and mosques and eliminate religion. They then begin their terrorist practices of creating deranged youth. This forces the residents to move. The communists take over part of a town and make it unpleasant for anyone who doesn't go along."

Thomas jumped into the conversation.

"First we have to go after their meeting places where terrorism is breeding. There are meeting places for not only indoctrination but future terrorists who are made to read and understand the principles of communism. Their churches are being fused with money straight from the Caribbean. Our money spent there is coming right back here."

"We have to take out the atheists who are sent here with one clear mission: to make communism the supreme rule within the United States," Weinstein added. "We take them down by treating them like a common criminal, subject to the laws of Alabama. We don't need special terrorist laws."

"We just use the Alabama Code of Criminal Law to criminalize the terrorist and make him subject to the rule of law," said Thomas.

"It's good to see both of you working together, and this time on the same team," Tatiana said.

Thomas smiled.

"I agree with everything you say," said Weinstein. "Their key is immigration. If they can keep importing their brand of terrorism through mass migration, then we will lose the country. That is how Mexico lost Texas. Mexico allowed foreigners to come to Texas to fight the Indians and soon they started identifying as Texians. Immigration is one thing. Mass migration is another."

"There are already have been two million immigrants enter this country this year under the 'catch and release program.' How could we win this war?" asked Brandeesha.

"I have a theory," Tatiana said.

Brandeesha looked surprised. "And what is that?"

"The government will retake the state the same way it won World War II. The Navy will launch an invasion and the Marines will come ashore. The barrage battalions will go ashore and launch their balloons. The Tuskegee Airmen will fly from Puerto Rico. The Buffalo Soldiers will invade from the East. The 761st Tank Division will invade from Texas. The Canadians will invade from the north. All these forces will fight until they liberate Birmingham."

They were all amazed with Tatiana's theory.

Chapter 49

"CHECK OUT SENATOR BLADE – he's Deep State," said Hans.

"How do you know?"

"His hair, what's left of it, is white."

Andre laughed. "I need more than that. I will be laughed off stage, literally, if I put that in print."

"He is now wearing a patch over one eye."

"That means nothing."

"Brown told Blade to write a letter to Deep State Director Bongino to ask the GCJ to investigate Card for Russian collusion. He wanted to make it look legitimate."

"Why would a U.S. senator write a letter to Director Bongino to investigate Card? How would a U.S. senator have more information than the Director of the GCJ? How would he know to even ask?"

"The Deep State gave him the paper work to give to Bongino to try to make it look like a legitimate request. The Deep State does that all the time."

"What did Bongino do with the letter?" Andre asked.

"Who knows? Bongino knew it was coming. Senator John McElhaney was given a copy of the dossier also."

"How can two U.S. senators from different political parties obtain the same dossier? Who gave them the information? For what purpose?"

Hans looked at him.

"I have to start writing this story," Andre said.

"I'm telling you kid, you are on to one of the biggest scandals in your country's history. It has to be exposed."

Chapter 50

TATIANA LAY ON HER BED. Brandeesha began to snore. Tatiana could make anything come true in her dreams. The past was right in front of her – energy rearranged. But she could not calibrate her mind to a certain day. She was investigating the fire at Andre's home but could not figure out the exact day to get there.

"I wish I could go to sleep that easily. At least she's human," said to herself.

The modern human was evolving. Modern man lived in different worlds that could be merged by meditation. Man's thoughts and dreams could become reality by raw brain power if a person was willing to understand it. This power was always available but no one knew how to use it because they were always processing multiple thoughts at the same time. The key was to concentrate on one thought for more than five minutes – to the exclusion of all other thoughts. Soon there would be books written on how much time to mediate, what music to listen to, and how to make thoughts specific. Because man could not travel in outerspace, man would learn to travel through other dimensions based on the mind power of thought.

That evening in her bunk an angel came to Tatiana. "I was called by Saint Michael to tell you to take up arms to restore the Dauphin to power," the angel said.

The most unlikely candidate, Tatiana, who did not attend church, who questioned whether she could have a relationship with Jesus, whom Brandeesha called an atheist, had been called to restore Governor Card to power, a politician whom she despised, and to remove the communists from Alabama. All for the purpose of restoring the Rule of Law. A civil society could not exist without the Rule of Law.

Tatiana awoke in the middle of the night. She went to the bathroom and looked in the mirror. She was dressed as "Tatiana the Great," as Brandeesha nicknamed her.

"Thoughts are things. Now thoughts are reality," Tatiana said to herself.

Tatiana was a modern-day wonder woman just as Cub had shown her on the comic book. Wonder Woman won World War II. Now Tatiana the Great would win the war to save Alabama.

"Oh, my gosh," she said.

Brandeesha woke up. "What is it?"

"I thought I saw a ghost."

"Is it gone?"

"Don't be funny."

Tatiana dreamed she was in bed with Oliver in their home.

"I'm having some serious dreams."

"In what way?" he asked, sitting up.

"I'm too embarrassed to say."

"I'm not going to laugh at you."

"You promise?"

"I promise," he said as he kissed her.

"I received a calling from St. Michael."

Oliver smiled.

"I thought you were going to laugh."

"I'm not laughing."

"Yes, you laughed."

"No, I did not," Oliver said.

"Yes, you did."

"Tell me what happened."

"I was called to restore the governor to power," Tatiana said.

"He isn't out of power. He's in the governor's mansion with his wife. He is safe and sound."

"I know, but in my dream, I am to rescue him and restore him to power. My God, I loathe Card and all of his so called "Basket of Horribles." I am told to rescue him, but I also wanted Rodderman to win the election by a million votes to nothing."

"Card? You mean Governor Card in the Griddle Iron Show?"

"Yes. Isn't this stupid. I'm to restore him to the governorship."

"That is because you are Tatiana the Great," Oliver said. "You are not dreaming. You are learning your lines."

Tatiana woke again. "Are you there, Brandeesha?"

Brandeesha was snoring.

Chapter 51

MARK TWAIN'S POWERFUL AND GRIPPING novel *Joan of Arc* was now on Tatiana's mind. She had become so powerful that reality could become whatever she read and then visualized.

Sister Camille, Sister Laurie, and Sister Aude equipped Tatiana the Great for her mission to restore Governor Card to power as the rightful Alabama governor. He had been removed by Deep State seditionists. Rodderman's hoax of Russian collusion had been successfully pinned on Card. The public had no idea that Rodderman reported to Zoros. Zoros' plan had worked so far.

Tatiana wore the most current military uniform worn by men so she could travel freely through the country. As a woman she would have been stopped. Tatiana's armor was in place and she had a white flag.

"How will you make it through the country to get to your uncle's home?" asked Sister Camille.

"The fairies will help me. They will show me the way. They always have. I've talked to them since I was fourteen."

"The fairies?" asked Sister Laurie.

"Yes. They were on the trees until they were banned by the communists. But they will help me."

"You really are Tatiana the Great," said Sister Aude.

"I knew you would do great things," said Sister Camille.

St. Peter's Catholic School was taken over by the communists. Father Webster, Father Sanders, Sister Camille, Sister Laurie, and

Sister Aude had no choice but to leave. They found safe haven at the *Birmingham Defender*.

"You can stay here for now. You can stay here until the state can regain the church," Nelms said. "All the reporters are either covering the war or serving in it. I will be leaving soon for Mobile. The paper will not operate while the war is on."

"I do not like to see war but there is precedent in taking back Christian land," said Father Webster.

A few days later they took refuge in the Birmingham City Performance Hall, where the Griddle Iron would take place Saturday night.

The Griddle Iron Show would perform for all the townspeople, the homeless, and news reporters with a guaranteed full house.

Chapter 52

"THIS IS GOING TO BE a hard practice tonight. Plan to stay an hour longer," Betty said.

"Great," Tatiana said.

"Yea!" Brandeesha said. "You go, girl."

Betty continued: "As I understand it, the Deep State refuses to hold accountable the politicians that they like," Betty said. "Is that right?"

Groans from the cast.

"YES!" Brandeesha said. "We have a two-tiered justice system in the United States."

"NO! That is not true, Brandeesha. That is a terrible thing to say," Tatiana said. "We do not have a two-tiered justice system. The Deep State is not real."

"We have to protest the system of government. That is how they protested things in the days of Shakespeare."

"To be or not to be, that is the question," said John as he stood up.

"Be quiet, John," said Betty.

"Okay," said John. John sat down.

"Now, Brandeesha and I will play reasonable prosecutors in the play. We will ask the Deep State characters why they deliberately exonerated Rodderman when there was sufficient evidence to prosecute her and then they opened up a counter-intelligence investigation against Governor Card for alleged collusion with

Russia when there was no evidence to open up that investigation when it was Rodderman who created the entire Russia collusion hoax and then leaked it their horizontal press to run with. And of course, the Deep State media ran with it and won Pulitzer Prize awards for their reporting. Did I say it right?"

More groans from the cast.

"No one in our government today would do that, Betty. We all know this is a joke, don't we?" asked Tatiana.

No one responded.

"Tell us about your character and read your lines," said Betty, playing the part of Pearl.

The character playing John Miller responded: "First of all, I know what you want to ask me. Am I Deep State?"

"I haven't asked you that … yet," said Satin.

"For the record. I AM NOT DEEP STATE!" said the Miller character.

Everyone in the cast reacted.

"Wow. That was good," said Satin.

"Thank you. My name is John Miller. I am conducting what you in the vertical media say is a 'witch hunt' on Governor Card. John Silverstein limited my investigation to Governor Card only and said to not look at Crooked Rodderman because Bongino and Strozinski exonerated her before investigating her. That is what reasonable prosecutors do. Isn't that right?"

No one said anything.

"We all know that Bongino conducted a thorough investigation of her."

Laughs from Satin and Pearl.

"This is not a laughing matter," said the Miller character.

"No, it is not," said Pearl.

"They told me to call it a 'matter,' not a criminal investigation. I get it."

"This is terrible," said Tatiana, interrupting.

"I think it is funny," Brandeesha said.

"Now, tell me, Mr. Miller, did you approve the sale of twenty percent of U.S. plutonium to the Soviets?"

"Yes."

"Did Jill Rodderman's foundation receive over $145 million in donations after the sale was approved?"

"Yes, it did."

"Was that legal?"

"Yes, it was legal. I know what you are asking. There was no quid pro quo and there was no 'pay for play.' All of that was legal," said the Miller character.

"Ok. That's good," Brandeesha said as Satin.

"Mr. Miller, have you actually indicted anyone for 'collusion with Russia' based on actions for which you were appointed to prosecute or have all of your indictments been based on 'process crimes' – crimes as a result of your investigation after you were appointed."

"No. I have no indictments based on Russian collusion."

"So you just prosecute what they call 'process crimes'?" asked Pearl.

"Yes. That's what we do. If we can't prosecute someone on the crime, we prosecute you for a process crime," said the Miller character.

Betty continued as Pearl: "Mr. Miller, I don't understand why you wanted to be the GCJ director a second time after you had completed your prior term. Can you explain that?"

"No one turns me down after a job interview!"

"And when you didn't get your old job back, you agreed to be appointed special counsel to investigate Russian collusion during the election of then candidate Card, whom you sought an appointment from?"

"Yes," said the Miller character. "And once again. I AM NOT DEEP STATE!"

"He's not Deep State," said Pearl.

"Ok. He's not Deep State. I get it," said Satin.

"Do you have a conflict in this case?" asked Pearl.

"No."

"You found no evidence of collusion?"

"Yes. I mean, no. We found no evidence that the Card campaign colluded with Russia, but we did not exonerate him either."

"Did you investigate whether the Rodderman campaign colluded with Russia?"

"No. I was not asked to do that. I only do what I am asked."

"Did you find that Card obstructed justice?"

"I could not make up my mind," said the Miller character.

"So you wanted to give a roadmap for impeachment for Governor Card?"

"Yes."

"Are you ready to answer questions on that issue?" asked Pearl.

"No. I can't get into that," said the Miller character.

"Thank you, Mr. Miller," Brandeesha said as Satin.

"John, you play Paul Strozinski in the play," said Betty.

"I have no bias," said John playing Strozinski.

"Wait, John … for my line first," said Betty.

"Now what did you do wrong in the Rodderman-Card investigation?" asked Betty to Peter.

"Nothing. I have no bias whatsoever. I hate Card, but I want you to know that in no way, shape, or form did my bias or hatred of Card ever interfere with or affect my decision in my responsibilities in investigating Rodderman, and in no way, shape or form did my hatred or bias, I mean did my opinions of Card, affect my decision to open up a counter-intelligence investigation of then-candidate Card when there was no evidence to open up that investigation, not was there any approval for me to open up that investigation."

"Let me see if I understand you. You said you had no bias in opening up an investigation of Governor Card when there was no evidence of a crime to open up that counter-intelligence investigation and you had no approval to open up that investigation?" said Pearl.

"Did he really do that?" said Satin.

"Yes, I had no bias in opening up a counter-intelligence investigation against Card when I had no evidence to open up that investigation and I had no approval to open up that investigation," said Peter.

"That's what I thought you said," said Satin.

"That's what he said," said Pearl.

"Yeah, that's what he said," said Satin.

"Now let me see, wasn't it you who changed the terms 'grossly negligent' to 'extremely careless' in the exoneration letter of Jill Rodderman and you told your boss Director Bongino to sign that letter?" asked Pearl.

"Yes. He works for me, but I have no bias," said Paul.

"Did you write that letter before you interviewed her?" asked Satin.

"Yes. I cleared her before interviewing her," said Paul.

"I thought you did that," said Satin.

"It's okay for a Navy enlisted sailor to go to jail for taking photographs of a submarine while Rodderman got off after thousands of classified documents were subpoenaed by a congressional committee and destroyed by her aides and lawyers?"

"Yes."

"Did you and Lisa Scheetz with EPK agree to leak to the press about the counter-intelligence investigation of Carter Scheetz?"

"Yes."

"Paul, do you remember George Pappadeux? He was the aide to Card that you set up in England with your two informants -- to see if he would take dirt on Rodderman?" asked Pearl.

"Yes. We set that up too. Then the pathetic and hopelessly biased vertical media exposed the identity of our agents."

"Did you and Lisa Scheetz come up with a leak strategy with the media?" asked Satin.

"Yes, but that strategy was to prevent leaks," said Pearl.

"But you congratulated Lisa Scheetz after two articles were leaked to the press confirming the counter-intelligence investigation on Carter Scheetz," asked Satin. "Does the GCJ normally confirm counter-intelligence investigations in the press?"

"No."

"Brandeesha, this play is horrible. I think you need to take your medication," Tatiana said, interrupting the scene. "We are really going to be in trouble for making fun of these people in this play. These are honorable people who thought they were doing the right thing. They live by a higher honor. This is truly disgusting to make light of such a serious topic."

"This is just a play. Tatiana. These people are not real."

"I know but how they are being portrayed in this skit affects the GCJ and that reflects poorly on our government."

"You mean we can't criticize the way our government does business? These are not real people. What's wrong with you?" asked Betty.

"Betty, I ask that this play be postponed so that we have time to read more information about it," Tatiana said.

"You are out of order," said Betty. "We will continue."

"I move that we adjourn," Tatiana said.

"Let's go to Mr. Bongino,' Brandeesha said.

"Now, Mr. Bongino. Did you do anything wrong in the Rodderman-Card investigation?" said Satin, turning to the character playing GCJ Director Bongino.

"No. I operate from a higher honor."

"Did Paul Strozinski write the letter reopening the Rodderman investigation?"

"Yes. I signed it. At least I did something right."

"They say you lost the election for Rodderman," said Pearl.

"Yes. I pissed everyone off," said the Bongino character.

Tatiana turned to Betty and said: "Betty, *this play is so stupid. It has to end..*"

"They are marsh creatures!" Brandeesha said.

"Drain the marsh!" said John.

"John, be quiet and sit down," said Betty.

"Yes," said John.

"Tatiana, take a deep breath and give your husband a hug," said Betty.

Tatiana did nothing.

Betty continued. "Let me ask this question: Who among the Deep State characters leaked false information about Card during the Card-Rodderman campaign?"

No one raised a hand.

"I will ask each of you. Mr. Bongino, did you leak false information to the press about Governor Card?" asked Satin.

"Yes. I leaked my notes with the governor to a law professor friend so he would leak it to the press. I wanted to trigger the appointment of a special prosecutor," said the Bongino character.

"Mr. Bongino, what exactly did the Governor say to you that would cause you to leak your notes to your law professor friend?" asked Satin.

"He didn't want us to prosecute a four-star general, whose conversations we secretly listened in on. I didn't think he lied but we prosecuted him for lying anyway. I sent two agents to his office to set him up."

"Did he lie?" asked Pearl.

"Of course not," said the Bongino character, lowering his head.

"Let me understand this, the Governor didn't want you to prosecute a four-star general for lying when the general did not lie to the GCJ?" asked Satin.

"Yes, its true; the general did not lie, but the Governor has no right to interfere in our ability to conduct investigations. If he does, then it's obstruction of justice. I want a GCJ report!" said the Bongino character.

"Now the last thing I will point out is that – the next person who says an GCJ report is worth anything obviously doesn't understand anything. The GCJ explicitly does not, in this or any other case, reach a *CONCLUSION,*" said Pearl, looking around at the group. *"PERIOD,"* she said, and she looked around once more, then said again: *"PERIOD."*[40]

"You wanted Jill Rodderman to be governor of Alabama?" asked Satin.

"Yes," said the Bongino character. "Card is morally unfit to be governor. He looks like a mob boss."[41]

"You cleared Rodderman deliberately when you had sufficient evidence to prosecute her, and you and Paul Strozinski, a Russian immigrant, opened up a counter-intelligence investigation against candidate Card when you had no evidence to open up that investigation. Then you used a dirty dossier to secure a warrant from a federal court to place a wiretap on one of his aides without telling the federal court the dossier was false and unverified and that it was campaign opposition research paid for by Jill Rodderman's campaign? Is that what you did, Mr. Bongino?" asked Pearl.

"Yes."

"Mr. Bongino, have you heard of a man named Ivan Danchenko?"

"I can't get into that."

"I'm sure you won't because you gave him CHS status and withheld his name from the public."

Bongino did not respond.

"He's no longer answering so I will save everyone time. Danchenko was the sub-source to the dirty dossier. He was a confidential source for the GCJ who made up the stories in the dirty dossier. He was a russian agent who the GCJ paid for the information in the dirty dossier. His name was withheld by Mr. Bongino who then carried on with the russian collusion investigation knowing that the information was false and had been paid for by the GCJ. Then he withheld the name from Mr. Miller and the Inspector General. Did you do that Mr. Bongino?"

"Yes. I admit it."

"It is good that you finally have this out of your system," said Satin.

"Oliver, would you play Governor Card in this session?" asked Betty.

"Yes," Oliver said.

"Mr. Bongino, would you walk over and give Governor Card a hug?" asked Betty.

"Do I have to do that?" asked the Bongino character.

"Yes, you do," said Betty.

"I can't do that," said the Bongino character.

"Get over there, Director Bongino!" said Betty.

They walked over and hugged. The entire cast clapped.

"That wasn't so hard, was it, Mr. Bongino?" asked Pearl.

"No," said the Bongino character.

"Mr. Brown?" asked Satin.

"Yes," said the character playing DJB Director Brown.

"Did you leak information to the press to try to damage the Card campaign against Jill Rodderman?" asked Satin.

"Yes," he said. "He committed treason. I mean he committed treasonous acts."

"Now, Mr. Brown. That is an awful thing to say. Do you think your security clearance should be pulled for a director who leaks to the press?" asked Satin.

"No."

"Mr. Brown, did you vote for a communist for president of the United States?"

"Yes," said the Brown character.

"Mr. Brown, you voted for a communist for president, you leak to the press, you peddled the dirty dossier to the GCJ and you said that Governor Card committed treasonous acts when he did not commit treason. Is that true?" asked Satin.

"Yes," said the Brown character, looking down.

"And you should keep your security clearance?"

"Yes, and so should fifty other military intelligence officials who stand behind me!"

"Well, I'm sure they do, and during this war when the bullets are flying at you, I'm sure they will stand right behind you. Thank you, Mr. Brown," said Satin.

"Now let me go to Lisa Scheetz. Lisa, what do you have to say for yourself?" asked Pearl.

"Tell me that he's not going to be governor of Alabama," said the character playing Lisa Scheetz.

"He won't. I will stop it. We have an insurance policy. Andrew Alexander and I discussed that in his office," Paul Strozinski interrupted.

"Paul, it is not your turn. We just talked with you. Thank you, Paul. You can now go back to your job at the GCJ WITH THE HUMAN RELATIONS DEPARTMENT!" said Pearl.

"I was not demoted," said Paul.

"Thank you, Paul," said Betty.

"Paul," asked Satin.

"Yes," said Peter.

"YOU'RE FIRED!" said Satin.

"Now, one other question, Lisa."

"Are you related to Carter Scheetz?"

"No. There is no way we could be related," she said.

"Ms. Scheetz, did you leak information to the press as an EPK employee?"

"Yes. Paul Strozinski and I had a media leak strategy. *The Morning News* was mad that I gave information to *The Herald* and not them first."

"Now let's get back to the rest of the leakers. Will the rest of you who leaked information to the press, please raise your hand?" asked Pearl.

No response.

"Come on now, all you Deep Staters. Let's try again. How many of you leaked information to the press during the Card-Rodderman campaign to damage Governor Card so you could help Jill Rodderman be elected?" asked Satin.

They all raised their hands reluctantly.

"See, that wasn't so hard," said Pearl. "Now raise those little hands and say 'To the Deep State!'"

"TO THE DEEP STATE!" they all yelled.

"And who of you peddled the false Russia collusion story to damage the governor's election and to drum up support for impeachment after he took office?" asked Satin.

No response.

"Come on, free yourselves of guilt. Mr. Bongino, you can't wiggle out of this one," said Pearl.

"I operate from a higher honor," said the Bongino character.

"Insubordination! You're fired!" said Satin to the Bongino character.

"Now I want all of you to come over here and tell Governor Card that you're sorry for what you did to him and that you apologize to him; give him a hug and tell him you will never do it again," said Pearl.

"I'm not going to do that," said the Brown character.

"You have to do that, Mr. Brown," said Satin.

"Okay, as long as he won't revoke my security clearance," said Brown.

"He would never do that to you," said Pearl.

The Brown character gave Oliver, playing Governor Card, a hug.

"I don't think I can do that," said John, playing the Paul Strozinski character.

"You can do it, Paul," said Satin.

Then John as the Paul Strozinski character walked over and gave Oliver a hug. John got his hug from "No Hugs Oliver."

"I will do that only because this is in a play," Oliver said.

"See, that wasn't so bad, was it, Paul?" said Pearl.

"No, it wasn't," said John. "I've always wanted to know what Card support smelled like."

"Stay on script," said Betty to John.

"I can't do it, either," said the Bongino character.

"Yes, you can, Mr. Bongino," said Satin. "You have to forgive the governor."

The Bongino character walked over and gave Governor Card a hug.

"See, I knew you could do it," said Satin.

"Now for penance, all of you Deep State characters will fight with Miss Tatiana the Great, who is actually Joan of Arc, and will fight to restore Governor Card to power after Zoros declares war on the state of Alabama and the vertical media," said Pearl.

"You know that Zoros has flooded the U.S. with four million immigrants. He wants them to vote in the next election even if they do not have any identification."

"I can't do that," said the Bongino character.

"I can't do that, either," said the Paul Strozinski character.

"Don't argue with the script," said Betty. "All of you Deep State characters will have to go to war to restore Governor Card to power, because you were seditious actors who overthrew the governor from office. As penance you will have to restore Alabama and the Rule of Law. That includes both of you – Mr. Silverstein and Mr. Miller."

"I am not Deep State," said the Miller character.

"I am not Deep State either," said the Silverstein character. Then he said, "I have only one line in this play?"

"Do you mind if I tape record my conversation with you, Mr. Silverstein?" said Satin. "Did you tape record your conversations with Governor Card?"

"I deny that," said Silverstein.

No one said anything.

"Let's end the skit after the war is won and Tatiana the Great, as Joan of Arc is tried and convicted. We need to end this play with something big. Some kind of explosive ending. One that will blast everyone out of their seats."

Tatiana heard Betty's request and then for a split second re-called her conversation with Oliver about Truman dropping the bomb on Japan to end World War II. Tatiana thought to herself: *That is exactly what I want to do to this play.* She would find a way to stop the ridiculous Griddle Iron play.

Chapter 53

"HELLO, MRS. PHILLIPS. I AM Dr. LaSalle. I wanted to update you briefly on your condition."

"Is it serious?"

"No. Certainly not."

"We had to delay your leaving the hospital because of certain tests that we had to perform. The facility room for that test was not available yesterday. Your husband says that you have been having some interesting dreams during your stay here. Can you tell me about them?"

"Doctor, they are quite embarrassing. I'm sure they have nothing to do with my stay here."

"You are quite right, of course, but if you wouldn't mind telling me more about them."

"You really want to know?"

"I do."

Tatiana told the doctor about her dreams which were from scenes from the books that she had read that included her friends and colleagues playing the roles in the book.

"Its is common to read a book and visualize what is happening and placing people you know in those roles is done often in the movies and theater."

"My boss did ask me to cover entertainment. Could that be it?"

"Perhaps. Have you had these dreams prior to your visit to the hospital?"

"No."

"When did they start?"

"After I came to the hospital."

"What do you think prompted them?"

"I don't know."

"What do these dreams do? I mean what is it that you are doing that you can't do in real life?"

"I am whatever character I read about."

"Are all the dreams based on what you read?"

"I think so ... actually, no." Tatiana thought about her vision with Sister Camille. "The visions tell me we can combine thought, feeling, and emotion and when we do that, we can ..."

"What?" asked the doctor.

"We can ..."

"Yes."

"We can move mountains...I'm embarrassed doctor. Don't laugh at me."

"I'm not laughing. What I want to know is precisely what you have been reading."

"It's all here on the desk by my bed."

Tatiana handed Dr. LaSalle the sack of books from Oliver, the Learner's Digest, and the script from the Griddle Iron play.

"Where did you get these?" asked the doctor.

"My husband brought me the novels. They were from Book Call at work. Everyone on the staff were to read their books by a certain time period. Then we would get together and discuss them and make reviews of them. I'm a fast reader. I've had visions after reading each one of those."

"What is the Learner's Digest magazine about?"

"A discovery about the lost gospel of Thomas."

"Why are you reading it?"

"It was given to me by another reporter. It was not part of Book Call."

"For a story?"

"No. He was reading it so I borrowed his copy to find out what he was working on."

"Working on? The lost gospel of Thomas?"

"I meant what he was reading."

"The lost gospel of Thomas," the doctor repeated as he looked through it.

"That one says you can move mountains," said Tatiana.

"Move mountains in what way?"

"By emotion and thoughts."

"Interesting. Very interesting."

"What is this?"

"It's a script about a Griddle Iron play."

"What is the Griddle Iron play?"

"It's an annual play that journalists put on to spoof the government. I'm sure you have heard of it."

"I have. Are you in the play?"

"Yes. I have the lead."

"Have you had a practice yet?"

"Not really. We've only had one meeting so far."

"Can you tell me about any other visions you have had?"

Tatiana was too embarrassed to tell him about his vision from Sister Camille. She was not going to go that far. She was not in the hospital for counseling.

"When do you think I can go home, Doctor LaSalle?"

"Soon my dear. Today, I'm sure. Do you have a regular doctor?"

"No. We can give you a referral."

"Thank you, Doctor."

"Thank you, Mrs. Phillips, and you take care."

Chapter 54

"THIS IS OUR LAST MEETING," said Hans.

"Why?" asked Andre.

"It's over."

"What is?"

"I've been discovered. I've been ratted out. The Deep State knows about me."

"What is going to happen?"

"The Deep State has removed Card from power and will stop anyone who gets in their way. The communist invasion will continue."

"I can't imagine that," Andre said.

"The Deep State has to be stopped. It will be up to the press to stop them. It's up to you, kid, because none of the other media outlets will touch it. I can't help you any longer. The entire world rests on your shoulders now."

"What should I do?"

"Talk to someone at the paper you trust. Do you know anyone?"

"Yes. Oliver Smith and Tatiana Smith. Mr. Nelms, Cub Miller."

"I'm sorry, kid. I thought you knew."

"What do you mean?"

"The future of the entire country and the world rests on you and your paper. The *Birmingham Defender* will finally expose the Deep State. I hate to tell you, kid, but I think your paper is Deep State. You may be the only one who is not compromised."

"What?"

"You heard me. Your two journalists Tatiana and Oliver have been communists for a long time. They were indoctrinated when they were in Europe together during World War II. The Russians got to them when they were in Europe. Did you ever wonder why they took an interest in you and covered your court-martial? Why they brought you into their newspaper without an education?"

"No."

"How many people get the chance you were given? And the other reporter, Cub Miller? How does a shoeshine man become a journalist and then is sent overseas to cover World War II? They are all Russian spies. That's why they don't believe your story about the Deep State. They will never let you publish it."

Andre was stunned. He had never heard this before. "I know there are communists trying to infiltrate the government, but I don't believe there is a Deep State."

"Your owner, Ed Nelms, is probably not Deep State. You have to get to him before they do. It might be your only chance. The communists have almost taken the entire state. It's just a matter of time before they take Birmingham. The entire city is fortified. Nothing's working."

"Do you know anything else?"

"There's more. That Tatiana Phillips is practicing some kind of mind control. The Russians are trying to develop the power and are trying to get to her to understand the power."

"What is it?"

"It's some kind of deep trance that allows people to go back and forth in the space-time continuum into the past and future. The theory is that your imagination is really a God-like force.

What you see here is the human experience. Once you're able to merge your imagination with the real world, you have joined with God. I know it sounds crazy. That is why the Pentagon has a dozen priests and ministers on a secret panel examining what is going on at the St. Peter's church out there in the country. That was until the communists took over the church and all the priests and nuns had to vacate. They are now in Birmingham. This power unleashes all kinds of abilities like levitation, telekinesis, astral projection, pyrokinesis, neural manipulation, and so forth. If the military could use that, they could defeat any enemy and they could use power in a positive way like propelling humans into space. It is some kind of force that can be harnessed for peaceful purposes. No more wars or poverty. I didn't think the people here were that advanced. I was sent to investigate."

Andre listened.

"You don't believe me, do you?" Hans asked.

"I don't know what to believe anymore."

"I know this sounds crazy, but listen up because this is the last time I can talk to you. According to this theory, if your mind is strong enough then it can merge your imagination with reality and they become one. What we can imagine in our mind we can really do in real life. That is the secret. Our imagination is a God-like force. That is where we talk to God. We all live in multidimensional realities. We can travel through space and time and change the world simply by viewing it. Everything changes based solely on our observation of it. No more work, struggle, poverty. You can fix every mistake you ever made in the past because this new power allows you to go back into the past or into the future or anywhere you can imagine. Once you imagine it, then it is created into a new reality. But you also have to have an emotional feeling – a feeling that you already have what you wish for or are imagining. You have to get to a certain frequency. When you combine your thoughts and emotions you can literally do anything. Move mountains, as they say."

"Is this on the up and up?"

"It's true. We have been monitoring that church up there – St. Peter's – for quite some time. Before the communists captured the St. Peter's church it was wired for sound and had cameras installed. One of the priests up there told one of the nuns to stop putting ideas in people's heads but she kept right on and started telling the homeless about it and unleashing this new power on the poorest in this country who were not ready for it. She was leading them to believe that they could do whatever they wanted to do if they believed. Then it turned out to be true. After Mrs. Tatiana Phillips made her visit at the church she fell and after that she started reading books and began to change reality. She really is a Wonder Woman. That is why she is still in the hospital. No one stays in the hospital for just a fall."

"How did you know that?" asked Andre.

"I know. The cover is that she fell and hurt her head, but the real story is that they're doing all kinds of tests on her until they figure out what is going on. Go check out the doctor at the hospital. He is no doctor. His real name is not LaSalle. He is a Russian and his real name is Reikovitch. He has been studying some kind of mind power that will enable you to do things you couldn't do before. He works for the DJB. They are trying to figure out what is going on in your fellow journalist, Tatiana Phillip's mind. She and her husband think they are going through some routine examination but it has going on for way too long. Boy, are they in for a surprise. The Pentagon is watching her right now as we speak."

Andre couldn't believe it. "What have they found out?"

"They think that man is on the verge of being able to unleash some awesome power based on his mind. If small atoms can unleash the explosion at Hiroshima and Nagasaki, imagine what a person can do if they can harness that kind of energy in their own mind. This is a big deal according to your government. It's nothing to me. No big deal."

Andre was stunned.

"Why do you think Lanny Ellis was here to see you? I mean it's not like you two were friends. He has been working on this project since the war. Did he take you to a Barons game?"[42]

"He didn't take me. I was covering it."

"How convenient. He made it your idea. Did you see Willie Mays?"

"No. He didn't play in that game."

"Let's see, after the game both of you walked by a lady who asked you the million-dollar question?"

"Yes."

"Then afterwards you had some wild dream that you couldn't tell what was real and what was your imagination? All your thoughts and dreams are merged together in some strange ending?"

"Yes."

"You read a book about Andrew Johnson and then you visualized being with him, right?"

"That's the same thing that Tatiana Phillips is experiencing."

"I see."

"That was really great, kid. I had to read up about your president Andrew Johnson in your history books just to figure out what you were doing. I had heard about Washington, Lincoln and Roosevelt, but not Johnson. And that interview of him was classic – right out of the future. Have you heard of Barack Obama?"

"Of course you haven't. He won't be born until August 5, 1961. I can see someone really interviewing a president just like that."

"How would you know that was a dream?" asked Andre.

"I just do."

"What else can you tell me?" asked Andre.

"Ellis placed a device near the clock on the dresser next to the bed that began to speak to you in a recording. Then he placed a monitor device on your head. That's how we monitored your dream on a program. He removed it after he found you on the stairs after you went outside. That was a scare. You could have gotten yourself killed. You are not the only one. We are monitoring other returning soldiers from the war with this new technology."

"I don't believe it," Andre said.

"Believe it," said Hans.

Andre said nothing.

"Why were you prosecuted and then your case was reversed on appeal so quickly and then you were returned to the battlefield? Didn't that seem strange that all of that could happen so fast?"

"Yes. It was fast," Andre said.

"The Deep State ordered it."

Andre smiled as if he wanted to laugh but didn't know if he should. "Why are you in Birmingham?"

"Think man. There are courts galore in D.C. Why would the Deep State need to come all the way to a federal court in Birmingham, Alabama, to get a warrant like that? Think. Who prosecuted you during the war?"

"Captain Thomas."

"Who is the federal judge in Birmingham?"

"Judge Thomas."

Andre's eyes opened wide.

Judge Thomas.

"Here, take this," said Hans. He pulled from his back pocket a brown envelope. "Open it."

Andre found three pages of a memo that referenced Judge Thomas. It was marked Confidential – Official Use Only.

"Here is the dirty dossier on Judge Thomas. It shows how Judge Thomas bungled the case of *U.S. v Perlaza* with his arguments to the jury that the presumption of innocence will disappear and the presumption of guilt will appear when they go into the jury room."

"The presumption of guilt?"

"Yes, sounds crazy from a U.S. prosecutor. When word got out about his closing argument, we began investigating him. This is not a typical statement for a normal prosecuting attorney with the Department of Justice. It sounded Deep State. His closing and actions he took in that case and others shows that he has Deep State tendencies. Some litigants are moving to recuse him from hearing their cases based on his judicial misconduct in that case."

"Like what?"

"There is no presumption of guilt. That is definitely a Deep State strategy to change the rule of law to the presumption of guilt. Thomas slipped up and openly said that in a criminal case. Then he tried to correct the record like he was a judge giving the jury instructions. Does this sound familiar?"

"Yes."

"Then it shows that he was suspended for not paying his bar dues in one state and then blamed it on being sick while serving in the war. His name was posted in the state bar journal as being suspended.

"Then there is the case of *U.S. v Armenta* a federal judge found him to be negligent in not responding to a defense counsel's request to make witnesses available at a hearing. Thomas knew the witnesses were being transferred out of the court's jurisdiction. Then by not responding to a request to make them available, they could not be compelled to return to testify by the defense counsel."

"Then there is *Rodriguez v Cash* where he presided over a case where a prosecutor made a mistake that was similar to the mistake he made in *U.S. v Perlaza*. The *Perlaza* case that Judge Thomas handled as a young federal prosecutor was reversed on appeal. But when Judge Thomas was presiding over the habeas corpus case in *Rodriguez v Cash* he sympathized with the prosecutor and found no constitutional violation by the prosecutor. He should have recused himself in the *Rodriguez* case because he had committed a similar error when he was prosecutor. Does any of this sound familiar to you?"

"Yes, All of the things that you talk about in this report are the same things that happened in my trial," Andre said.

"You got it. The guy can never admit a mistake. He always has an excuse for his behavior. Now you know the secret of Judge Thomas. If you decide to go with this story then wait twenty-four hours to let me get my family out of town. That is secret I will keep to myself. The Deep State will figure out where you are getting your information. My family and I are leaving Birmingham for France. I've heard there are ships coming into Mobile offering passage to Marseille. From there I can find safe passage to Bora Bora in the South Pacific. When they start dropping nuclear bombs I want to be as far away from this place as possible. Take care, kid," said Hans as he left. "That is the last tip I can give you."

"Hans," Andre said as he was walking off. "What is your wife's name?"

Hans turned around. "I can't tell you. Being with the agency and with this war going on, I have to protect my family."

Chapter 55

Tatiana began to travel through time with her new powers. She could now investigate Andre's life story and see firsthand how the fire at Andre's home happened in 1930 on that extremely hot that day in Mountain Springs.

Tatiana saw the Williams' home. In the distance she could see St. Peter's Catholic Church and the ongoing construction on the church grounds.

The Williams' home was old with wood slats and porches on two sides. It had wood shingles and was surrounded by trees. She looked around and there were other homes not far from each other. People were coming and going, working, laughing, sleeping, sweeping, walking, talking, and taking care of their farms, property, and homes. It was a community living together, working together, and growing together.

"Are you lost?" asked Kyle Williams.

"Hello," she said startled by his sudden presence.

"My name is Tatiana Phillips. I'm with the *Birmingham Defender*. I would like to interview you."

"Interview me? Perhaps it is you who should be interviewed."

"Me be interviewed? Why would you say that?"

"Is it not you who is on a journey?"

"I'm always looking for a new story. Tell me about your family. What is the secret of your family's success?"

"It is the long concentration of the mind. There is a force unseen. You cannot tell just what this force is, but it brings up the thing we long for from the cosmos. We only know that it exists. The force around us consists of unseen possibilities. This intelligence attracts to its own and brings you what you ask."

Tatiana was stunned listening to him.

"This worries me," she said.

"Why are you worried?"

"This seems like a dream. Is this a dream?"

"This is not a dream; it is a new horizon?"

"If this is not a dream then I am lost here," Tatiana said.

"Do you not recognize a dream when you see one? Can you not imagine what you want and think about? A dream is reality once you think it and feel it. All you do is ask for it and believe, and assume the felling that you already have it."

"That is pretty deep state to be in. So, what does your family like to do here?"

"We have time for thinking, wonderment, reflection, music. Our health is good, and we live to a long and very old age."

"Indeed," Tatiana said. "And would that apply to me?"

"Yes."

"Everyone is living here together and growing together. This seems real sappy to me. Is this for real?"

"Yes, that is how it is here."

"I see."

"You have written so much in your newspaper about how the world will never be the same. You create divisiveness among your people. Your horizontals, your verticals; have you never seen such a pitiful site? There is no distinction here. There is no future. There is no past. There is only now."

"I'm writing. Keep talking," Tatiana said.

"Can you not recognize the good faith in everyone? You fail to recognize the beauty in life before you, in the existence of God, in his creation, and our relationship to the universe. You pursue only that which will divide and conquer and will ultimately fail."

"What do you mean?"

"Here life flows through us. The most infinite particle in the universe is not a wave or a vibration or a tiny piece of gold or of mass. The universe consists of nothing but a relationship. That was what Jesus was telling us. We are part of the creator. The creator is God. We are all gods because we are part of the creator."

"Oh, my gosh. I can't believe I'm hearing this," Tatiana said. "Where have I heard that?"

"I am sure you have heard this before."

"Somehow I feel like it is me who is on trial here."

"It is you who are on a journey; just like everyone else, trying to find the creator before you die; the longing to know God before you die; to have that absolute confirmation that you are not alone; to have a relationship with Jesus before you die; that your life was not for nothing but that it had a purpose, a meaning, a truth, a basis in fact and was not a game. My dear, you are not investigating us. You are investigating yourself."

Tatiana was stunned.

"So, what is the answer to the universe?" asked Tatiana after gaining her composure.

"Love is the answer."

"And how is that found?"

"By combining thought, emotion, and feelings; when you do that, you can move mountains. Part of your journey is here. Isn't that why you are here? I have been waiting or you."

"Mr. Williams, I can't lose sight of why I am here. Where is your family?"

"See, over there," Kyle said, pointing to a stage where the children would sing and perform plays. "We have all been waiting for you."

All of the Williams children were standing on the stage ready to sing. Booker Thompson sat on the ground watching and grinning. There was no way he would be on stage. Deanna, Franklin, LaVonda, Andre, and Ben began to sing:

> *My Shepherd will supply my need*
> *Jehovah is his name*
> *In pastures fresh you make me feed,*
> *Beside the living stream*

When it was over Deanna said, "I don't think we got that one right. Let's try it again and pick it up a bit."

After the song ended, Kyle invited Tatiana inside to meet the family.

"This is Tatiana Phillips with the *Birmingham Defender*. She will be asking questions." Kyle went to the barn where Ben and Booker were looking for eggs.

In the home, Deanna began playing the song "My Shepherd Will Supply My Need" on the piano.

Andre went upstairs. You could hear the guitar being played in Franklin's room. Franklin was not strumming the guitar. He was playing a chord for every note in the song.

"Where's Booker? He's your friend and you should be playing with him," said Franklin.

"He's outside with Ben. He hates music. He says we sing the worst songs he has ever heard."

"We're ready," called Bertha, the mother of five children. She was in the kitchen putting icing on the cake. LaVonda was assisting and Deanna was still playing the piano.

Outside, Ben was running to his father, Kyle: "I found five eggs, Daddy!"

"Good job."

"I have two eggs," said Booker.

"Good boy," said Kyle. "Let's go inside now."

Tatiana walked outside and saw Clara Thompson approaching. Clara Thompson was Booker's aunt. Tatiana remembered it was later determined Clara started the fire in the home. Tatiana realized she had returned to the day of the fire. She would watch the house burn down and find out the cause.

Booker ran to Clara with his arms open wide. "Aunt Clara!" he yelled.

"Nice to see you, Clara," greeted Kyle as they walked up to the house.

"Hello, Mr. Kyle. How was my precious Booker last night?"

"We told him we were not going to church and he didn't have to sing at Andre's party, so he was a happy camper all night."

"Which church?" Clara asked.

"What do you mean which church?" said Kyle.

"Nothing," said Clara.

Tatiana walked back into the home. Bertha and LaVonda were finishing the last bit of icing when they heard the knock.

"Who is it?" asked LaVonda.

"It's Clara," said Bertha. "I invited her."

"You invited Booker's aunt?" asked LaVonda, surprised.

"I did. She can take Booker home after the party." As Clara walked in, Deanna played the piano.

"Here are some party napkins and candles, in case you need some," Clara said, walking into the kitchen.

Tatiana followed. Clara didn't realize she was there.

"Thank you. I do have candles, but thanks."

"So, you didn't go up to the new church today?" asked Clara.

"Shush," said Bertha. "I haven't told Kyle about that. I was going to tell him after lunch and see if we could go to the 5:30 service."

It was time for lunch.

"Sit here, Booker," said Bertha. "Andre, you can sit next to Booker."

Kyle said the blessing. "Let us be thankful for what we have."

"All right. Just get to it. No big speeches," said Franklin.

"Franklin," reprimanded Bertha.

Andre had worn a tie to the table on his birthday.

"Andre, you look like you're going to a wedding," his father said.

Everyone laughed.

"I'm going to a birthday party," he said. Then he put mashed potatoes on his plate.

"Well, are you going to eat 'em or climb 'em?" asked Kyle.

"He's going to climb 'em," said Ben. "I found five eggs."

"That's great, Ben," said Bertha.

"I found two eggs," said Booker.

"That is great, Booker," said Clara. "How were the boys yesterday? Did they play all day?"

"They tore up my room," said Deanna.

"Booker needs a bath," said LaVonda. "He stinks."

Everyone laughed.

Tatiana fell asleep after she finished the book *Lost Horizon*.

Chapter 56

Tatiana looked at Booker at the table. She looked at Clara and imagined Clara walking back to her home where she lived with Booker. Tatiana followed her. It was the day before the fire when Booker came to stay with the Williams'.

She walked into a filthy and pathetic house. Curled up in a corner of the room among piles of dirt and dirty clothes she saw Booker on the floor. She went over to look at him. He had been beaten all over with his belt. There were marks on his back. He had no shoes on. His feet were bruised. She looked over and saw a rumpled couch with a guitar on the floor. She picked it up and it had the inscription "Andre" written on it. The guitar had been used as a weapon to hit Booker. Booker used his feet to stop the blow of the guitar. The back of the guitar was shattered. Booker was crying on the floor. You could see the bruises on his feet.

Tatiana wanted to cry. She picked up Booker and took him to the Williams' home and into the barn and laid him down on a pile of hay.

"I know who you are," he said.

"You do?"

"Yes. You are an angel. You came to rescue me."

"I'm no angel."

"I have to go back," he said. "She will find me here."

Booker got up and walked out of the barn. Then he came back in and said: "See you sometime."

"You will. I promise you, you will. I want you to remember something."

"What?"

"You will grow up and will go to war and fight in France during the Great War. They will call it World War II. At one point in time, you and your friend Andre will come across a house. You will want to go in and clear the people out of the house. I want you to stay away from that house. Do not go into the house. You and Andre need to walk away from that house and get away as far as possible. Can you remember that?"

"I will remember," said Booker.

Booker walked back home. The next day Clara brought him to the Williams' home to stay the weekend.

Back at the house with the Williams family, Tatiana could now see what happened on the day of the fire. She saw Aunt Clara and Booker and Andre go upstairs into the attic. Then Aunt Clara came back down and went back up with matches.

"I have to get in there," Tatiana said.

She went into the attic and saw Aunt Clara light the candles. The boys played and then went downstairs. Aunt Clara followed. Nothing happened.

Tatiana went downstairs. They couldn't see her. There was no fire in the attic. Andre and Booker went in the room on the first floor where the other children were playing. Franklin left the front room to go graze the horses. Deanna went to the bathroom to take a bath. She turned the water on to run in the bathtub.

Franklin went outside and around to the barn and saddled a horse and walked it to the back door of the house. He knocked on the door and asked Deanna to bring him a towel for his neck. She took a rag and rinsed it in the sink and gave it to him and went back to the bathroom.

Tatiana walked into the room where LaVonda, Andre, and Ben were playing. Andre looked out the window. Franklin had walked the horse around the front of the house and was motioning to Andre to come outside to graze the horse on the side of the road. Then an old-fashioned fan that was running in the downstairs suddenly stopped. There was no more electricity in the house.

This was the clue she sought. Tatiana went to the attic and saw the electrical wire that had sparked and set the attic on fire. The house was frequented by a squirrel that would get in the attic and chew on the electrical cables. The house was so old and hot, that the wood was like a tinderbox ready to explode. The spark from the electrical short caused a fire on the wood slats that spread along the floor of the attic and began to rage. All this time Clara thought she caused the fire at the home and tried to blame it on Andre and Booker. If she only knew that it was the squirrel who caused the fire by chewing on the electrical wires.

Andre walked outside to get on one of the horses with Franklin. Tatiana went back downstairs and walked outside and saw Andre get on the horse and turn around and see the smoke coming from the roof. Franklin got off his horse and went into the home and got everyone out, but he could not get out of the house. Tatiana couldn't look any longer. She knew what was coming. She imagined herself back to the time when she came. She had just met Kyle Williams.

"Mr. Williams, I need to tell you something. Today I want you to take your entire family and leave today and drive to the coast to get away for a few days. I want you to drive to Mobile, Alabama, and get as far away from this place as you can."

"I will do as you say," said Kyle.

Chapter 57

WITH THE WAR CONTINUING TO rage across Alabama, Andre went to the *Birmingham Defender* and began his story to expose the Deep State. This story could end the war if he could convince the the paper to publish it.

He began his story: "Some people say it doesn't exist. Some say it has always existed …" His story charged that the Deep State had infiltrated the federal government and media outlets who were unwittingly working as Deed State actors. The media had become divided between the horizontals and the verticals after they were infiltrated by a worldwide conspiratorial organization run by Zoros, who was determined to take over the world.

Zoros' operation was run by members who were embedded in these organizations. The Deep State plan was to take control of the United States through mass migrations of communists into each state to shift the voting pattern to from orange to green and to control the government after controlling the media.

Alabama was the first state in the plan. But the plan came to a halt when the state unexpectedly elected Ronald Card, who took on the Deep State and Zoros, only to be removed from power by the Deep State, and this resulted in the war beginning in Alabama. This was the beginning of open borders, the abandonment of the rule of law, search and destroy and the end of the presumption of innocence.

Andre stopped typing. Tatiana's dream was so powerful, it had affected everyone around her. He asked himself: *Who is the governor of Alabama?*

He went to the paper's library and pulled out a bound volume of the state directory. He went to the governor's page. It said "James Folsom."

"Folsom? Why does my article read Card?" he asked.

He turned the page and there was a picture of the governor's wife and the governor at a reception. He turned the page back and the name on the page was now "Ronald Card."

"I thought I had it correct the first time. For a minute there I thought it said Folsom. I don't know where I got that."

Tatiana's power to visualize after reading had changed the world. The Griddle Iron play was now reality and what was once Alabama was lost to history. Andre was part of the new fabric of reality, one that had emerged because Tatiana had observed it and her observation changed that world and everyone around her. Tatiana and her colleagues were part of a new world order.

No one will believe this, thought Andre.

"Brandeesha, have young Andre come to my office," Nelms said.

"Yes, sir," she said. She called Andre.

"What does he want?" he asked.

"I don't know. Go find out."

Andre entered.

"Have a seat," Nelms said. "How's it going?"

"Good. I'm working on a story but I'm not sure I will turn it in. I'm still thinking about it."

"Better than proofreading?"

"Yes."

"And you're still in school?"

"Yes."

"What are you working on?"

"Oliver has me researching the election for him. Tatiana has me looking at a few things for her … she wants to investigate the fire at my home. I have another story. I'm going to interview the federal judge who prosecuted me during the war."

"Very good. Very good indeed."

"Thank you."

"You can't go down there looking like that," Nelms said.

He opened his wallet and pulled out two $100 bills. Nelms was wealthy, the first black millionaire in Alabama. He was making so much money that the IRS made him cut back on his salary.

"Go down to Tim James' and buy yourself a new brown double-breasted suit. And buy a brown hat. Tell them I sent you. You can't be seen looking like that in a federal court. Be respectful and treat the judge with the dignity and respect that he deserves. You may not agree with him but he made it to that point being appointed by the president. Don't ask any 'I got you' questions. Make our profession proud of you. Make yourself trusted. Gain his confidence and he will talk to you. If you don't, he will never have anything to do with you. A good journalist is respected. We are neutral. We don't favor one side or the other. If a journalist loses that respect, he will be vilified by everyone. The public can tell if a journalist is biased. If he's biased then he's not a journalist. He is a peddler of disinformation and lower than the lowest at the bottom of the ocean. That is where you will sink."

"Yes, sir."

"What are you working on?" asked Nelms.

"I have a real source that I'm talking with. I haven't written the story. I don't know if it's true."

"What is it about? Who is your source?"

Andre didn't say anything.

"You won't tell me? That is good. I respect that. That's what journalists are supposed to do."

"Let me ask you, Mr. Nelms. Is there such a thing called the Deep State?"

"The what?"

"The Deep State."

"There is no Deep State and never has been."

Andre did not respond. "May I ask another question?"

"Yes."

"When Mr. and Mrs. Smith and Mr. Miller were reporters in Europe, who paid their expenses?"

"We paid for Oliver and Cub. We paid for their food and lodging. Tatiana was not with this paper then."

"Okay. Thank you."

Chapter 58

ANDRE APPEARED AT THE COURTHOUSE of Judge Thomas in his new suit and hat. He took off his hat in the federal courtroom, which was majestic with a large hand-carved eagle above the judge's bench. On the side were pictures of former judges. He had studied the dossier on Judge Thomas and was prepared. The dossier must have been written by a lawyer because the issues raised in it involved extremely narrow legal issues. The bailiff called the judge. "Judge, there is a reporter here, says he wants to talk to you."

Andre went to Judge Thomas' office.

"Have a seat."

"Do you remember me?" asked Andre.

"No. Should I?"

"I am Private Andre Williams. You tried me in Paris in 1944." Judge Thomas was stunned. "Are you still holding court during the war?"

"I come back one day a week. The rest I spend at the Rule of Law Task Force at the edge of Birmingham. The rule of law goes on despite the war. You have five minutes. I will do that because you fought in the Great War."

"How do you like the bench?"

"It is comfortable," the judge said.

"When did you come off of active duty?"

"In 1946. I was in private practice. Then a state district judge before being appointed to this bench."

"Do you keep in contact with Captain Jesse Weinstein?"

"Not really. He tried a few cases in my court."

"Can we talk about my trial during the war?"

"Yes. Why not. The case is over."

"What happened when you misplaced the burden of proof at my trial in your closing arguments?"

"You remember that? Don't bring that up. That lives with me forever. I will never forget that. I was recently asked to recuse myself from a case based on that case. The case is a reported opinion and studied all the time in law schools. I have to explain that every time I go to a criminal law seminar."

"My case was reversed on appeal."

"I know that." said Judge Thomas.

"Did you misplace the burden of proof in your closing argument on purpose or by accident in my case?"

"Accident. That was an unfortunate remark during the heat of trial. I would never have done that on purpose."

"But the transcript of the trial says that you intentionally made the statement that the presumption of innocence will disappear and there is presumption of guilt ..."

"That was a mistake There isn't a presumption of guilt.. I'm sorry about that but it helped you win the case. As far as 'intentionally' making the statement, that meant that I did make the statement but I didn't mean what I said."

"My attorney thought you made all those mistakes in the trial on purpose so that the case would get reversed on appeal."

"I see."

"When you were with the Department of Justice, did you handle the case of *U.S. v Perlaza* where you told the jury that

when they went into the jury room that would be when the presumption of innocence would disappear and the presumption of
guilt would take over, or something like that. How could you
have made the same mistake in my trial?"

"I would never have done that. That would be like throwing a
case deliberately just to let you off. That would be unethical. The
DOJ, no matter how powerful they might be, is not unethical."

"Does not putting someone on trial who shouldn't be on
trial, unethical?"

"No, it was not in your case."

"Judge, I have the case of *Rodriguez v Cash* where the defendant alleged that his rights were violated when the prosecutor commented on the defense counsel's failure to rebut certain
evidence? The argument was that the state prosecutor's pointing
out the defense counsel's failure to rebut evidence violated the
Fifth Amendment right against self- incrimination."

"Yes, what about it?"

"You presided over that trial."

"So what?"

"The prosecutor made the same mistake that you did in that
trial."

"That was not the same mistake."

"You seem to sympathize with the prosecution."

"I do not."

"In the recent case of *Roe v City of San Diego*, a motion to
recuse was filed to have you recuse yourself from a case based on
a breach of ethics, your have a pro-law enforcement philosophy,
and you make condesending remarks during a hearing, that you
mocked a party during a hearing..."

"Stop it. This court takes its responsibilities very seriously
to be fair and impartial to all parties. In the *U.S. v Perlaza* case

in a heated moment at trial, during a rebuttal closing argument, I made an injudicious remark and inarticulate comment to the jury. While the court on appeals found it to be prosecutorial misconduct you fail to address the body of my work which has never been characterized as improper, except in that one instance."

"Should you have recused yourself in the other case?"

"Which case?"

"The case where the prosecutor made the same mistake as you?

"I did not need to recuse myself. That was not the same type of case as yours," said Judge Thomas.

"At my trial, were there witnesses who could have testified, but you allowed them to be transferred out of the theater and therefore my attorney could not call them as witnesses?"

"I did not do that. I could not change their military orders if they were to be transferred out of theater."

"You were accused of doing the same thing in the case of *U.S. v Armenta* when you were a U.S. Attorney and witnesses were somehow transferred out of the state and not available to testify. The federal judge said that you were negligent in not responding to the defense counsel."

"Yes, I was negligent, but I did not intentionally violate the law."

"I was told that you were disbarred in California for not paying your bar dues."

"I was not disbarred. I was suspended for not paying the dues. That was a mistake on my part and I admitted my mistake."

"Why did you not pay your bar dues after you left the state?" asked Andre.

"That was a mistake. I was practicing law in another state and moved and forgot to keep up my bar dues in the other state. I accepted responsibility."

"Let me ask you. Have you had many cases against the Ku Klux Klan in your court?"

"Those come here sometimes."

"Are you familiar with the Klan activities in the South?"

"Just what I read in the papers."

"But you have no knowledge of Klan activity?"

"What kind of question is that? No, I have 'no knowledge' of Klan activity."

"What about Russians influencing the government?"

"That is a fact. Congress has been investigating that for years. There is a committee doing that in Washington. They are about to go public and investigate the State Department and Hollywood. That's in the newspapers. That's all I am going to talk about. Good luck to you. I wish you well."

Thomas getting up was a sign for Andre to leave.

"Finally, have you ever heard of the Deep State?"

"The what?"

"The Deep State."

Thomas laughed. "There is no Deep State."

"I know this sounds strange, Judge Thomas, but there is a theory floating around, just a working theory, that the campaign of Jill Rodderman paid for political opposition research on Governor Card. It is what they call the 'dirty dossier' and it was nothing but salacious lies about Governor Card paid for by Nexus, a political research company. They say that a U.S. senator gave a copy of it to the GCJ. They say that the DJB director snookered the GCJ into opening up a counterintelligence investigation of the governor to spy on one of his aides hoping to find some kind of Russian collusion between Governor Card and his campaign to defeat Jill Rodderman."

"That's totally ridiculous. I know Director Bongino, and he would never do such a thing."

"There's more," Andre said.

"Next you'll tell me that the GCJ cleared Jill Rodderman deliberately and then opened up the counterintelligence investigation to investigate Card as an 'insurance policy' to make sure that if he was elected he would be impeached," said Judge Thomas.

"How did you know?"

"I watch the *Font News*. I watch Brandeesha Yancey railing every night. I'm not a potted plant."

"There is one other thing," Andre said.

"What is it?"

"They say there is a secret federal court that signs counterintelligence search warrants and that one federal judge signed off on the warrant to spy on the Card campaign based on the 'dirty dossier' – the one that Bongino verified as true and that John Silverstein never disclosed to the court that the dossier was unverified opposition research paid for by Jill Rodderman."

"That's ridiculous. Surely the FBI would have informed the district judge of that."

"They say they didn't. They say that they placed a long and complicated footnote designed not to disclose where the dirty dossier came from."

"If the judge would have seen that, then the judge would not have signed the warrant."

"That's what everyone thinks," Andre said.

"Who is the federal district judge who signed the warrant to spy on the Card campaign without knowing that it contained the dirty dossier paid for by the Jill Rodderman campaign?"

"Judge, the word is that it … it was you."

"What?"

"I have one last question Judge. Judge … are you part of the Deep State?"

"Thank you, Mr. Williams. The bailiff will show you out."

"Judge, is there a question about your character?"

"No."

"I wish you well," Andre said. "I am going public with our story in twenty-four hours."

Judge Thomas did not respond.

Andre returned to his desk at work to finish his final story. The Deep State existed and Brown, Bongino, and others used the dirty dossier paid for by the Rodderman campaign to frame Governor Card for collusion with the communists in the Soviet Union when there was no evidence of collusion, and they deliberately cleared Jill Rodderman of violations of the law that would have been charged against any other citizen. Federal Judge Thomas signed the search warrant that authorized the counter-intelligence operation against the governor based on the dirty dossier.

It was an unbelievable story, the biggest story of the twentieth century, and it was handed to Andre as his first story for the *Birmingham Defender* by whistleblower Hans McClannahan, who gave the story to him because no other media outlet would touch it. Andre's story would end World War III, save Alabama and the United States, and save the world.

Chapter 59

TATIANA FINISHED READING *JOAN OF Arc* by Mark Twain. She would, as Tatiana the Great, rid Alabama of all communists and restore the governor to power – like Joan of Arc tried to rid all of France of the English and restore the rightful heir to the throne to power. She would restore the governor to power, because the Rule of Law commanded it, even though she personally despised the governor.

Tatiana rode to Uncle Laxalt, where she hoped to obtain his support to lead a force to conquer New Orleans. Once at his home, her uncle sent for the local priest to determine if Tatiana were really called or was a witch. The priest performed an exorcism. Soon word got around that she was truly called and the local county judge came to visit with her.

Others in town came to see the African American woman who sought to restore the rightful governor. Many townspeople from the local hamlets came to see the delightful and unassuming Tatiana. After witnessing the burning and killing across Alabama, they were impressed that Tatiana had been called to restore the seat of the governor.

Tatiana had never engaged in war planning, but from covering the Canadian Army during World War II she had some understanding of the tactics of war. She would ride south with the Buffalo Soldiers cavalry and cross Alabama into Louisiana and free New Orleans. Then she would ride back into Alabama and liberate Montgomery, Huntsville, and Birmingham. She would be joined by the 761st Tank Battalion, which would leave Texas and cross the border of Louisiana and Alabama and drive out the Russians. From the east, the U.S. Army would charge across the border from Georgia. The Canadians would cross from the north until they liberated Birmingham.

From the sea, the United States Navy would carry Army and Marines and launch an amphibious landing across the coast of Alabama. As soon as the shores were safe, the 320th Barrage Balloon Battalion would install balloons along the coast to protect the Tuskegee Airmen who would fly from Puerto Rico to Alabama, bombing the Russians across the state. The state would be retaken from all sides. All these events were repeated events from World War II that she, Oliver, and Cub had covered during their days as combat journalists.

For Tatiana, thoughts were things. It did not matter where or when those thoughts entered her mind. Tatiana would restore the rule of law, the presumption of innocence, the right of free speech, the right to be safe in one's home and free from invasion, robbery, or burglary. The communist insurgent in Alabama leading the invasion, Aleksandr Putaineue, would be captured and taken to the Rule of Law Task Force and tried by a military trial for his crimes. That was her plan.

"Tatiana the Great, here are your men. We were called by your uncle. We will escort you," said Maj. Kirk Kirkpatrick.

"Who are you?" she asked. "Why are you helping me?"

"Madam, we are the Buffalo Soldiers and other volunteers here to assist you. We ought together during World War II."

"Here with me are Second Lieutenants Trimmer, Saller, Hawkins, Adkerson, Ellis and Williams. And over here are our newest recruits." Kirkpatrick pointed to John Brown, John Bongino, John Clapton, Paul Strozinski, Lisa Scheetz, and the rest of the Deep State characters. "They are doing penance for trying to remove the governor while they were members of the Deep State. They are now fighting for Alabama and against the Deep State. They have been absolved of all of their sins."

"I am not Deep State," said the Miller character.

"Okay. He's not Deep State," said Maj. Kirkpatrick.

"Thank you, Major," Tatiana said. "Jesus forgives all sin. There is no crime that cannot be forgiven."

"Madam," said Trimmer, who bowed to her presence, pulling off his feathered hat, as did the rest of the group.

"Representatives from all countries," she said. "And a woman in battle with me. That is good." Tatiana was referring to Lisa Scheetz.

"I am coming," said Jim Ayacostu, representing an embedded combat journalist credentialed to cover the war.

"And who are you?" asked Tatiana the Great.

"I'm the free press. I am embedded with this integrated unit who fought bravely during the Great War," said Ayacostu.

"Then may God be with us," said Tatiana the Great, who, sword in hand, turned her horse around and with her armor gleaming off the sun pushed her sword into the air and took off with her white flag. The Russians were intimidated by her.

"Where are we heading?" Williams asked Ellis.

"God only knows," said Ellis.

"I've been wanting to cover you guys for years and I finally have my chance," said Ayacostu, riding the last horse.

"So, this is what it's like to fight against communists," said the Brown character as he was riding his horse into combat. They rode for twenty miles and stopped by a stream and let the horses get water and feed.

"We will camp here," said Tatiana the Great.

Trimmer had a copper pot in his saddlebags and began a fire with his flint rock after he whittled the wood with the knife he always kept in his pocket along with other items on his leather belt.

"We need a rabbit," said Saller.

"How about a three-legged deer? Hey, Williams, go shoot us a three-legged deer," said Hawkins.

"With a bow and arrow?" asked Williams.

Saller shot a squirrel in a tree and brought it to the camp. Trimmer took his knife and skinned it and put the meat in the pan with water that he had already boiled. Kirkpatrick found mushrooms in the forest and soon they all found edible vegetables that they brought to the camp and boiled in a stew.

Kirkpatrick took out the first serving and gave it to Tatiana the Great.

"Thank you," she said.

"Madam," he responded.

They savored the meat, tasting the food as it went down their throats. Ellis began to roll a cigarette.

"Don't do that," said Hawkins. "The enemy can see that and then pick you off when they see the flame."

"Where have I heard that before?" asked Ellis. "All of this seems strangely familiar to me."

Tatiana left to go into the forest to pray.

"So, tell me, Mr. Brown, did you really vote for a communist for president?" asked Trimmer.

"No. That was fake news," said the Brown character.

"No, it wasn't," said Ayacostu.

"Hey, you," said Saller, referring to Ayacostu. "You come over here and stay in this box. Saller drew a box for Ayacostu to remain.

"Hey Bongino, why did you go on national television and condemn Rodderman and then clear her at the same time? Then you said 'no reasonable prosecutor would bring such a case,'" said Kirkpatrick. "Was that your job to clear her? There are plenty of reasonable prosecutors who would have convened a grand jury and subpoenaed witnesses."

"I know. It was a joint enterprise. I couldn't let her be indicted during the election against Card so I decided to fall on my sword. I hated Card. We hated Card so much that we lost sight of who we worked for. It's as simple as that."

"Hate is a strong emotion," said Trimmer.

"You would prefer this country go through a recession just to make sure Card could be defeated?" asked Kirkpatrick.

"Yes. If it came to that. Yes, of course," said Bongino. "I would wear a mask for as long as it takes to make sure he did not win."

"Even if the mask does not work?" asked Trimmer.

"Even if it didn't work," said Bongino.

"Card didn't want you to indict a four-star general who did nothing wrong and you said that he was obstructing justice. But when the president wants Rodderman cleared you took that as an order and you cleared her. Why isn't that obstruction of justice. What is the difference? When someone has an opinion, is that obstruction of justice?" asked Kirkpatrick.

"That's different. It depends which political party makes the order. There is a double standard going on in this country. I am partly responsible for that," said Bongino.

"Didn't you go after Martha Wayne for lying to the GCJ and she spent six months in prison?" asked Trimmer.

"Yes. She lied to the GCJ."

"So did Rodderman."

"But that is different. I have prosecutorial discretion," said Bongino.

"Didn't you prosecute a Navy sailor and he spent a year in jail for taking some photographs of a submarine?" asked Andre.

"Yes. That was top secret information. He violated the law."

"Isn't that what Rodderman did?" asked Kirkpatrick.

"Yes," said the Bongino character.

"And you let her go," asked Kirkpatrick.

"Yes, because I have prosecutorial discretion."

"You prosecuted a four-star general for having classified information in his home but not Rodderman? What is the difference?"

"Prosecutorial discretion," said Bongino.

"You destroyed his career."

"Yes."

"But you let Rodderman off," said Trimmer.

"Yes."

"You pick and choose whom you want to prosecute," said Saller.

"No. We have prosecutorial discretion," said Bongino.

"You have unfettered discretion," said Saller.

"You have no accountability," said Trimmer.

"There is a two-tiered justice system going on," said Kirkpatrick.

"No, there isn't," said Bongino.

"We have no bias," said Paul Strozinski.

"He doesn't have bias," said Jim Ayacostu.

"Let me ask Director Clapton a question," said Trimmer.

"Yes," said Clapton.

"When you testified in Congress about the PMJ program and you were asked about the program, you said 'no.' So that is a lie."

"I made a mistake," Clapton said. "I didn't lie. I was thinking about something else, another program."

"Uh-huh," said Trimmer.

"I have been trotting up the Hill testifying for 25 years. Gee, just for a change of pace. I think I will, on this one question, and by the way, do it on live television and do it in front of one of my oversight committees. So, I made a mistake, but I did not lie."[43]

"But did you leak the dirty dossier to the press?" asked Trimmer of the Clapton character.

"No."

"Yes, he did," said Ayacostu, looking on from his box.

"Hey you, shut up," Clapton said to Ayacostu.

"Did you give the dirty dossier to Senator Blade?" asked Trimmer to John Brown.

"No," said the Brown character.

"Yes, he did," said Ayacostu.

"Hey you, shut up! These are security matters. It's none of your business," said Brown to Ayacostu.

"Don't ask me any questions," said Paul Strozinski. "I testified for nine hours in Congress. I'm done."

Then for the next hour the characters from the play confessed all their sins about their deliberate effort to clear Rodderman and to bring down Governor Card. They were ready to fight to restore the governor to power and end the Deep State. The Deep State characters as a group sang from the Griddle Iron play.

"You know, you guys, despite what you did, are okay," said Kirkpatrick to the Deep State characters after the song was over.

"I'm glad we talked this out. I don't think we're really that far apart. We just disagree politically but why can't we talk to each other anymore?" asked Trimmer.

"That was a long time ago. It will take time to be able to do that again," said Saller.

"Time is what we have," said Kirkpatrick.

"I'm done with the Deep State," said Bongino.

"Me, too," said the Brown character.

"Me, too. I'm not lying again," said the Clapton character.

"I'm done, too," said the Strozinski character.

The rest followed suit until the Miller character said: "Don't look at me. The author of this play knows I'm not Deep State."

"He's not Deep State," said Kirkpatrick.

"Are you guys ready to fight?" asked Trimmer.

Tatiana came back and saw her men and the Deep State characters talking with each other and bonding during wartime. War brings out the real character of a man or woman.

"What a woman," said Kirkpatrick when he saw Tatiana approach.

"Can you define what a woman is?" asked Ayacostu.

"Hey you," Saller said to Ayacostu, "you are not going there in this play. Go back and sit down where I told you."

Tatiana paced around and then turned to them and said: "Men and women, we are on a mission. I have been called to save the great state of Alabama from the communist invasion. I saw what the English did to France. For over 100 years, France fought against England and claimed France as part of its territory, removing the rightful dauphin from power. I restored the dauphin to power. I wanted all English removed from France. I will restore the governor to his rightful place and remove all of the communists from Alabama."

"Here, here!" said Trimmer.

"What is she talking about?" asked Ayacostu.

"Shut up," said Saller. "Stay right where you are and say nothing."

The men continued to drink and carouse the rest of the night, listening to Tatiana the Great tell how she would restore the governor and the rule of law.

"Where are we headed tomorrow?" asked Hawkins.

Kirkpatrick piped up, "Don't ask her the plans. We will know when she knows."

"We will take New Orleans," said Tatiana.

"We are with you to the end," said Trimmer.

"Here, here," said Kirkpatrick, as did the rest of the men and women.

"Tomorrow we ride to the governor and then we take New Orleans," Tatiana said. Her troops were amazed at her and her determination. Now there was no difference between them. They were one fighting force now. What happened in the past was in the past.

Chapter 60

TATIANA AND HER SOLDIERS FOUND where the governor was stay-
ing. Her white horse shone with brilliance and her heavy armor
reflected the sun. She would recognize the governor no matter
what he was wearing. She knew he would be disguised for his
own protection. She was taken to see him but once in the room
there were many people. No one pointed out the governor to her
but she spotted him with his back to her. He was standing next to
a nice-looking black woman who appeared to be guarding him.

"My name is Tatiana Phillips. I work for the *Birmingham Defender*. I am here to save you from the Deep State and restore you to power," Tatiana said.

"I know who you are. I've done my research on you," boomed Governor Card as he turned around. He was dressed like King Henry VI. "You are Tatiana the Great. The lady who interviewed Eleanor Roosevelt. You followed her all day and then walked into a meeting late! You were late then and you are late now!"

The men in the room roared with laughter and boos.

"I am here to help." Tatiana said.

The governor and his staff laughed.

"She came to rescue me," he said.

More laughter.

"Allow me to introduce my own personal assistant, Ogerosa," said Governor Card.

Tatiana nodded her head. Ogerosa held out her hand, expecting Tatiana to kiss it.

"I want to run for president someday," Ogerosa said. "I've had senators come up to me, I've had congressmen and women come up to me, I've had lobbyists and, of course, you-know-who is probably watching. Without a doubt he is watching right now. I might write a book someday."[44]

Tatiana ignored the remark and looked to Governor Card. "I know this sounds incredible, Governor, but you are in serious danger and I intend to install you back into power as governor of Alabama."

More laughter.

"You – the fake news media who has been attacking me every day in the press, trying to have me impeached before I took office, promoting fake stories, collusion with the communists, with Bongino using false evidence in a warrant with a federal court, refusing to cover the deliberate exoneration of Rodderman by the Deep State heroes – now you are trying to bring me back to power? It is because of you that I am out of power! You have been spying on my organization. I demand an investigation!"

His voice thundered across the room.

"I know, Governor. You are trying to expose the Deep State and the two-tiered justice system. Zoros and the Deep State will kill you before you expose them. You are in great danger."

"I have brought the lowest in black unemployment in the history of Alabama and this is the thanks that I get. I am in danger thanks to YOU!"

"I know you must hate me and hate what I said about you. I really don't hate you as a person. But you have to know that you can't continue to lash out at people you disagree with and make fun of them with nicknames. You have to rise above that. You have to unify, not divide. I am here to rid the country and the press of the Deep State and Zoros and restore you to power."

"Why don't you let me run the state and you run the newspaper? You should not be working for the *Birmingham Defender*. You should be ashamed of yourself. The way you treat my press secretary is a disgrace. You are a terrible person."[45]

"As a member of the press, I am here to rescue you from the Deep State, even though I don't agree with you and did not vote for you. I believe in the rule of law."

"The media saving the State of Alabama? Somehow I find that hard to believe."

Tatiana said nothing.

"I have no problem with the media in general. They are controlled by six conglomerates by billionaires who are not living in this country. They are a corporate monopoly and need to be trust busted just like Big Tech that censors free speech and are communists. Otherwise, there will be no more First Amendment. We have to make our state great again!"

"The press did not spy on you, Governor," said Tatiana. "I didn't believe anyone spied on you but they did. A Navy admiral figured out that the Deep State was unmasking your people."

"I know."

"They were using the top-secret data base to query names to figure out who we were talking to. I moved my offices after he warned me," said the Governor.

"They unmasked your people and illegally wire tapped them and entrapped some of them."

"Do you despise me?" asked Tatiana.

Laughter in the room.

"There is a two-tiered justice system in our government, thanks to Bongino. It refuses to believe that. It has to be stopped."

"Yes, but this is about the rule of law," Tatiana said. "The law says you are the governor. You have to return to power to govern this state. This is the only way to defeat Zoros."

After having Tatiana's story checked out by his aides, Tatiana was given the governor's army and they rode with her men to New Orleans. Before leaving, she sent a letter to the Deep State bogeyman, Zoros, demanding that he and his men surrender, or "I shall have them all killed."

Tatiana and the governor's army reclaimed New Orleans.

Tatiana and her men went on to fight thirteen battles to restore Alabama and its governor to his rightful place after the coup of his administration by the Deep State. She inspired the men with her white banner, and her approach frightened the communists.

During an attack trying to retake Birmingham, an arrow struck her above her breast. The governor's forces retreated but Tatiana returned to the battle and put her flag and said, "There shall be no retreat." The governor's forces returned to battle. More than thirty cities in Alabama occupied by Deep State Russians surrendered to Tatiana the Great.

Tatiana restored Governor Card to power but they lacked the supplies for her to continue her campaign to remove all communists from Alabama. The governor decided it was time to make peace with the communists and agreed to reopen the government, but Tatiana wanted all communists removed from Alabama. Finally, during the battle to retake Birmingham, she was captured by the communists on the first day of the siege. Tatiana's frequent use of offense was her weakness.

Chapter 61

Oliver volunteered to serve in Mobile, Alabama, in the Red Cross. He had no idea that Tatiana had been captured or her whereabouts. It had been sometime since they had communicated. His immediate job was to drive ambulances of wounded soldiers.

Oliver and Nelms were roommates. In their room, Nelms pulled out a bottle of Dewar's whiskey. "Let's have a drink. To your return to service."

"Not Dewar's. Glenfiddich," Oliver said.

Nelms poured two glasses. "How about another?" he said.

They drank another and then Nelms left the room. After putting on his uniform, Oliver went downstairs. Nelms was at the bar having a drink.

"Let's go downtown," Oliver said. "I hear British nurses will be there after work."

They left, and while walking down the sidewalk two nurses walked by. Nelms was the oldest journalist covering the war in Alabama against the Deep State. He hadn't worn a uniform since World War I, when he covered the Harlem Hellfighters.

"How are you?" he said to the nurses.

One was Brandeesha. She had been transferred from the Rule of Law Task Force to the hospital.

"I'm fine. How are you?" she said to Nelms. "And to you?" she said to Oliver.

Oliver looked at her. Nurse Brandeesha Yancey was tall and thin and beautiful.

"You look good in your uniform," she said to Oliver.

"It's not really the military. I just drive an ambulance for the Red Cross."

After a few minutes they departed.

"Did you get her name?" asked Nelms.

"Yancey. Brandeesha Yancey."

"I don't know her but I do know her. I don't know why. But I know her. She has a distinctive voice."

"I know her already."

"You aren't going downtown with me, are you?"

"No," Oliver said.

"You are going to the hospital," Nelms said.

Oliver said nothing.

"You are going to see Miss Yancey," Nelms said.

Oliver went to the hospital and asked for her at the front desk. "She is on duty. She cannot have any visitors," said the lady at the front desk.

"Would you tell her that Oliver ..."

"No, I will not," said the lady at the front desk.

Oliver left and walked outside and stood around looking. "Where am I and what is this? How can Alabama be taken over by Russians fighting on our own soil, and where is the United States government? Why is this a state-run war against a foreign power?"

A few seconds later Brandeesha walked out. "I only have a minute," she said.

They walked to a park bench and sat down.

"Do you like New Orleans?"

"Very much so," Brandeesha said.

"Why did you join up with the Alabamans?"

"I was in Alabama and I spoke Alabamian."

"Oh. That is funny. Do you speak any languages?"

"Je parle francais un peu. J'etudie francaise huit ans. And I'm learning Italian. It is so wonderful."

"Are you a nurse?" Oliver asked.

"I'm an LVN, a licensed vocational nurse. The nurses don't trust us."

Oliver looked at her and decided to give her a kiss.

"I can't," she said.

"No?"

"No."

"I thought I was getting somewhere," Oliver said.

"You are a sweet boy," she said.

They talked some more and then they kissed. He put his arms around her. She was nervous and her heart beat against his body, and then they were together.

"You will be nice to me, won't you?" she asked.

"Of course, I will. You are a nice girl."

"You like my voice, don't you?" she asked.

"I do."

"I mean, some people say that my voice is like a missile attack that will knock the paint off of walls. That is so mean. My voice doesn't sound like that?"

"No, it doesn't. Don't say anything."

Brandeesha was crying. "This is going to be strange. No one is going to believe us together."

Oliver walked her back to the hospital and they said goodbye.

Back at his room Nelms was still up. He was smoking a cigar and reading the newspaper.

"Did you have any luck with Miss Yancey?"

"We're good friends."

"You're like a lion looking for your next meal to devour."

"Shut up, Ed."

The next day Oliver was wounded when his ambulance was attacked by an improvised explosive device. His right knee was injured. There were over fifty pieces of shrapnel to remove from his leg. All he could do was stay in his room until he could walk again. He had not seen Brandeesha for weeks.

Finally, she came to see him.

"What do you have under your bed, darling?"

Brandeesha found several empty bottles of whiskey.

"Now I see what the problem is," she said.

"That's not me. That was Ed."

"Right."

Before long, Oliver was walking with crutches and Brandeesha would take him out for long walks. They were in love. Soon he could walk again. Brandeesha was pregnant.

Oliver decided he would not return to the ambulance service. He would leave Alabama and head for France and lead his life in France as a foreign correspondent. He had to make it out of Alabama while the war was still on and take his pregnant girl-friend with him.

"I will marry you, Oliver," Brandeesha said. "Oh, Oliver, I will marry you. You will make me happy."

"Don't say anything," he said.

They had to make it to Mobile where they could take a ship to Europe. They stayed in a small hotel the night before their ship was to leave.

Before heading to the hotel Oliver stopped at a pawnshop and purchased a new weapon. "This is a good one," said the storekeeper. "Just came in from the war from an officer. I know it will work."

"I will take that and one extra clip and one box of shells."

They went to a restaurant. Brandeesha was noticeably pregnant.

"It could be any time," she said. "You want a boy. I know you want a boy."

"I want a girl."

"You do want a girl," she said. "I am famished."

"What's on the menu?" Oliver asked.

"You can have chicken or I could shoot you a duck by dinner," said the waiter.

The waiter came back and said, "Excuse me, sir, but I have to tell you that you haven't much time."

"What do you mean?"

"I know who you are. You are an officer. You won't be able to leave during the war. The military knows where you are and they will arrest you. Come with me after dinner and we can give you safe passage out of Mobile."

After dinner Oliver and Brandeesha left through the back door of the restaurant. The owner had a small boat with a paddle. "Take the boat to Little Sand Island. There you will find a wrecked ship. You can hide there. Another ship will dock shortly and you can leave from there. They will give you passage to Europe."

Oliver and Brandeesha left and went to the boat but Brandeesha's labor pains began. Oliver decided to turn back and paddle up the channel to downtown Mobile and take his chances. There he found a hospital for Brandeesha.

"You are the father?" said the emergency room nurse.

"I am," Oliver said.

After hours of labor, Oliver was told that the baby was born dead and that Brandeesha had died. Oliver cried. He had thought to himself earlier: What if she dies? No. It can't happen.

Then Tatiana woke up.

"How disgusting," she said, getting up.

"What is?" Oliver asked. "The doctor will be back in a few minutes."

"Just seeing that disgusting Brandeesha pregnant was enough to wake me up."

"What?"

"Thank God she's dead. This is what they call a 'pregnant pause.' Oh, I didn't mean that, but that girl drives me crazy."

Tatiana went to take a shower and afterwards she came back in her white robe.

"Oliver, do you want children?" she asked. "I know it will make your mother happy. I wish you would just tell me that. I never know what you're thinking."

"Are you dreaming?" he said.

"Yes. I read *A Farewell to Arms* and now you are serving in the Red Cross in Mobile with Brandeesha."

"You know what they say: dreams are reality."

"No, they're not. They are two different worlds."

"What if that were true?" Oliver said. "That dreams and reality merge?"

Tatiana looked at him.

Oliver perused through the envelopes that were delivered to Tatiana. He noticed the second envelope that had not been opened.

"Did you open this envelope earlier?" Oliver asked.

"I forgot. I went to sleep and never opened it."

Oliver opened the envelope and read the materials.

Chapter 62

After the capture of Tatiana the Great, the communist soldiers paraded around her. They put her inside a steel-cage carriage driven by a horse and a driver. The communist troops yelled obscenities at her as her carriage was leaving. They spread lies that she was a witch.

She was taken captive by the communist leader Aleksandr Putaineue and brought to his headquarters in a secret hidden cave in the Quary Valley mountains of Alabama. Once out of the carriage, she had to bow and kiss his ring.

"You are the one who interfered in the 1946 election and prevented Jill Rodderman from defeating Ronald Card?" Tatiana said.

"There was no collusion," he said.

"I have a copy of the indictment that was presented by special counsel Robert Miller about twelve members of Russian military intelligence, the GRU, and it talks specifically about units 26165 and 75455; they say …"[46] Tatiana said before stopping.

Putaineue smiled.

"You smile. Let me finish. They say that these units were specifically involved in burglarizing the Democratic Party headquarters and taking their information and spreading it to the world to disrupt the Card-Rodderman election."[47]

Putaineue said nothing.

"I have a copy of the indictment. I can give it to you."

"Let me start answering your question with something a little bit different. Let's look at it this way. I mentioned it in 1942 and I want to say it again now, and I really wish that the Americans would listen to what I say. First, all Russia as a state has never interfered in the internal affairs of the United States, let alone its elections."[48]

"The Russians have been fomenting revolution everywhere from Southeast Asia, Latin America to Africa," Tatiana said. "Just like you started the war in Ukraine. You will have to leave some-day. You will never take it forcibly."

Putaineue ignored her remark. Then he said: "We did not elect Card, your voters did."

"The Miller investigation indicted twelve of your intelligence officers," Tatiana said.

"This is not the case. You are fighting to restore Card to power. This is against the Deep State. The Deep State will se-cure all arms of the government and the press and then we will be civil. My question to you is why is a horizontal wing media journalist fighting to restore Card to power? You are supposed to be fighting with us."

"Because I believe in the rule of law and not mob rule and the presumption of innocence and not search and destroy. I believe that the media should be neutral and not pick sides."

"The media should be neutral and not pick sides? All your press picks sides. All of your newspapers operate as political arms of one party or the other. Even the *Birmingham Defender* is part of the Deep State. Why do you resist?"

"Because I believe in a free press."

"Resistance is futile," said Putaineue, interrupting her.

"I want all communists out of Alabama," Tatiana said.

"You will submit to our rule of law. This world of yours here in America is decadent and perverted. Look at you. You act like a man. You wear a man's military uniform. You will always serve man."

Tatiana was disgusted listening to a man living in the seventh century. She had lost her powers and was a servant to Alexandre Puaineueu in hiding.

Chapter 63

Brig. Gen. Sengleton was an Australian who volunteered to be serve in Alabama to fight to restore Alabama from the communists. He served at the U.S. Embassy in Birmingham and was placed in charge of the Hostage Rescue Committee to rescue American military personnel who were kidnapped by the Russians in occupied Alabama territory.

BG Sengleton grilled the representatives each week intensely on his vision of rescuing one hostage. Each week representatives were asked if they had new information on the same cases that were brought up each week. Each week Cub had to stand up and brief the possible whereabouts of Tatiana. The ROLTF planned an invasion of an area where they believed Tatiana was being held captive.

It would be up to BG Sengleton and his committee to bring her home. Cub worked on the FRAGO (fragmentary order) that would be approved by Commanding General Payton to authorize that mission. To find her they first needed to send an intelligence scout who could infiltrate the communists fighting in the mountains of Alabama. They could target the communist insurgents based on evidence developed through military intelligence that could be declassified and used as unclassified information in an Alabama court of law.

"I find myself driven towards evidentiary-based targets," BG Sengleton told the group. Then he had all the representatives to the group go around the room and advise what new information they had to bring home American hostages who had been captured by the Russians. Each week members cringed having to attend the meeting unless they had new information to share.

After discovering that Tatiana might be in the mountains of Quary Valley, Cub volunteered to be taken close to enemy lines where he could hope to cross over and find local resistance fighters fighting against Zoros and the Deep State and possibly bring her home.

"Do you know how to read a map?" BG Sengleton asked.

"Yes. I covered Africa and Europe and was at the invasion of Normandy," Cub said. After settling in with the locals in the mountains, his job would be to blow up a bridge that would cut off supplies of the communists and then bring Tatiana home. The FRAGO was approved by BG Sengleton and then the commanding general. The mission: Operation Quary Valley. Cub was taken by a jeep with his supplies to the edge of the mountain and then was dropped off. He had food, a handgun, rifle, ammunition, and dynamite that he carried in his bag.

He found the cave in the mountains where the resistance fighters were located. He saw a man standing outside the cave talking to a woman, and it was Tatiana. The man struck Tatiana in the face. She was the slave of Aleksandr Putaineue, who was in hiding with the resistance group after being ousted from power by the Deep State and its bogeyman, Zoros. What better place than to hide than in the enemy's midst?

Cub moved behind a tree and pulled out his Colt 1911 pistol, aimed it at Putaineue, and shot him. It hit him in the back of his right shoulder. The bullet went through his chest and out the other side. Tatiana screamed.

Cub went up to them. "He won't die. Let's get him into the cave."

Cub and Tatiana dragged Putaineue into the cave. There were John and Betty. Betty and Tatiana were dressed as gypsies.

"You have killed our leader," said Betty.

"I don't think you know who he really is," Tatiana said.

They set him up against the wall of the cave.

"Leave him here and attend to his needs," Cub said to Betty. Betty got a wet cloth and placed it on Putaineue's head. He was unconscious.

"You brought dynamite," said John. "We can help you."

On the first evening Cub slept outside in his sleeping bag in the cold and on top of pine needles and rocks in the mountains. Tatiana left the cave and came outside to get inside Cub's sleeping bag.

"You were so brave. You killed Putaineue just like that. No one resisted. Not one shot was fired. Putaineue had no protection. He was alone with us. I am amazed how you killed him so easily. You are such a warrior," said Tatiana.

"The author of this play can make anything happen."

"I will make you a good woman," she said. "As God is my witness, I will make you a good woman."

"Don't say anything."

Tatiana said to Cub, feeling the full length of his body, "I need to kiss you."

"You don't have to."

"I don't know how. I must do all that a wife is to do. I can go with you to your home. I will be your woman."

Cub had not had a woman like Tatiana. He needed a woman. The soft touch, the embracing of bodies and souls. They lay together in the sleeping bag, the warmth of their bodies contrasting the coolness of the night. With no cloud cover, the stars in the Milky Way stretched across the sky.

"Have you been in love with anyone else?" asked Tatiana.

"No way. Not with you around."

"But I cannot love you."

"Why not?"

"Somethings happened in my past."

"Like what?"

"You should not ask."

"It doesn't matter," Cub said. "I love you."

"I have never kissed a man," she said.

"Don't say anything," Cub said.

They kissed.

"Where do my hands go?" she asked.

"Who worries about where their hands go?" Cub said.

Then Cub kissed Tatiana again and again. They were pressed together, and he was the happiest he had ever been. But what would Oliver think? How could he explain it? Where was Oliver? What would Brandeesha think if she knew he was with Tatiana the Great?

"Look out there," Cub said, pointing to the land in the distance. They could see rockets being launched into downtown Birmingham and exploding like fireworks. Each night the communists would launch twenty to thirty rockets into the city, bombing all parts of it indiscriminately. The insurgents could pull out a rocket launcher, fire a rocket, then move the launcher back into a garage to hide it. The U.S. military could not respond fast enough.

"They are already setting up the barrage balloons all around Birmingham. See the balloon go up? I saw that at D-Day in '41."

Tatiana looked and said nothing while they watch the sky being lit up with explosions across the entire night sky.

Cub was reliving his days as a combat journalist. There were no real barrage balloons going up. The Deep State had no aircraft. He was reliving his war time experiences along with the other combat journalists in Tatiana's dream.

Zoros was ordering daily attacks of Birmingham to conquer Alabama but he was losing. Tatiana, prior to her capture, had rescued most of the state. The last fight was for Birmingham. It was only a matter of time before the U.S. finally defeated Zoros and would put an end to his stranglehold over the federal government and the media.

The only ones left standing up to Zoros and the Deep State were Card and the Basket of Deplorables, who were always armed and prepared to fight.

"I remember when we had peace and everyone could go about their lives without fear for their safety, no mob violence, there was the presumption of innocence and the rule of law," Cub said. "We could walk down the streets without being harmed. All of that is gone. The horizontals and verticals cannot coexist."

"That's not true," Tatiana said. "I wouldn't be here if that were true. We can coexist. It is possible. You and I have to go out there and prove it and end this war. Cub, what do you think is causing all of this violence?"

"Zoros can no longer shape public opinion. He has the governor and the vertical media to contend with. They are not going to let Zoros decide how this country will be ruled."

"We have to stop Zoros. This has to end," said Tatiana.

"This war has gone on for four years. Longer than World War II. I remember when the media was neutral and dug up its own stories by genuine shoe leather reporting. I shined those shoes. We haven't seen that in years. Now everything is opinion and how to frame the narrative with operatives from political parties posing as journalists. This is a fight within our own country. It is over the ideals of this country. Journalism is dead."

"This was nothing like covering World War II," Tatiana said. "There was a war between good and evil. We were fighting against Hitler to destroy the Nazis. This is a civil war that is destroying journalism and politics. It's part of Zoros's plan to pit the media and the people against each other until one side final wins. How is this going to end?"

"I don't know."

"All I know is that when this war is over I'm going to go back to being a neutral reporter," Tatiana said. "No axes to grind. No more favorites for one political party. No more trashing the conservatives or liberals based on their beliefs. No more covering hastily called news conferences on Sunday night to influence the narrative on Monday morning without giving the other side a chance to respond. No more leaks to me by people who shouldn't be leaking just to print dirt on a candidate. I just want things back like they used to be. I'm tired of fighting," said Tatiana.

Chapter 64

THEY SLEPT THE NIGHT, AND when Cub awoke the next morning Tatiana was gone. He saw John come out from the woods smoking a cigarette. John went into the cave, saying nothing to Cub. Then John and Betty came out and were standing looking into the new morning wind. Three planes went by. Everyone looked in the sky.

"Have you seen planes like this before?" Cub asked.

"Never," said John. "Get in the cave. They can see you."

Cub pulled out his stopwatch and counted eight seconds. There was no bombing sound afterwards, and there had never been this many planes. Soon it would be time to blow up the bridge. He would have to rely on John to help him.

Cub took out a notebook and told John to go down the mountain to see if he could see any tanks. If he did, then mark the tanks with a slant and a mark for each. If there were trucks, then make a mark. If they had troops, then make this kind of mark. Mark for troops on foot by companies, for cavalry. Find out how often the guards change shifts.

"I know that," said John. "Eight hours."

"Take my watch," Cub said.

"I know. Eight o'clock. Noon, eat. Six o'clock, eat. Ten o'clock, sleep."

"Don't be a clown. Finish your breakfast and go."

"You know what the problem is with you?" John said. "It's not me who needs a woman. It's you who needs a woman."

John left the mountain to go down near the bridge to make a report on the military he observed.

He returned in two hours.

"Let me see what you have," Cub said. "Yes, trucks and personnel. Nothing else?"

"No."

"How many men?"

"Eight, maybe ten."

"Did you see any civilians? Any women?"

"No."

John thought of the Griddle Iron Show. So did Cub.

"What are you thinking about?" asked John.

"Nothing I want to be a part of," Cub said.

In their minds they were in the Griddle Iron show, but this time the setting was in the hills of Alabama where they were about to blow up a bridge.

John and Cub went into the cave. Betty turned around as they came in.

"I know what you were thinking," she said. Cub sat down at the table and Betty gave him an empty cup. "Take this," she said to Cub.

"John, sing your song," she said as she poured a cup of wine from the wine skin into Cub's cup and then John's cup.

"That is good wine," said John.

"Yeah," Cub said. "But we don't have time for this."

Then John stood on top of the table and began to sing his song in the Griddle Iron Show. It was a song about how Cub would find a woman for John and once he did he would "get me one, too," except that he used his real name, LeRoy in the song.

Then Cub and John were at a rehearsal for the Griddle Iron play. "That is really great," said Betty. "Now we will have to change the words to make it fit the play. I think we will have the character playing Paul Strozinski sing it to his boss, Mr. Bongino. Let's change the word 'woman' to 'warrant.' Get it? 'We gotta get you a warrant.' In other words, Strozinski is telling Director Bongino that we will get him a warrant to spy on Governor Card."

Groans from the cast.

Then Cub and John were back in the mountains and it was time to make the move to the bridge to blow it up. Betty was gone. Cub grabbed his sack of dynamite but the dynamite was gone. Betty had fled the camp. Putaineue had died under her care and she knew there would be violence afterwards and she did not believe in violence. She took the dynamite with her to stop further violence. To her, there were no enemies and there was no reason to destroy life. There were only Broadway plays and more Broadway plays. Life was a play and life was played out on the stage as a play. A play on stage was reality. She had no place in a war zone and would not help out the war effort.

"We will have to blow the bridge up in the morning after I figure out what to do," Cub said.

"I will stand guard tonight," said John.

The next morning Cub was ready to leave. He had hand grenades that he could use for the dynamite if he could figure out how to trigger them. It would take two people to wire the grenades to the bridge. Cub looked around and could not find John. The planes flew overhead. It was the Tuskegee Airmen. Eight seconds later Cub heard the bombs drop. That was his clue to blow up the bridge. He had to leave now. But John was gone. Where was he?

John left his post. He was so hungry he couldn't wait any longer. Cub had to leave. "The hell with him," he muttered.

On his way to the bridge Cub saw John chasing two squirrels.

"Where did you go? We have a bridge to blow up now. We have no dynamite."

"I had to go after them," John said. "Do you know what it would be like to have two squirrels at the same time? These are big and plenty of meat."

"We've lost the dynamite. How did that happen?"

"I don't know."

"I know. Betty took the dynamite. She doesn't believe in violence. How did I ever get mixed up with her? Let's go."

They walked down the mountain, making sure they were not seen.

"Did you hear the planes?" Cub asked.

"No."

"They already came. That was the sign. When the plane comes it is just a matter of time before you blow up the bridge. To blow it up you have to blow it up right. You blow it up when the Russian train is on the bridge."

"But we have no dynamite."

"We will use hand grenades and tie them together. If you see anyone, kill him. Don't fire your rifle. They will hear us. Kill him with your bayonet."

Cub and John went to the bridge and wired it to blow up using the hand grenades that Cub had with him.

Then two Russian soldiers came walking by.

John had a rifle and a bayonet. He had never been to war. Cub was 100 yards away and motioned to John to kill them. John froze. He couldn't do it. Then they came closer, but John had no strength. The wimp whom Cub would make fun of couldn't kill them. Cub motioned again. John grimaced. Then he gathered his strength and jumped out in front of the men and stabbed both of them with his bayonet. One fired his weapon before John stabbed him a second time.

Cub ran to help and stabbed them one more time with the bayonet on his rifle. Then he took out his pistol and shot both of the men.

"Good job," Cub said. "You are a real man."

John froze. He had never seen death. Cub put his hand on John's shoulder and said, "Come on. They know we're here. We have to blow up the bridge at the right time."

It was less than an hour before the train came. Cub pulled the wires that would trigger the hand grenades to go off. The bridge blew when the train rolled on it, and it fell to the bottom of the valley into the stream.

Cub and John congratulated themselves.

"I knew we could do it," Cub said.

"We did it, Mr. Miller," said John.

"It's Cub."

"Let's go find Tatiana and leave before they find her."

When they returned Tatiana was gone. The communists had raided the cave and taken her prisoner.

Cub's short relationship with Tatiana was over. He had not found a woman. He returned to the Rule of Law Task Force and told BG Sengleton that the bridge was blown up but Tatiana was taken prisoner by the communists. The communists spread lies that Tatiana was a witch, a spy, and part of the Deep State. She would be tried as a spy.

Chapter 65

THE COMMUNISTS STRAPPED HER TO a stake and put wood around her to burn her while chanting "Lock her up! Lock her up! Execute her! Burn her! As the communists lit the fire beneath her feet to burn her at the stake, Tatiana called out to Jesus to save her. Never before religious, she had no choice.

"I am prepared to die. I was called to restore Governor Card to power after being overthrown by the Deep State."

This was real. She remembered traveling through Rouen, France on her way to Paris making her way for the liberation of France. Joan of Arc was burned at the stake in Rouen, she remembered. She remembered she and Oliver talking about Joan of Arc while at dinner while in Paris. Thoughts ran through her mind..

"My thoughts are causing this. Everything I think about is playing out. Thoughts are things. They create reality. I have to get out of here," she said in anguish.

"Burn, witch, burn!" said the men around the fire.

"If thoughts create the thing we imagine then all I have to do is think my way out of this." Tatiana imagined herself escaping the fire and returning to the *Birmingham Defender*.

Still strapped and tied to the wood, the communists put Tatiana the Great on trial. All the men said, "Execute her! Execute her! She's a witch. Burn!"

"How will she be tried?" asked one of the communists.

Word got out that the governor was seeking to make peace in the land. To make peace the communists agreed to turn over Tatiana to the ROLTF as long as she was tried under local tribal communist rule.

"How will she be tried?" asked Jesse Weinstein.

"She was captured in the Quary Valley Section of Alabama which is under Russian control. That means we have to try her under the law of that tribal section. If she is a witch and caught posing as a military man then the penalty is death. Rather than subjecting her to a military tribunal for crimes of terrorism under U.S. federal law because she became a combatant, she could be tried under the law of the communists where she was arrested," said Judge Thomas.

"That doesn't make sense. She is an American," said Weinstein. "We can't try under some local custom that is 700 years old. Who do you think she is? Joan of Arc?"

"She became a spy and a witch and turned on the Americans and is treated like a local combatant. She is not entitled to the benefit of U.S. law. The presumption of innocence has disappeared and the presumption of guilt has taken over" said Judge Thomas.

"Objection! There can never be a presumption of guilt!" said Weinstein.

"Overruled," said the presiding Priest. "This is not an American trial."

"You don't believe in the presumption of innocence?" asked Weinstein.

"No. According to Zoros, there is no rule of law, no presumption of innocence. There is only search and destroy and the presumption of guilt. We have searched and found her. Now we will try here where the presumption of innocence has disappeared and the presumption of guilt has appeared," said Thomas.

"You don't believe that women should be believed?" asked Weinstein.

"Men need to shut up," said Thomas. "Shut up."

"There is something rotten here," said Weinstein.

"Begin your prosecution," said the priest.

"I call Brandeesha Yancey," said Thomas.

"State your name."

"I am Brandeesha Yancey," she said.

"Do you know the defendant?"

"I do."

"And how do you know her."

"We worked together."

"What do you know of the Defendant?"

"She's a witch."

"How certain are you of that?"

"One hundred percent."

"What did she say or do that made you to believe that she was a witch?" asked Thomas.

"She has this notion that the world will bring you what you want simply by thinking about it. Instead of asking Jesus for what you want in his name, she thinks the world is some kind of magnet and you attract to yourself what you think about – like there is a law of attraction. It is like she has fired Jesus. You are fired!"

"She said that?"

"No, not exactly, but that is what she thinks."

"What else does she do or say?"

"She thinks that anyone who has a personal relationship with Jesus has mental illness."

"So, the rest of us are mentally ill?"

"And she talks to a magnet?"

"It would appear so," Brandeesha.

"I rest our case," said Thomas.

"No questions," said Weinstein.

"You may step down," said the presiding priest.

Weinstein chose to put Tatiana on the witness stand.

"State your name."

"I am Tatiana, the Great."

"Who called you to battle?" asked Weinstein.

"I was called by Michael the Archangel," said Tatiana.

"No further questions," said Weinstein.

On cross examination Thomas asked: "Tatiana the Great, did St. Michael speak English or French?"

"He spoke French."

"Did you do what he said?"

"Yes."

"You took his orders as a form of personal command?"

"Yes," she said.

"And did you understand his orders? You know a good military officer acknowledges and understands orders," said Thomas.

"Yes, I know that, " said Tatiana.

"Tatiana, do you speak French?"

Tatiana was stunned. She didn't know what to say. Then she had to reluctantly admit. "No. I do not speak French."

"Then how is it possible that you took orders from St. Michael in French if you do not understand French?"

Tatiana said nothing.

"Not saying anything is a response," said Thomas.

"Objection," said Weinstein. "I move we adjourn. We need more time to examine documents."

"Your objection is out of order. We will proceed," said the priest.

"Tatiana, is it true that you led your forces into battle with a flag of Jesus, the Mother Mary and two angels?"

"Yes, as a servant of God I did," said Tatiana.

"Mrs. Phillips, do you go to church?" asked Thomas.

Tatiana was mortified. She had to admit that she did not attend church.

"No."

"Are you Catholic?"

"What?" Tatiana asked.

"Have you ever been baptized in the Catholic Church?"

"No."

"I'm sorry. I didn't hear you," said Thomas.

"No. I have not been baptized in the Catholic Church."

"Don't you think it is odd that you would lead the forces into battle under the name of Jesus when you don't go to church and are not Catholic?"

Tatiana said nothing.

"Tatiana, are you an atheist?"

"You don't have to answer that," said Weinstein.

"I would like to hear her answer," said the priest.

"Objection. This is out of order. She should not have to answer a question like that. We have freedom of religion in this country."

"And freedom not to have religion," said the priest. "I would like to hear her answer. I would like to know if an atheist is carrying the flag of Jesus, Mother Mary, and two angels into battle."

"I am not an atheist. God has called me."

"Are you mentally ill?" asked Judge Thomas.

"No," said Tatiana.

"Do you believe in Jesus?"

"Yes."

"Do you know Brandeesha Yancey?"

"Yes."

"Do you recall a conversation where you said that people who speak to Jesus have mental illness?"

Tatiana didn't know what to say.

"Can you answer the question?" asked Judge Thomas.

"I didn't mean it like that. I was questioning," said Tatiana.

"Did you ever say that you have never spoken to God and that nothing comes back?"

"Yes," said Tatiana reluctantly and after a few seconds and looking around for a response.

"So how is it that God would choose you to lead the armed forces into battle to defeat the Deep State if you believe that talking to Jesus means that you have mental illness?"

"Jesus called on Saint Paul," said Tatiana. "He is always calling on the most unlikely people to do His work."

"Mrs. Phillips, Tatiana Phillips, Tatiana the Great, as you are called. Do you speak Russian?"

There were gasps in the crowd watching the trial.

"Burn her, burn her," they said.

"Last question. Mrs. Phillips, are you a witch?"

Tatiana was mortified. She wanted to be able to have a relationship with Jesus but could not make it happen. She was secretly jealous of those who claim they could communicate with the Son of God. Tatiana began to understand how Andre had been destroyed on the witness stand during his court martial during World War II by almost the same questions during his trial by then Captain Thomas.

Tatiana woke up.

Chapter 66

Andre couldn't wait to deliver his article.

He finished it Friday and delivered it to Nelms, who read it on Saturday prior to the Griddle Iron play. They met in his office before the play.

"Come in, Andre."

"Did you read it?"

"I did. It's quite a story."

"Are you going to run it?"

"No."

"Why not? I mean, this is the biggest story there is. There could be no story bigger than this."

"We can't run with it because it is not true. I don't think you have recovered from the war. Same thing with Oliver, Tatiana, and Cub. After those presentations at the Catholic Church, it stirred all those memories again. I remember covering the Harlem Hellfighters during World War I – same thing with me. Other reporters had the same thing. Pyle, Hemingway, all the rest. All experienced the same kind of shell shock. The mind does funny things sometimes."

"What are you saying, Mr. Nelms?"

"I'm saying that with counseling you and the others will get through your war experience. It is no discredit to you. I should have realized there was a problem. My mistake. When you came home, I assumed that you would return to work like before, but you couldn't. You needed time to decompress and to collect your thoughts."

"I feel fine," Andre said. "And it has been three years since the war."

"You will be carrying the war with you for the rest of your life," Nelms said.

"What is it about the story that you don't agree with?"

"I don't even know where to begin. First, no CIA director would target a sitting governor and peddle a false dossier to the press and give it to the FBI to snooker them into opening a counter-intelligence investigation and then use a false affidavit to secure a warrant to spy on a political campaign from a federal court. The FBI does not take sides. A real FBI director would never sign off on an unverified campaign "garbage document" like that. No, he wouldn't. I know J. Edgar Hoover. We have our differences but he would not do that. Neither the CIA nor the FBI leak information to the press. The Justice Department keeps a tight reign on criminal investigations. Leaking to the press by the Department of Justice never happens. Why all the codes? It took me a while to figure it out that DJB meant CIA, the Central Intelligence Agency, GCJ meant FBI, Federal Bureau of Investigation and EPK meant DOJ, Department of Justice."

"But these agencies leak to the press."

"Someone is fooling you. They don't do that. Second, no FBI director would knowingly clear a candidate who committed the kind of acts that you say this Rodderman character committed. The FBI doesn't exonerate people in advance and then investigate. The FBI investigates and delivers their investigation report to the DOJ so it can make a decision to prosecute. The FBI director does not go on national television to chastise someone and then announce that 'no reasonable prosecutor would bring such a case.'

No that does not happen. Then FBI doesn't engage in cover ups. And, what is this Navy sailor going to prison for taking photographs of a submarine about?"

"He did."

"Show me the proof that in 1948 a Navy sailor was sent to prison for one year for taking photographs of a submarine. If that happened, then I'm sure President Truman would have pardoned him."

"I don't have proof. I'm relying on what my source said."

"And the FBI does not draft exoneration letters before investigating people, either. That didn't happen – never could happen."

"Ok," said Andre.

"Then here comes this Miller character you write about and he turns a blind eye towards Rodderman and then investigates the Card character ad nauseam and drafts a report that is a roadmap for impeachment. Why would the U.S. sell twenty percent of the country's plutonium to Russia who is engaged in a war in Ukraine? That makes no sense. And this lady's husband made almost a million dollars giving speeches in Russia and her foundation made over $100 million to a charity after the sale went through. That's corruption. This is not a banana republic.

"And then this Deep State stuff. There is no Deep State. And then a newspaper publishing an opinion piece that there is a 'Steady State' of bureaucrats who are circumventing the president? The opinion piece should have identified the source. That is gutless. Newspapers don't do that. That's why there is a House Un-American Activities Committee right now investigating the government and Hollywood. That guy has to be routed out of the government.

"The FBI and DOJ don't target one party and go after the other party. That is a myth. They don't try to trap targets into lying so they can prosecute them for lying. That is entrapment. They don't do that."

"But there is a two-tiered justice system in the United States," Andre said. "My source says that DOJ has a Soviet-style prosecutorial system where they appoint a special prosecutor to go after people to find crimes when they had no basis for the crime."

"They don't do that," Nelms said.

"He said that special prosecutors now are named to find evidence against presidents or other politicians they want removed from office even if there is no crime. If they lose at the ballot box, then the Deep State operatives open up criminal investigations to run off politicians or political appointees they disagree with, then they use a media leak strategy to tickle the wires. The DOJ is not accountable to anyone."

"That's preposterous. That doesn't happen. There are no orange or green states. There is no vertical or horizontal media outlets." Nelms continued. "The media has never been part of a Russian worldwide criminal enterprise known as the Deep State run by a man named Zoros. They don't leak classified information in their papers. The press consists only of neutral journalists and opinion writers who favor neither political party. They give equal weight and time to both political candidates and parties. The press has no dog in these political fights. We are like judges on the court. Some call us the Fourth Estate."

"I know what you're thinking," Nelms said. "There is no Deep State – there never was – and there is no organization that practices mind control to take over all of the religious groups and to replace religion with the concept called the 'Law of Attraction.' I'm surprised you would write something like that after the St. Peter's church rescued you as a child."

"From what I understand there was the Book of Thomas that was found recently where a sentence or two was left out that said to surround yourself with your answer and believe that you already have it," said Andre.

"That's not new," said Nelms, standing up and walking over to reach his Bible off of a desk on the opposite side of the room. He handed it to Andre. "Here. Look up Mark 11:24."

Andre opened up the Bible to Mark. Then he found the chapter and the verse: "Therefore I tell you, whatever you ask for in prayer, believe that you have received it, and it will be yours."

"You see, a good reporter wouldn't need a source uncovered after 2,000 years when the truth is already staring you right in your face."

"It really says that?" Andre asked.

"Believe me, it says that," said Nelms.

"They knew what they were doing in the 300s when they put together the Bible."

"Huh," said Andre.

"Using some book they uncovered to use it to justify a text today reminds me of courts that look to legislative intent before examining the exact text in a statute. They should read the statute first before looking at what was debated. You have to check all your sources if you want to be a reporter."

Andre looked at him.

"Then that term 'Basket of Deplorables' – that is a terrible thing to say. No modern-day politician would say that about the opponents' voters."

"What about calling his opponent 'Crooked Rodderman?'"

"That is bad too. No politician would do that. Believe me, these politicians fight all the time in public but after 6 pm they are friends," Nelms said.

"What about Brown? He's a communist or he voted for a communist. That makes him a communist sympathizer," Andre said.

"Andre, the CIA director is Rear Admiral Roscoe Hillenkoetter, who was appointed by Harry Truman. The CIA is only one year old. There is no such person known as John Brown and there is no way that the U.S. president would ever appoint a man as CIA director who voted for a communist. That could never happen. A person like that could never get a security clearance. That was just your imagination playing tricks on you, like what happened when you were on trial during the war."

"What about Bongino and how he deliberately cleared Rodderman and began spying on Card?"

"None of those people exist. I saw the same script. Brandeesha showed it to me. Brandeesha ran with it. Someone out there played all of you. The people you describe in your article are not real. They are fake characters in the Griddle Iron play. You are confusing the Griddle Iron play with reality. If we published your article, even in the funnies – thank goodness for Tatiana and Cub for coming up with the funnies – we would be accused of promoting ..."

"Promoting what?"

Nelms looked at Andre.

"Fake news."

Andre said nothing.

Nelms continued. "So, I'm not running this article of yours."

Nelms dropped the article in the trash. "Are you covering the Alabama-Auburn game?"

"Yes. Alabama will win big time."

"Good. That's the real story. Now let's get over to the Griddle Iron Show and have fun tonight."

Chapter 67

On Saturday night, Hans drove Lanny to the performance hall in his 1940 two-door Plymouth Road King that he borrowed from a friend at the agency.

"You sure this thing will work?" asked Lanny.

Hans was driving them to the Griddle Iron play. Lanny was looking at a contraption Hans purchased. It had a device that you could point in a direction and it would pick up sound and transmit it to earphones.

"Yes. It will work. Whatever is going on in that performance hall, we will hear it."

"Just what exactly will that thing do?"

"It is an electromagnetic sensor. All of my data tells me that whatever is going to happen will happen at the performance hall on Saturday night, and whatever it is, I'm going to be there."

"How do you know that?"

"I know. It looks like they took the bait."

"The what?" asked Lanny.

"The script," said Hans.

"That thing you wrote about the Deep State? That was a joke," Lanny said. "You're crazy, man."

Hans parked the car across from the performance hall.

"Can you go in there and monitor it and let me know if you see something unusual, then report back," said Hans.

Lanny looked at him funny. "Are you crazy, man? Thanks for the ride. Pick me up at 10."

Lanny left the car and walked to the performance hall. Hans got out and put the sensor machine in the front passenger seat.

"If this is going to work, I need to point it right there."

He put on what looked like earmuffs that had an electrical wire leading to the machine. He pointed the machine toward Lanny walking to the performance hall.

Lanny was talking to himself: "What the hell is wrong with that dude? Man, what a piece of work."

Hans heard it all and smiled.

Chapter 68

Nelms told Father Webster he received wire reports that the Pentagon was launching an invasion of Alabama that would finally free the state from the communists and end the war.

He said that Aleksandr Putaineue was found dead in the mountains of Quary Valley in Alabama, and that while he was the enemy, we should pray for our enemies.

Tatiana visualized a massive D-Day invasion repeated like the invasion of Normandy along the Alabama coast, just as she briefed Brandeesha and the others at the Rule of Law Task Force. The good news was that they could destroy the terrorists. The bad news was that they would have to drop the largest non-conventional bomb on terrorist camps near Birmingham and it could possibly destroy much of the city. Father Webster was to prepare the group that they could possibly die. .

"Prepare yourself. There will only be a short pain and then you will be with the Lord," he said. "With that in mind, I'm told there won't be a Griddle Iron Show this evening."

The audience said nothing.

"We have plenty of food and water for those who want to stay here tonight," he said. "I'm told that there is no exit from the city, which is completely fortified at this point."

In response to Father Webster's announcement, the old lady in the wheelchair who attended Sister Camille's seminar stood up. The audience gasped. She had been an invalid most of her life.

"I want to thank Sister Camille for opening my eyes and making me understand. She told us to pray to Jesus and ask for what we wanted in his name. I could not see, and now I see. I could not walk, and now I can walk."

The people in the room cheered and clapped.

"One of the hardest Bible stories for me to accept is in Matthew 13:10-17, where Jesus explained why he spoke in parables. One of the disciples asked: 'Why do you speak to the crowd in parables?' He said in reply, 'Because knowledge of the mysteries of the kingdom of heaven has been granted to you, but to them it has not been granted. To anyone who has, more will be given and he will grow rich; from anyone who has not, even what he has will be taken away. This is why I speak to them in parables, because *they look but do not see and hear but do not listen or understand.*'"

No one responded.

"I did not understand why Jesus would take from me when I had nothing to give and why would he give more to someone else and allow them to grow rich while I was starving in the streets and begging? Now I understand. It is about belief. For those who believe that Jesus will grant what they ask, more will be given to them. For those who think negative that nothing will become of them, then they will be given what they ask for. It was that simple."

The crowd was silent.

The old lady continued: "Blessed are your eyes, because they see, and your ears, because they hear. Amen. I say to you, many prophets and righteous people longed to see what you see but did not see it, and to hear what you hear but did not hear it."

Chapter 69

"Burn the witch! Burn the witch!"

The Russian soldiers busily gathered more wood to place under the feet of Tatiana the Great. One man started the fire and shortly it raged out of control.

Tatiana remembered that Oliver had promised to rescue her. In the distance came Oliver on horseback in full armor. Her mind powers worked. He was embedded with the Buffalo Soldiers. The soldiers arrived and began to fight with lances and swords to kill all the Russians.

Oliver reached the burning flames and went to Tatiana.

"Oliver, help me, I'm so glad you rescue me."

"I am too," as he took his knife and cut the ropes around her hands. Tatiana, none of this is real but if we don't get out of here it will become real. Your thoughts create things. Thoughts are things. You create what you think about, but you are going about it the wrong way."

"What do you mean?," said Tatiana.

"There is lesson here. This is what happens when journalists take sides. Instead of reporting the news, you are creating the news. You will end up disappointed in the end," said Oliver while taking knife and cutting the rope around her hands. The fire was roaring.

"What do you mean?" asked Tatiana.

"Get on the horse."

Oliver helped her on his horse behind his seat and then he mounted and they rode off in a swift gallop.

"You didn't read all of the script. While you were in the hospital another envelope was delivered to you. I intercepted it. Governor Card is defeated for reelection. He is impeached not once, but twice. He is impeached after he leaves office. A man named Bowden ran against him and won the election by thousands more votes, more than any prior vote cast in the history of Alabama. Card and his deplorables promote that the election was stolen by voter fraud and 2,000 people used as mules to stuff the ballot boxes. The courts decline to hear the cases. His supporters try to take over the Capitol to prevent Bowden from being elected. It was ugly. They called it an insurrection. Card left office and took classified documents with him and got himself in the same kind of trouble that his opponent Rodderman found herself in. You can't take sides, because when you do, you will be disappointed."

"That really happened?" asked Tatiana.

"Yes."

"But I was not supporting him, I was supporting the Rule of Law. The Deep State tried to remove him from office without giving him a chance."

"Yes, but he is not a real person. None of this is real, but if we don't get out of here, it will become real. Thoughts are things and we can create our own reality."

"Oliver, what are we doing?" The fire was raging.

"Taking sides, but no longer. Don't you see, whoever sent us that script was not intending for us to put on a play. They were sending us a message."

Tatiana was stunned.

Kirkpatrick, Trimmer, Saller, and the Deep State characters fought with their swords like they were fighting in World War II again, but this time they fought until all communists were dead and the fields were red. They won.

"Oliver, how can you rescue me if Joan of Arc dies in real life?"

"Anything is possible in your dreams. We are living in a world with multiple universes and possibilities. You figured out how to move from one universe to the other. The rest of us haven't figured out how to do that. You represent where man is heading, the ability to travel the universe in your mind and to use your mind powers. You are Wonder Woman."

"That is great. Can you define what a woman is?"

"Not today," said Oliver.

"I have to imagine us back to the *Birmingham Defender*," she said.

"Do something quickly. We haven't much time. There is a second army in the woods," Oliver said. Oliver rode the horse directly toward the woods looking for cover.

Tatiana peered around Oliver as she held on tightly and saw thousands of communist soldiers coming from the woods. There was no escape. "The horse is galloping so much, I cannot concentrate."

"Just find a way," Oliver said.

After the fighting ended, Trimmer saw Oliver and Tatiana ride directly into the second army and then disappear.

"She really is Tatiana the Great," Trimmer said.

Chapter 70

AFTER THE OLD WOMAN SANG the song, the sisters continued to serve chili to the homeless at the performance hall.

Andre saw Lanny Ellis sitting at one of the seats.

"You played me, man," Andre said.

"What?" asked Lanny, surprised.

"You know what I'm talking about. Your friend, Hans McClannahan, the FBI agent. He came up with this story about Jill Rodderman and the Deep State."

"I didn't do that, man. You fell for it," Lanny said.

"Thanks a lot. Where is he tonight?"

"Who knows. Probably taking pictures of the night sky."

"How did you get here tonight?" asked Andre.

"He drove me."

"What was he driving?"

"A black two-door Road King."

Andre thought for a moment and walked outside, and across from the performance hall was a car with a man in it. Andre went over to the car and there was Hans with his electromagnetic machine in the front passenger seat.

"Hans. I thought that was you. What are you doing out here? Why didn't you go to the play with Lanny? What do you have there? I saw one of those down at Montgomery Wards on sale. Does it work?"

"I think it does. I'm checking it out tonight. It's a gift for my son."

"Hans," Andre said to him as he fiddled with the machine, "you aren't married, are you? There are no kids, are there?"

Hans looked at him and said nothing.

"You can tell me. Anything you tell me is confidential. No one can make me reveal my sources."

Hans looked down for a moment and then looked up at Andre. He began to stutter. "It's just me. It has always been just me. There is no one for me. There never will be."

"There won't be if you think like that. You have to think just the opposite," Andre said.

Hans said nothing.

"You are the one who sent all the scripts to the newspaper staff aren't you?"

Hans looked at him and said nothing. Then a shooting star passed along the night sky. Hans looked at it.

"You aren't from this planet, are you? That's why you keep looking into the sky and talk about outer space."

Hans said nothing.

"You are the one who has been causing all the havoc in the world aren't you? There are no horizontals or verticals. Zoros doesn't exist, does he? None of this war is real is it?"

Hans said nothing.

"Come inside and watch the play."

Hans opened up the door and got out of the car. They walked to the performance hall.

"How did you get here?" Andre asked.

"Your nuclear explosions three years ago sent a signal. I was sent to investigate. Thoughts are things. You can go anywhere in this universe and you can have whatever you imagine. You have to work and work hard to get what you desire. Your people are about to figure that out. But the power is not perfect. You have to know what you are doing. I can't figure out how to land at the right time. I landed here in 2016 and it took three years after that to figure out how to get back to 1948. I was supposed to be here prior to the bombing in 1945 and missed it by three years. I haven't figured out how to go home, yet but when I do, I won't be late because I can set it to land at a right time so I won't miss anything."

"You have no wife or family, do you?"

"No. I'm jealous of what you have here on this planet of yours. You should be grateful for what you have."

"How do you do it?"

"Meditation. That's where you should do your work. You have to be on the right frequency. It is a vibrational frequency that transcends the universe. Your people have a term for it."

"What is it?"

"You call it love. When your human body is in a love state it is vibrating at a certain frequency. That is the frequency that you have to achieve in order to do, have, or achieve whatever you want, or go wherever you want to go. That is the frequency that God communicates with his universe. Your people have been told this many, many times but no one believes it. My gosh, how many times did Jesus say that to you and you never believed. I guess the only thing that will convince you is a second coming."

Andre looked at him. "Let's go see the play."

Andre brought Hans into the performance hall and they sat next to Lanny.

"Let me introduce you to my friend, Hans McClannahan. He works in maintenance at the FBI."

"Nice to meet you," said Hans to people around him. Hans always stuttered when he talked to other people besides Andre.

"You are not going to believe who this guy really is," Andre said to Lanny.

"I know what you're thinking," Lanny said. "I never said he was an FBI agent. I said he works at the GCJ, I mean FBI and knows what he's talking about as long as he's talking about Saturn and Jupiter. I told you that."

"There is no Deep State?"

"There is no Deep State. I told you that from day one."

"You were telling the truth."

Maryellen noticed one of the homeless. He looked strikingly like former President Andrew Johnson. He was penniless, ragged, and sitting at a table by himself eating chili.

"Who are you?" asked Sister Laurie. "For some reason I feel like I know you."

"Please, madam, can I have some water?"

"Sure."

He drank it. "Can I have some more?"

"More? Of course, you can."

Andre walked over to him. "I've seen you before. Who are you?"

"President Andrew Johnson. I have no idea why I'm here or where I am."

"Do you recognize him?" Maryellen asked her 106-year-old Aunt Myrtle, who would have been only twenty-three years old when Johnson was president.

"Yep, that's Andy Johnson."

Father Sanders got up in front of the group and said it would be good if everyone went around the room and said their names and what they accomplished in life. Then they would gather together and pray to end the war. People stood up and said who they were. Some chose not to speak.

Cub stood up. "My name is Cub Miller. I shined shoes in Mountain Creek before moving to Birmingham and set up a stand at the *Birmingham Defender*. Later Mr. Nelms gave me a job as a reporter. In those days you took anyone you could get. I was glad to see my name in print, and my parents, bless their soul, were glad that it was a byline and that I didn't kill nobody. I don't want to die, either. I wish it hadn't come to this, but I guess if you have to go out, then you might as well go out with a bang."

"Cub," Tatiana said.

"My only regret is that I wanted to do more fishing and I liked cooking outside."

There was laughter but no one was in the mood for laughing.

"My name is Andrew Phillips. My daughter is Tatiana Phillips. She is my delight. She grew up at the newspaper and I sent her off as a reporter. She interviewed Eleanor Roosevelt and was at the opening day of the Pentagon. Then she went to Europe to cover the war and went through Paris and then came back to the paper. Later, Oliver Smith snatched her from us and brought her to Birmingham. I guess that was my doing. I showed him a picture of her on December 8, 1941, at a meeting in the Pentagon. Let's see, what I would like to do. Well first, I don't want to die. I want to live so I pray that President Truman finds a way to end this without another nuclear war."

"My name is Ethyl Phillips. Tatiana is my daughter. I echo my husband's sentiments. I don't want to die either, but all I know is to pray. God answers prayers." She sat down.

"I am Second Lieutenant Trimmer. I served in the war with Andre Williams. He calls me 'Jim' all the time and is always asking me to come over. I don't know how I got here or why I'm here but I'm here. We served in the war together. We had some good times duck hunting and smoking cigars. I wish everyone well."

"What would you like to do?" someone yelled.

"Let's see. I would like to have a few kids."

"Maybe you will," yelled someone.

"My name is Lanny Ellis. I was a private in the army with Andre Williams and the rest of these jokers and no, I did not shoot Booker Thompson and I don't know who did."

No one laughed.

"That was supposed to be funny," he said.

"What are you working on?" said someone in the crowd.

"I worked as a contract employee for the FBI and currently I'm working to kill the Deep State and the Klan."

"The Deep what?" asked someone in the group.

"Nothing. It doesn't exist. It's made up," Lanny said. "The government is run on imagination and paranoia. I'm just kidding."

"What do you like to do?" asked someone in the crowd.

"Well, Andre and I like to take in the Birmingham Barons on occasion as long as I don't buy him too many beers."

"My name is Major Kirkpatrick. I served with Andre Williams in the war. I was sorry to hear about his conviction but glad it was reversed on appeal. After his trial he joined our unit and we took out a German battery near the end of the war."

"I am Second Lieutenant Adkerson. I would like to be a lawyer someday and have my own law firm in Dallas."

"I'm Second Lieutenant Saller, and I'm moving to Texas to go in the oil business. I like to work out. I help the poor through the Society of Vincent DePaul. I like to go to mass on Saturdays. I'm Catholic so I bet I'll have thirteen grandkids someday."

"Anyone else?" asked Sister Camille.

No one said anything.

"There's plenty of food, and we will have a prayer session afterwards."

"Daddy, I don't want to die," said a child.

"I can assure you that God answers prayers and that we are not going to die tonight, but if we do then we will be with our God," said Father Webster. "Either way, everything works out for a reason."

The dessert was a choice of chocolate chip cookies and chocolate pudding.

"I promise I won't eat all of the cookies," said the Rev. George Williams.

"No, you will not," said Aunt Clara.

"My name is Jesse Weinstein. I am an attorney in private practice in Birmingham – that is, until we were all called back into the service to fight the Russians at the Rule of Law Task Force. We have tonight off so we decided to come see the play. I defended Andre Williams during his trial in Paris back in 1944. This man over here is the guy who prosecuted him."

There were boos in the crowd.

"I am Federal Judge John Thomas. I am a United States district judge in Birmingham. I served in World War II. Some of you know me. I was a JAG officer then, and yes, it's true, I run the Rule of Law Task Force at the edge of town. I was a good prosecutor with the U.S. Attorney's office and distinguished myself. I am proud of my service. Forgive me for carrying my weapons in here and my helmet. We have to be armed at all times during the war. We came in on Saturday night to watch the play. I prosecuted Andre Williams during the war."

There were many boos.

"I know you think that was bad ..."

More boos.

"But if you hear me out, I did the right thing."

More boos.

"If you are interested, I didn't put him on the witness stand. His lawyer did, but since he was up there, it was my job to cross examine him."

Thomas turned to Weinstein and asked: "Why did you put him on the witness stand?"

Silence.

He continued, "I would like to continue my service as a federal judge. For all the attorneys out there, one thing I can tell you if you work for the FBI or DOJ, then don't file applications for search warrants based on false campaign opposition research. Make sure you pay your bar dues. Don't misplace the burden of proof in a criminal case during closing arguments. I made that mistake. Don't slander your fellow attorneys, and since this looks like it is going to be the end, the truth is that I grew up in a dysfunctional home. My three sisters were divorced six times between them, and my brother killed himself by suicide. When I was a kid I was teased and bullied. Truth is, I hate bullies. I just do. I became a judge so I could use my past experiences to rectify some wrongs."

Silence. He sat down. Then he stood up. "I needed to get that off my chest. I felt like I was on trial and being hung here."

Judge Thomas was abused and bullied as a child and grew up being the thing he hated the most. The abused child became the bully. He prosecuted Andre because he thought Andre was weak. Bullies always pick on weaker kids, and then when they have the weaker kid cornered the weaker kid either is destroyed or punches back and becomes the master over the bully. The bully becomes the hunted and ends up being bullied. It is an abusive and repeated cycle.

Andre stood up. "I thought you prosecuted me because you were a racist and the head of the Ku Klux Klan."

The people were stunned when they heard that, and they reacted. It was a slander of a federal judge.

"I'm not a racist and I'm not a member of the Klan," said Judge Thomas.

"Some day you will hang for what you did to me," Andre said.

"Andre, you must forgive," said Sister Camille. "Have you forgotten everything I taught you?"

Sister Laurie walked up to Andre. "This is all going to be over soon and you don't want to go to your grave without forgiving Judge Thomas. It is time to forgive Judge Thomas and put an end to this private war between both of you. This has to come to an end." No one said anything.

Sister Laurie continued: "From what I know of this, he did not prosecute you because he was a racist. From what I understand went on in the trial he didn't believe your story on the witness stand, and quite frankly if someone gave me a photo of a white priest and I said he was a black priest, then I would have questioned my own sanity, because I would not have believed that story, either. That's why you were convicted. But it is over because Judge Thomas bungled the trial – some say deliberately – and you got off, so it worked out in the end. Everything works out in the end. But as for Judge Thomas, you must forgive him to shut down the pain."

Andre looked at him. At least a minute went by. "I forgive you," he said.

Sherry walked up to Andre and said, "I knew you could do it."

The crowd clapped and cheered. Andre put his hands up in the air in praise. The crowd cheered louder.

"It's finally over," he said.

"I have a confession to make," said Judge Thomas.

The people stopped and looked at him.

Judge Thomas took a moment to crawl on top of the table and to stand up. Then he looked around the room and announced: **"I AM ZOROS!"**

"What?" said someone in the crowd.

"What did he say?" said another.

"I AM THE DEEP STATE!" proclaimed Judge Thomas.

Gasps went through the entire room.

"The what?" said an old man sitting on the floor.

"Oh my gosh," Oliver said.

"There is no Deep State," Lanny said.

"The what?" said a homeless man on the floor.

"The Deep State, stupid. Don't you know what the Deep State is?" said another old man sitting next to him.

"Oh," the first man said, then he went back to sleep.

No one reacted.

"Another pint!" said an old British gentleman.

"My goodness," said Sister Camille. "What have we done here?"

Someone in the crowd looked at what was going on and said, "I don't know what that was all about, but this is one crazy play."

Former President Andrew Johnson said to himself under his breath, "I thought he said he was a racist."

"Okay, now it's my turn," Brandeesha said. "I know I didn't get along with the liberal newspaper media elites who think they know it all and they want the rest of us 'Basket of Deplorables' … they can just rot in the sun …"

The paint began to fall off the wall.

"Incoming," Cub said.

"Brandeesha," Nelms said, "tell them what you were going to say."

"Okay, Mr. Nelms, but this is hard. The truth is that I hate the liberal media. All of the Basket of Deplorables, like me, hate the liberal media, the liberal media elites who know everything, and I wish they would go straight to …"

"Brandeesha," Nelms said.

"Okay. The truth is. The truth is. Well, the truth is that I believe we all want the same thing. While we don't agree on the methods on how it is done, we all must come together and agree that we are all acting in good faith. Like the election between President Truman and Mr. Dewey. I have no idea who's going to win, but regardless of who wins, that person has a big job ahead and he or she – there might be a woman president someday – needs our support. And yes, I know what a woman is. We don't need to be trashing these people on a daily basis. They are just human beings like us. They get up and go to work like the rest of us. If we make it so difficult for them to seek public office then many good qualified candidates will not seek office. We must respect their privacy and dignity as humans and the office they hold. Now I said it."

The crowd clapped.

"Here, here! How about another pint!" said a homeless man.

"What is with all of this alcohol!" said Sister Camille.

"I agree with that and I'm a liberal," said one of the members in the group.

"Well done," Nelms said.

"I would have voted for her if she ran in 1860," said President Andrew Johnson.

After a while Stefan the teacher got up. Someone clicked the glasses on the table. "I have an announcement," he said. "Sister Aude and I have decided to get married."

"What?" said Sister Laurie.

"It's true," Sister Aude said. "I decided to leave the convent."

She walked over to Sister Camille to tell her. "I understand now what you were saying, Sister Camille. It is more than just climbing every mountain. From what I've learned from you is that if you marry your thoughts and emotions and feelings together, then we can move mountains. That is what I am doing by marrying. I am combining my thoughts and emotions. I will do more than climb mountains. I am going to move mountains."

"You are so right," said Sister Camille, giving her a hug.

"Here, here!" said one of the homeless men. The crowd clapped. "How about another pint."

"And another," said another.

"My God. Where is all this coming from?" asked Sister Camille.

"You told us that if we wanted something then ask for it," said one of the men in the audience.

"I don't know what we are going to do now," said Sister Laurie. "It has always been just the three of us. Is this really the end?"

"It is not the end," said Sister Camille. "We will always be together."

Chapter 71

TATIANA RETURNED TO THE BIRMINGHAM Performance Hall, missing the confessions of the guests. This was not the correct time. She wanted to arrive right after her presentation at St. Peter's. Since there was no Griddle Iron play, some in the audience were performing their own acts and singing to keep the crowd entertained. The cast finally convinced Nelms to sing.

"Our world is going to end soon, so why not give it a try," he said.

"Another pint!" said the British man.

"Sister Laurie, can you do something with him?" asked Sister Camille. "He is going to be the end of us."

Ed Nelms went on stage and grabbed the microphone. "I told Tatiana that I would never be in the Griddle Iron Show, but seeing that we might not have much time, I agreed to sing. I want to thank all of our soldiers who are here tonight and who are fighting the war. I want to thank all of our journalists who covered the war right alongside of them. You did this country a great service. You know, I covered the Harlem Hellfighters during World War I, and then I did a stint in Mobile with Oliver Smith, one of our foreign correspondents, driving ambulances for the Red Cross. Oliver is still down there. So, let's see for my song. I'll give it a try."

The orchestra began and Nelms sang a song about the love he has for the common man.

"Andre, look who showed up to see the play!" said Sister Camille. Andre turned around; it was Lew and Alvin from Second Street Barbershop.

"This is Andre?" asked Lew.

"It is," said Sister Camille. "And this is his wife, Sherry."

"It has been a while," said Sherry.

"You have grown up," said Lew.

"He has grown up," said Alvin.

"Andre doesn't like girls," said Lew to Sherry.

"No, he doesn't like girls. You must be his sister," said Alvin.

"Okay. Stop. What are you guys doing here? How did you find out about the play?" asked Andre.

"Same as you; Mountain Springs was evacuated and we were sent here. The Birmingham Civic Center is where everyone is being sent until the war is over."

"It will be over soon," Andre said. "This Deep State war is not real. It's just a matter of time before things get back to like they were."

They looked at him.

Nelms was still singing his song.

"Sister Aude. Do you remember us?"

Sister Aude looked at them and immediately recognized them.

"I'm Leondra."

"Oh, my children," said Sister Aude.

"We are not going to die, are we?"

"Of course not," said Sister Aude. "Tasheeka, are you still taking Latin?"

"*Nec quicquam massa*," said Tasheeka in response. "Sister Aude, I've decided to be a nun."

"Oh, my child," said Sister Aude.

"*Soeur Aude, je suis si heureux de vous revoir*," said Violet.

"*Elegí el español como mi segundo idioma,*" said Leondra.

"Oh, my children," said Sister Aude as she began to cry and hugged them.

"There is Aunt Clara," said Violet as she saw her at one of the tables. Violet left and ran to Aunt Clara.

"Aunt Clara!" said Violet as she ran.

"The crazy aunt?" said Leondra. "I don't think we need any voodoo in Jackson. We need voodoo in Birmingham."

The entire cast and crew came up and everyone in the room at the *Birmingham Defender* and *Birmingham News*, including Tatiana, surrounded Nelms to congratulate him.

"I didn't know I could sing. Sure doesn't sound like something I would sing," he said.

"You were great, Mr. Nelms," Tatiana said.

"No, it was you who are great for putting this on."

"Oh, I'm not great."

"Yes, you are."

"He was wonderful," said Betty. "I'm going to cry. Oh John, wherefore art thou, John?"

"Here I am," said John. "I will never leave you."

"Oh, John."

"Oh, Betty."

"I guess he did get a woman," Cub said.

"Now it's time to leave," Tatiana said.

Tatiana imagined herself back at St. Peter's giving her presentation. This was the only way to reverse everything that had happened.

Chapter 72

ANDRE, CUB, NELMS, AND MANY in the audience reacted when Tatiana fell after her presentation at St. Peter's. They rushed to the podium.

"Lift her head up," Sister Camille said as she put her hands underneath Tatiana's head. Brandeesha gave her large purse to Sister Camille to support Tatiana's head.

"She will be fine," said Sister Camille.

"Where am I?" Tatiana said.

"You are at St. Peter's. You fell during your presentation."

"You mean I'm okay?"

"Of course, you are. You were out for just a moment."

"We were worried about you," said Sister Laurie.

"God has blessed us this very day with your presence," said Sister Aude.

"What happened?" Oliver asked.

"Oh, my gosh, I feel like I'm being burned at the stake," Tatiana said.

"You had us worried," Oliver said.

"Yes, you had the whole paper in a tizzy, except for …" Cub said.

"Cub," Oliver said, interrupting him.

"What he was about to say was that even Brandesha asked about you," Oliver said.

"She did?"

"Of course, I did," Brandeesha said.

"Thank you," Tatiana said.

"Girl, we were really worried about you," Brandeesha said. "I know we have our differences but we're on the same team. We care about each other. We might see things differently but we're still family. We're still God's family."

"Yes, we are," Tatiana said.

"What were you dreaming about while you were out?" Oliver asked.

"You won't believe it. Just be glad it was a dream."

"Dreams are reality," Andre said.

"I'm not going there," Tatiana said.

Tatiana got up and brushed herself off.

"Let's go home, Oliver. My parents and your parents are coming over tonight, and I promised I would cook dinner for all of us."

Chapter 73

BEFORE WORK, TATIANA DROVE TO Booker Thompson's grave to place flowers on it. She bent down to see his grave and prayed. Then she stood up and turned around and walked on the cemetery sidewalk to her car. For a moment she felt the presence of others. At the entrance she turned around to see the graves and headstones but she saw nothing. She cried all the way back to the newspaper.

Then she was at work and at her desk with her morning coffee, and she was relieved. She was safe, warm, comfortable. Eager to work. What a relief knowing that everything she dreamed was not real. All the battles she fought across Alabama to restore the governor to power, her trial, and the existence of the Russian invasion – a total dream. She sat back with her cup of coffee to think. She opened the file containing the photos of Andre and Booker and the fire.

"Dreams are reality. Isn't that what Andre says?" she said to herself. She remembered her first trip where she followed Eleanor Roosevelt, covering the Pentagon, traveling to Europe and being sick in London, following the Canadian Army through Rouen and seeing the city where Joan of Arc was burned at the stake. "Who said that dreams are reality? They don't know what they're talking about."

Then she thought about her meeting with Oliver in Paris and their long dinner conversation. He was so handsome. That's where she first brought up Joan of Arc.

Then she thought of Andre's trial: That was quite a tale he told on the witness stand. I'm still not over it. How could he say the white priests were black? I can't imagine how he can say things that are not true. He was just imagining that, I guess. Then she thought about the hastily arranged and awkward meeting in Nelms' office and her pursuit of Oliver after the war. The rest is history. These scenes were going through her mind.

Oliver walked in her office pushing a cart with a new 1948 Emerson-628 television set with a ten inch screen.

"The new television set for the news room. Now we can watch the election results. The governor is about to talk."

He plugged in the television and turned the dial and there was Governor Jim Folsom discussing the election.

"There he is. Safe and sound. He has been in the same place and nothing happened to him," said Oliver as he turned around to look at Tatiana.

"I want the people of the great state of Alabama to know that..." said the governor.

Tatiana smiled and said nothing.

"Feeling better now?"

"Yes. I'm ready to go back to work and report things as accurately as I can. So, what's going on in your world?"

"I know what you have been going through."

"You do?"

"Yes."

Brandeesha walked in. "Excuse me, but Mr. Nelms needs this book off your desk."

Brandeesha was not pregnant. She was thin as she always had been.

"Let me move over," Tatiana said.

"Excuse me, girl. Who do you think you are, Tatiana the Great?" Brandeesha asked, and she smiled.

"So, you were saying, Oliver?" asked Tatiana.

"Are you ready to cover the governor?"

"I am ready to cover the governor."

"Governor Folsom."

"Yes."

"I know everything now," he said. "You don't have to hide anything."

"Does everyone know what I have been going through? Oliver, you can't tell anyone about this."

"It's okay. They all know. It wasn't hard to figure out."

"Oh no, Oliver. I can't go to work. I will never be able to show my face around here. The idea that you can just think of something and it comes to you. Surely you didn't tell them about my dreams, did you? Those are embarrassing."

"There is nothing embarrassing about what you are going through. It is to be expected."

"What do you mean?"

"You don't know?"

"I don't."

"You don't remember what I told you when I rescued you at the fire?"

"Tell me again."

"The script was meant to tell the media not to take sides, to be ethical, accurate and fair and be a watchdog over public affairs and government. We should be fair to both sides. Quit hiring political operatives who pose as journalists. Just like a judge in a case in court is to be neutral, we need to be the same way. The script was to remind us how important our job is to remain objective."

"I will never take sides like that again," said Tatiana. "So, Oliver, what was all the religion stuff about?"

"That's simple. If you place your faith in men you will be disappointed. But if you place your faith in God, all things are possible."

"I can't believe it was that simple. We were ready to blow up the world in that stupid play," said Tatiana.

"We've all been suffering from the war. Remember Ernie Pyle? Same thing with him. All reporters who cover a war suffer from the same conditions that soldiers do when they come home. You are no different."

"So what else were you referring to?"

"You don't know, do you? I called the doctor yesterday, and the test came back positive!"

"What?"

"You're pregnant!" Oliver said, picking her up.

"What?" exclaimed Tatiana.

"That's why you fainted at the church during your presentation. He said the first trimester is actually the hardest."

"I can't believe it."

"My mother is going to be so happy," Oliver said.

"Well, the election is over," Cub said as he came in the office holding up the newspaper. "Look who won." The *Chicago Daily Tribune* headline read: "Dewey defeats Truman."

"That's fake news," Tatiana said.

"Congratulations on the baby," Cub said. "I hope it's a boy and you name it Leroy."

The buzzer rang. It was Brandeesha. "Miss Great. I mean Miss Pregnant Queen. Uh, Mrs. Smith, you have a lady visitor."

Tatiana and Oliver grimaced at Brandeesha, and then they smiled.

"Okay, send her in," Tatiana said.

It was Sister Camille.

"I will leave," Oliver said.

"Me, too," Cub said.

Sister Camille came in the office.

"Oh, Sister, I'm so glad you came here."

"Thank you, my dear, and how are you?"

"Oh, Sister Camille, I want to tell you that I understand everything you have been talking about. All the thoughts about how the world brings you want you want; that we are all energy vibrations and that our thoughts bring us what we think about. The attraction law, is that what it is called? Isn't that what you are preaching? Isn't that why you brought all the poor people into the church to try to get them to think about what they want and then the world brings it to you? Isn't that how you cure poverty?"

"My child, I have no idea what you are talking about. I teach no such thing. We seek the kingdom of God first. Jesus came to bring us the Good News that we can have eternal life with him and forgiveness of our sins. His new commandment is to love one another. I came to see if you were fine after your fall. We would like for you to finish your presentation."

Tatiana looked at her. "You mean …" She stopped. "What was I thinking?"

"Tatiana is pregnant," Oliver said.

"That is wonderful news!" said Sister Camille. "I am so happy for you."

Andre walked in the office. "Are you all ready for Griddle Iron practice tonight? Hello, Sister Camille."

"Hello, Andre. Is this a play?"

"Yes, Tatiana has the lead as Joan of Arc. She is going to restore Alabama to its rightful place in the United States. We have practice tonight. Are you sure you want to be burned at the stake?"

"I'm ready. Speaking of fires, Andre, I am convinced … wait, do you mind if I bring this up in front of Sister Camille?"

"Bring what up?"

"The fire at your home when you were a child."

"Who cares at this point? It's okay."

"You might as well hear this, too, Sister Camille, since you were there. Andre, the fire in your home was not started by your Aunt Clara. I know. I personally investigated it. It was an electrical fire in the attic caused by squirrels; they chewed on the electrical wires. It was just a matter of time before they would spark and cause a fire. Did your family feed the squirrels around the house?"

"We did. One squirrel we taught to take food from our hands when he was hungry. He would jump on the screen door to the house."

Brandeesha walked in. "Andre, your mother is on the line."

"Okay," he said as he walked out of the office.

Nelms was walking to Tatiana's office with a new reporter. Andre and the new reporter slapped hands as they passed each other.

Nelms walked in the office. "Sorry to bother all of you. What's going on? Hello, Sister."

"Hello," Sister Camille responded.

"Tatiana, are you busy?" Nelms asked.

He had a visitor with him.

"Tatiana, I want you to meet – I guess all of you can meet him. This is a new reporter who will be working at the paper with Andre."

The young reporter was handsome, healthy, and physically in shape. Tatiana stood up from her chair and walked around her desk to meet him.

"I'm always interested in meeting a new reporter in our field. I'm Tatiana Phillips," she said, extending her hand.

"Good morning," he said. "My name is Booker Thompson."

THE END

NOTES

Chapter 1

1 The reference to "far difference" comes from *Bryan Garner's Usage Tip of the Day* that "far distance is a redundancy. In most contexts, each word implies the other." Retrieved from: http://content.bridgemailsystem.com/pms/v/w/
BzAEqwsEk20Hm21Rn30Un33Kk26Bk17Ek20Mr21
Tp30BgyStRf/
BzAEqwsEk20Kp21Ok30Rk33Rr26Fo17BcdDZrt/

2 The reference "fall through the cracks" between Ed Nelms and Tatiana Phillips comes from *Bryan Garner's Usage Tip of the Day* referencing "fall through the cracks." Retrieved from: http://content.bridgemailsystem.com/pms/v/w/q
cWOc30Te33Nf26Ef17Ec20Fc21Oc30Yj33
Ph26qTy/qcWOc30Vg33Sk26Cd17Ig20Li21qNm/
(accessed 1/2019) ("The *cracks* in this idiom are the openings between slats, as on a boardwalk. Things can *fall through the cracks*, but nothing can fall *between* them, because that's where the slats are. Yet the idiom is often mangled into the illogical *fall between the cracks ...*").

Chapter 4

3 USS Shangri-La. (December 11, 2018). Retrieved from https://en.wikipedia.org/wiki/USS_Shangri-La.

4 In *A Private War II, Andre* visualizes a play directed by Betty based on the book *Clisson and Eugénie* by Napoleon Bonaparte. Andre is being facetious with this statement.

Chapter 6

5 The quiz in the journalism class comes from *The Quill, A Magazine by the Society of Professional Journalists* by Paula LaRocque. (July 2, 2018). Retrieved from https://quill.spjnetwork.org/2018/07/02/copy-editing-quiz-paula-larocque-july-column

6 Ibid.

7 "I Am Part of the Resistance Inside the Trump Administration," *The New York Times*, September 9, 2018. https://www.nytimes.com/2018/09/05/opinion/trump-white-house-anonymous-resistance.html.

Chapter 9

8 Windham, Ben. "Southern Lights: Wide smiles, wild stories tell story of 'Big Jim' Folsom," *Tuscaloosa News*, June 10, 2012. https://www.tuscaloosanews.com/opinion/20120610/southern-lights-wide-smiles-wild-stories-tell-story-of-big-jim-folsom.

9 Ibid.

Chapter 19

10 *54th Massachusetts Infantry Regiment.* (December 28, 2018). Retrieved from: https://en.wikipedia.org/wiki/54th_Massachusetts_Infantry_Regiment; *9th United States Colored Infantry* from: https://en.wikipedia.org/wiki/9th_United_States_Colored_Infantry *10th Cavalry Regiment* from: https://en.wikipedia.org/wiki/10th_Cavalry_Regiment_(United_States).

11 Military history of African Americans. (December 12, 2018). Retrieved from: https://en.wikipedia.org/wiki/Military_history_of_African_Americans#World_War_II.

12 Ollie Stewart. (November 13, 2018). Retrieved from: https://en.wikipedia.org/wiki/Ollie_Stewart.

13 Houston, Ivan J. & Cohn, Gordon. *Black Warriors: The Buffalo Soldiers of World War II Memories of the Only Negro Infantry Division to Fight in Europe During World War* (iUniverse, March 8, 2011).

14 See footnote #16, Linda Hervieux, *Forgotten: The Untold Story of D-Day's Black Heroes, at Home and at War.*

15 Ibid.
16 Ibid.
17 Ibid.

18 Ibid.
19 Ibid.
20 Ibid.
21 Ibid.
22 Ibid.

23 Dieppe Raid. Retrieved on January 8, 2019 from: https://en.wikipedia.org/wiki/Dieppe_Raid.

24 The reference to believing in God is mental illness is based on Joy Behar's mocking of Vice President Pence's belief in God on *The View*. Retrieved from:
https://www.realclearpolitics.com/video/2018/02/18/the_view_host_joy_behar_mocks_vp_pences_christian_faith_as_mental_illness.html.

Chapter 41

25 The statements in this chapter regarding the Mayor of Birmingham, England banning knives comes from London Mayor Sadiq Khan, who announced in April 2018 a tough crackdown on knives.

26 Ibid.
27 Ibid.
28 Ibid.
29 Ibid.
30 Ibid.
31 Ibid.

32 The reference that the police department has been shrunk is from an interview of London Mayor Sadiq Khan. "Where are the 400 known Jihadists in London," *Good Morning Britain*, June 7, 2017.

33 Based on similar statements made by Fox News commentator Sean Hannity about the MSNBC show *Morning Joe*.

34 Based on statements made by MSNBC commentators Joe Scarborough and Mika Brzezinski on *Morning Joe*.

35 The dialogue "[S]he is planning Christmas in July" and "these are child abusers" is from MSNBC commentator Mika Brzezinski on *Morning Joe*.

36 The scene between Brandeesha and Tatiana is based on the incident between Whoopi Goldberg and Judge Jeanine Pirro during an interview on *The View* in July 2018: "Whoopi Goldberg Blows Up, Ends 'The View' Interview with Judge Jeanine Pirro: Goodbye." Retrieved from: https://www.realclearpolitics.com/video/2018/07/19/whoopi_goldberg_blows_up_ends_the_view_interview_with_judge_jeanine_goodbye.html
Also, her interview commenting on the interview on *Hannity*: http://video.foxnews.com/v/5811450202001/?#sp=show-clips.

37 Ibid.
38 Ibid.
39 Ibid.

Chapter 52

40 Based on a statement made by then Senator Joe Biden during the confirmation hearing of Supreme Court nominee, Clarence Thomas in 1991.

41 Based on a statement made by James Comey, former Director of the Federal Bureau of Investigation referring to President Donald Trump.

42 Hans is describing a scene from *A Private War II* that occurred between Lanny and Andre when they went to see the Birmingham Barons play baseball.

Chapter 59

43 Chapter 59 is a parody of *Joan of Arc* by Mark Twain. Based on an interview of James Clapper on *The View* when asked a question by Meghan McCain in May 2018.

Chapter 60

44 The reference to Ogeroso and her running for president comes from Omarosa Manigault Newman. Retrieved from: https://www.etonline.com/omarosa-manigault-newman-says-she-would-consider-running-for-president-110182.
45 Based on the exchange at the White House between CNN reporter Jim Acosta and President Donald Trump in November 2018.

Chapter 62

46 Based on the interview of Fox News reporter Chris Wallace with Russian President Vladimir Putin in July 2018. Retrieved from:
https://www.youtube.com/watch?v=rHY8yG4mVzs

47 Ibid.
48 Ibid.

www.ingramcontent.com/pod-product-compliance
Lightning Source LLC
Chambersburg PA
CBHW070637180626
46817CB00006B/2145